WAITING
FOR THE SEA
TO BE BLUE

WAITING
FOR THE SEA
TO BE BLUE

Philippa Blake

[handwritten signature and inscription]

2·1·07

ORION

First published in Great Britain in 1996 by
Orion
An imprint of Orion Books Ltd
Orion House, 5 Upper St Martin's Lane, London WC2H 9EA

A CIP catalogue record for this book
is available from the British Library

ISBN 0 75280 157 0

Typeset at The Spartan Press Ltd,
Lymington, Hants

Printed in Great Britain by
Clays Ltd, St Ives plc

PREFACE

There is a code among thieves.
Thieves distinguish crimes between themselves, between theft which is honest, which makes no pretence, and theft which is sly and hidden.

The swift brutality of a burglar, with his smashed glass, broken locks, spaces left on a mantelpiece, has a certain logic, a kind of truth. So, too, the bank robber; his face is masked but his intention is plain. These are brothers in trade. Their business is clear.

Fraud has no such code, no such companions. There is no weapon, no mask. The essence is to mislead, to look innocent, even in the deed, to have the trappings of innocence. A burglar will say that fraud is dishonest.

A name among a list of names: the headed paper of an old City firm. A name appearing on such a list carries a presumption of rectitude, enough of itself to over-ride ordinary caution. If there is nothing in the face, in the discreet signature, the card slipped with a small measure of panache from a slim wallet into your hand, if there is nothing to warn, the fraud is easy.

Leonora Cohen fingered the collar of her black silk dress. She felt a rim of sweat. Her husband's funeral had been a formal, lengthy affair. She had drawn comfort from the crowds who had come; their presence and the hostess's instincts that they stirred in her had helped to blur the grief, the helpless panic that

1

threatened her composure. But now her energy was spent, she longed for the crowds to be gone. It was a relief to see her solicitor, Arthur Wright, coming across the drawing room towards her.

'I'm so sorry, Leonora. You have my deepest sympathy.'

'It was kind of you to come, Arthur, to give up your precious time to comfort an old widow.'

'Not at all,' said Arthur. 'Your husband's family have been clients of my firm for generations. Of course we will support you at a time like this.' He turned to a young man who had followed him, stood a pace behind. 'I want you to meet my assistant, Theodore Ransome.'

Leonora shook that young man's hand. 'You look barely old enough to have left school.'

Teddy smiled.

'He certainly has,' said Arthur. 'Theodore achieved distinction in his professional exams.'

Teddy's smile broadened. He blushed a little. Leonora Cohen decided that she liked him.

'I'm going to ask Teddy to deal with the probate of the will, my dear. Teddy is specialising in this sort of work, and I know he will do a good job for you.'

'If you recommend him to me, then I am perfectly satisfied,' said Leonora.

'And perhaps when that is done,' said Arthur, 'you should give some thought to making a new will yourself.'

Leonora had no qualms. The young Mr Ransome was efficient, polite. When the estate was distributed he prepared a full set of accounts and he took the trouble to go through them to her, explaining how every asset had been dealt with, the legacies paid and the balance transferred to her own bank account.

'You've done a very good job.' She patted his hand. 'I hope that when it is my turn, someone will do as good a job on my estate.'

Teddy cleared this throat. 'Do you remember that Mr Wright suggested that you should consider your will?'

'I do indeed,' said Leonora, 'and how efficient you are to

2

remember it.' She patted his hand once more. 'I should like you to be my Executor.'

'Oh, Mrs Cohen – '

'Is it not permitted?'

Teddy paused. 'There's no reason why I shouldn't be. Anyone may be appointed as Executor of a will. Usually two people are named.'

'Why two?'

'Well, one might die before the testator.'

'But this will not happen here. I am more than twice your age, Theodore. You will be a young man still, when I am taken.'

'I shall have to ask Mr Wright.'

Arthur Wright was not in his room. 'He's very busy,' said the secretary. 'There's a big case going on.'

Teddy retreated. I'll just prepare a draft, he thought. I'll show it to Arthur before she comes in to execute it.

The draft will sat on his desk for a week. He sent Arthur Wright a note. 'Could I have a word with you about Mrs Cohen?'

The secretary telephoned. 'He's left for his holiday. He won't see your note for a couple of weeks.'

Mrs Cohen came in to sign the will. Teddy arranged for two boys from the post room to act as witnesses. Leonora beamed and offered them a five-pound note each.

'Really, Mrs Cohen,' said Teddy when they had gone. 'There was no need.'

'But they had such nice manners,' said Leonora, 'for working-class boys.'

The will went down to the strong room. Arthur Wright returned from his holiday, peered round Teddy's door, tanned and smiling. 'You wanted to see me about Mrs Cohen?'

'It was nothing, really,' said Teddy. 'It was just to let you know that she has made a new will.'

'Good!' said Arthur. 'Important that she should, with all the old boy's money in her pocket.'

'Did you enjoy your holiday?'

'I certainly did,' said Arthur. 'And you know, Ransome, I do believe I enjoyed it all the more for knowing you've got everything in hand. Private clients aren't really my metier, as you know. Such a relief to know you're there, being so efficient and charming the old ladies.'

There were other old ladies. Teddy had a special skill with them; he was equally good with retired colonels and minor aristocracy, the wealthy, elderly clients who made up the bulk of the private clients of Harbour Lowe & Robbins.

ONE

Susan Ransome opened the oven door. The internal fan blew a draught of dry, barely warm air over her fingers, filling the open sleeve of her dress. Behind her on the counter, laid out on shallow trays lined with rice paper, were neat platters of whipped egg-white, delicately tinted by the addition of ground almonds, and so carefully piped and fripped they resembled the container of a very exclusive cosmetic.

She slid the trays into the oven and set the timer. The oven was electric. Behind her, interrupting the sweep of the counter to give the kitchen a pleasantly rustic air, was the brand new Aga that ran on bottled gas, its bright green enamel echoed in the colours of the hand-painted tiles.

'It's just a kitchen!' Winifred had cried, when she heard what Susan had planned to spend.

'It's an improvement,' said Susan. 'A good kitchen adds to the value of a property.'

Winifred sniffed. 'In my day a kitchen was a place for servants.'

It was sixteen years since Winifred had moved out of Chanting Hill and into the gardener's cottage at the end of the drive. Dear Winifred, *Aunt* Winifred as Teddy still called her sometimes, using the word as if it could draw something from the old lady, some extra nuance of the strange, stilted affection in which they held one another. The death of Hills, the gardener, had coincided with Susan's third pregnancy and Teddy being made an equity partner of Harbour Lowe & Robbins. The pregnancy was the excuse Winifred had waited for.

5

'You must come and live in the country,' she had said, patting Susan's swelling bump. 'Wandsworth is no place to bring up a family.'

Susan had come to Chanting Hill alone, a flying visit while the boys were at school and Teddy submerged in his new responsibilities at the office. Despite the brightness of the day the interior of the house was dark, gloom bouncing off the old, stained panelling, the dusty, faded curtains. She had come to announce her pregnancy, to seek Winifred's approval, to bathe in the pleasure that this time Teddy wouldn't or couldn't or simply didn't have time to share with her. Winifred's offer of Chanting Hill was unexpected, breathtaking. Susan stalled for time, wondering how she should react.

'But what about you, Auntie Win? Mr Hills' cottage will be a bit of a change from Chanting Hill.'

'The Lodge is quite big enough for me,' Winifred had said. 'Mr Hills was a tidy man, it will need no more than a lick of paint.'

'I don't know what Teddy will say.'

'He'll be delighted,' said Winifred firmly. 'It will suit him for you all to live here. He'll be able to show off as much as he likes.'

'It's too far for Teddy to commute,' said Susan.

'He can stay in his club.'

Susan hesitated. She did not know Winifred very well in those days, but she said what was in her mind, testing for a reaction.

'Is it wise? To have him living away like that?'

Winifred gave her a look. After a short silence she said, 'He's a good husband to you, Susan.'

'I know, it's just . . .'

Winifred raised her hand to tuck away a stray grey hair. 'It's no good expecting perfection. Teddy has done better than I ever thought he would.'

'I don't mean to criticise – '

'He got nothing from Hugo, you know. My brother cut him off without a penny. Everything you have he has earned.'

'What will Hugo say about us moving into Chanting Hill? Surely he – '

Winifred puffed her cheeks. 'Pah! What will he care? He'll never come back. He'll never admit he was wrong. He'll stay out there in Pentecost until we are both dead.'

6

Teddy had been wary, reluctant. 'Chanting Hill is a gloomy house, Susan. My memories of it aren't exactly happy.'

'But we can change all that. It's a lovely old place, and there's so much space –'

'It's impossibly old-fashioned.'

There were other objections, but Teddy having to stay in his club during the week wasn't one of them; that idea dismayed him not at all, though he did ask how she would manage on her own. And the boys – they would hardly ever see him.

'They rarely see you now, Teddy. You're always working late. At least if we live in the country we'll have you to ourselves at the weekends.'

Teddy put his arms around her. 'Do I detect a complaint?'

'No, of course not. I know you have to work. Winifred thinks Chanting Hill will really suit us. She says the country would be good for the children.'

'It wasn't much good to me as a child.'

Susan paused. She searched his face for clues but there was nothing. He was as inscrutable as he had always been, since she had first known him, first come upon the core, the place at the heart of him to which she had no access, could not comprehend. That core remained, a place that was frozen and at the same time burning, visible from time to time, as it was in the look that flitted now across his face, so brief it could be no more than her imagination.

He was smiling again, his usual calm, indulgent smile. She grasped his hands. 'If we sell the house in London we can use the money to improve Chanting Hill. It'll be marvellous, Teddy. We can transform the place.'

'It won't be ours, Susan.'

'That's just a technicality. Winifred says we can do what we like, we can treat it as if it were our own.'

'But she will never give it to us while she is alive. She will never go against Hugo's wishes.'

'And when he dies?'

'Well then, that will be a different story.'

As he spoke Teddy turned away, hiding his face, the look that had been there before, the old look – of hate and angry triumph.

Mama loves me better than anybody. She does. She gave me this Diary. She told me to take it with me when I go on the ship. She wrote in the front. Write something every day, my darling. Write down the things you see and do. I will keep a diary just like this, and one day we will show them to each other, and catch up with the time we have missed.

I don't want to go away. Mama says I will like school in England. All the boys live in the school. She says I will be happy because there will be boys to play with. When she says that she closes her eyes.

TWO

Hush. Tall windows hanging open, high glass panes leaning in, caught by hinges and long sash cords twisted into figures of eight, letting in the sounds of outside: birdsong, the cars on the road, a distant hammering. The interior of the church was still, as if the very purpose of the place made a defence, a blanket of serenity, calming the air, softening the play of sunlight and shadow on the simple wooden pews, the altar at the end where the vestments waited for the priest, the special clothing for the dead, and trestles draped in white cotton.

'Oh!' Honey allowed the sound. 'Oh!'

And then she was moving again, stepping briskly up the aisle, a brief pause before the altar, the sign of the cross and then on past the table with its drape of lace to the tall wooden stands holding vases of flowers left over from Sunday Mass. They would have to do. The master had ordered no flowers, nothing but a simple wooden coffin, the subject of the hammer that could be heard, louder at this end of the church.

The lilies were losing their whiteness, a smell of decay in the pot. Honey bustled about, fetching a jug of fresh water from the outside tap. The left-over lilies would have to be enough.

A swift flicking away of fallen pollen, of a dead fly on the altar lace. The parish register was on a side table, Clara's death already entered on the page.

The hammering ceased. In the carpenter's yard the coffin was complete. They would be taking it up to the house and she must

9

be there when it came. It would be she and Justine who would put Clara inside. They would do it together. There was no question of weight, of men needed. Honey had lifted that weight often enough: from the drawing room to the bedroom, from the floor to the bed, the feet dangling, too drunk to undress.

Lifting her now for the last time. Clara would drink no more, Clara would weep no more. The last of her tears were in the still water of the mangrove swamp.

Honey shut the church door. Bana had customers for his shop, filling their baskets. She hurried by. The truck was drawing out of the carpenter's yard, Sahilil himself at the wheel, taking the work of his son up to the house. He waited, the dust of the road settling on his load, while she clambered up into the cab and sat on the plastic seat, smoothing her skirt.

'It will be the master's car for you this afternoon.'

'Yes.'

'And a sad load following.'

'Yes.'

He gestured to the back. 'My son has made a good box for her, better than the master has paid for.'

'William is a good boy.'

'He is a good carpenter. It is what I wanted – and Justine – that he would not be a house-servant, sweeping the floors for a white man.' Sahilil pulled at the gear-stick, coaxing the ancient truck up the hill. 'But I did not think of this, when I asked for the fees for apprentice school. I did not think my son would be making a box for *her*.'

Seven months. Honey took a square of cotton from her pocket and gently blew her nose. Seven months since the child was sent. Seven months of Clara grieving, as Honey herself had grieved, as if little Teddy were dead. The whole falling-down plantation house creaking with grief and the silence of the little boy gone. And Clara with the grief of a mother bereft, more grim and more strident than ever her joy had been, drinking herself away. A mother bereft of her child, seized with anger, seized with hatred for the man who would do this thing, drinking to punish him, to make herself ugly, drinking herself at last into the grave of water where the sea and the river join at the edge of

10

the land and the mangroves crowd in to shut out the light.

There were men up from the compound to carry the box in; men who had never set foot in the master's house. Silent, vying to be the one who would carry the weight of the box up into the house and to the room where the body lay, pausing with it perched on their shoulders, at the closed door.

Honey led the way. She held the door wide and placed herself between them and the master. Hiding the master with her body so they would not know and would not go and tell the world, that here in this room with the smells of his wife's poor bloated body rising around him, here in this shuttered, stifling darkness, the master was slumped in a chair asleep, snoring.

And barely awake when the private, silent rituals of Honey and Justine were complete; barely awake to lean on Honey's arm, his stick knocking her ankles as they walked through the shaded house and out into the sunshine. He had not changed his clothes or washed; he wore the same blue shirt that he had worn to go to the police station to identify his drowned wife's body, the leeches still fastened to her skin.

The church was full. The people of Mahana had come as one. To pray and to stare. At the end of the service a woman from the village tapped Honey's arm. 'If there are any clothes to be thrown away – things not wanted?' Honey brushed the woman away. There would be no such looting. Nothing would be moved. She would guard the cupboards from their greed. The master would not be permitted to forget.

He stayed on beside the grave, sober enough now, to watch the earth going back, dry dust rattling on the better-than-paid-for coffin. On the journey home he asked Elias to drive along the coast, to where the mouth of the river spread out, the mangroves filling the spans.

'Why was it here?' His breath was foul.

They had no answer, Elias and she, there in the car, her feet in her new shoes, starting to rub a sore.

'Why here? She could have chosen another way – something less public.'

Honey shrank from him, from the bad breath that filled the car. It was a question she had asked herself, why a beautiful

11

woman would choose such a place – knowing how she would be found, her naked body swollen, her face a gargoyle, small water creatures nibbling at her white skin.

The old dairy had been unused for decades, since the days when Chanting Hill had its own estate.

'I used to play here with Hugo, when we were children,' said Winifred. 'We used to think it was haunted, filled with the ghosts of old dairymaids.'

Susan had no time for ghosts, especially not old Ransome ghosts. Teddy said she could have whatever she wanted and her aim was to have the kitchen finished before the baby came. A new kitchen was to be installed in the dairy, and the old kitchen become a laundry room. Susan was kept so busy, with the architect and the builder and the army of plumbers and carpenters and electricians, that she hardly noticed how little she saw of him. Distemper had to be stripped from the old walls and new dry linings installed; in place of the high, short windows went a wall of glass, in the latest double glazing, so that she could see all of the hill after which the house had been named, and beyond it, the rolling Salisbury Plain.

From time to time she phoned Harbour Lowe & Robbins. 'He's working very hard, Mrs Ransome,' his secretary, Phyllis, would say, 'I've told him he shouldn't do so much, but he takes no notice of me.'

'Me neither,' said Susan. 'But I mustn't complain.'

'I've made sure he'll be with you on the day the baby's due. His diary has a red line through and no-one may make an appointment.'

'Thank you, Phyllis.'

Susan longed to ask questions. 'What makes him so busy? What does he actually do all day long? What is he doing now, right now, out of the office in the middle of the afternoon?' But Phyllis was too loyal to Teddy for there to be any substance in her answer.

Winifred was more critical. 'It's too bad of him,' she complained. 'Teddy should be here, not gallivanting in London.'

'He has to be at the office, Winnie. It's part of the price of our being here at Chanting Hill, that I see less of him.'

The old lady sniffed. 'That's all very well as a rule, but you're about to have a child. Look at the size of you.'

Susan smiled. She was learning to enjoy Winifred's fierceness. The old lady came up to the house every day, her bag filled with small temptations; pots of home-made soup, slices of ham from the delicatessen, tangerines and small squares of chocolate, tutting about the workmen in the dairy, the noisy afternoons when a woman in her condition should be resting.

Of the day Crystal was born, Susan remembered every detail, all the differences from the days that the boys were born. For Graham's birth Teddy had taken a fortnight's leave. He drove to the hospital holding her hand, wore a green gown and mask and stayed with her for all the hours of her labour; breathed with her, counted with her, cried tears with her when Graham was finally born. For Lucian there had been less time, but still Teddy came to the hospital, held her through the worst of it.

Crystal arrived a week early. For her there were only the ambulance men. Winifred at her bridge club, a pot of soup left on the Aga. Even the cleaning girl had been and gone, shouting her goodbye up the stairs. Chanting Hill was empty and silent. Susan phoned for the ambulance herself, her voice calm. 'This is not the first.'

An hour and a half alone in the house. She soiled a sheet, tried to take it down to the laundry, a moment on the stairs when it was difficult to move: and then stuck there, like a spider on her back, her legs blindly waving. The ambulance man broke the glass in the door.

'You all on your tod, love? Where's your governor?'

'He'll be here soon.'

No need to tell them that Teddy was in London, that he saw his wife only at weekends.

She heard herself panting, chattering between breaths. 'I've had two already. I know the form. I've got two boys at school.'

They weren't listening: too concerned with whisking her discharging body up the stairs and on to the bed, rolling long gloves that smelled of rubber bands up their solid forearms. Crystal came swiftly and messily and travelled to the hospital in

Susan's arms, barely wiped, a smeary pink-and-yellow ball nudging blindly at her breasts. Susan hung on, tired beyond belief (the thought in her mind, I am too old for this), but full of joy: a daughter, a child that would be more than the boys had been, a friend, hers. The nurses helped her bathe the child and then herself and then she slept, her body squeezed like a spent balloon between crisp white hospital sheets, the child in a cot beside her, a shock of black hair on the pillow.

At visiting time there was Winifred, Lucian and Graham trailing behind, scrubbed, unfamiliar angels.

First they peered into the cot.

'Will it talk?'

'No darling, not yet.'

Lucian put a tentative finger on the child's nose. 'It moved!'

'Ugh!' They backed away – and then came forward again. A small hand waved in the air.

'It's alive!'

'I should hope so.' Winifred's voice reminded them of their surroundings. They came to the bedside. Seeing her there, their mother, looking about the same as usual, the boys hugged her in a perfunctory way before wandering out into the corridor.

'Theodore should be here.' Winifred's voice was sharp, unforgiving.

Susan turned her head on the pillow. The cradle was within reach. She could see a little fist beating the air. 'He's catching the first train. Something was happening in the office – he couldn't get away immediately.'

'There's something happening here!'

'Don't Winifred, please, not now.' Susan felt tears on her cheeks.

Immediately there was a handkerchief, a large, square hand patting hers. 'Don't worry about crying, my dear. Your hormones are upside down.'

They were interrupted by the door. The boys' faces were alight. 'Papa's here!'

Flowers: red roses, carnations the colour of apricots frilled with butter yellow, clouds of gypsophila – even a pair of vases, spheres of cut glass that winked in the bright clinical light.

'How are you, Winifred?' His aunt was kissed first; the flowers thrust into her arms. Then Teddy was there by the bed, scooping her up from the pillows, surrounding her with his scent, the smell of cigar smoke and red wine. She felt herself relax, the old safe feeling. 'And what have you been up to today, my darling?'

Turning from her he reached into the cot. She saw him lift their daughter, with infinite care, as if she were made of glass.

Susan said, 'She's all right. I'm sorry she wasn't quite on schedule, but there's nothing wrong.'

'Of course she's all right!' Teddy answered, in a hoarse whisper. 'She's perfect. Aren't you, my lovely, my little Crystal?'

'There are far too many flowers here, Theodore,' said Winifred. 'It's a shocking waste, and you know they'll steal these vases. I'll have to ask the nurse for another.' She went out; they could hear her voice in the corridor, chastising Graham.

'We shouldn't let the boys roam around the hospital.'

Teddy sat on the bed. 'I'll take them for a pizza in a moment.'

He unbuttoned the front of her nightdress and lifted the baby into the crook of her arm. The child's mouth opened, swallowed blindly and closed itself greedily on her nipple.

Susan looked up. Teddy was standing back, like an artist stepping back from his easel. On his face was an expression of softness and delight that she had never seen before.

'She is truly perfect,' he said. 'Exquisite.'

The moment that should have been long and quiet between them was broken by the creak of the door and a shriek from Graham. Lucian was behind him, his mouth wide with astonishment. They stared at her breasts, at the child sucking and swallowing.

Lucian recovered first. 'It's eating you, Mum!'

'She's not eating me, silly. You know what breast-feeding is. You saw it all when the kittens were born.'

'But they were cats.'

'You did the same, you know.' Winifred had come in behind them, a plastic vase in each hand.

'I never did that!' said Lucian.

'Now then.' Teddy was gathering them towards him. 'I think it's time you boys were having some supper yourselves.'

Graham looked at him in horror. Laughter bubbled from Susan's lips, pulling all the stretched muscles of her body. 'He doesn't mean me. He's going to take you for a pizza.'

'Susan's had quite enough, Theodore,' said Winifred. The vases were set out in neat rows on the windowsill. She turned to Susan. 'You shouldn't feed the baby again so soon, dear, the child must have a routine.'

No-one took any notice. The boys craned towards their mother, holding their bodies clear of the bed, to give her a small dry kiss, one on either cheek. From Teddy there was another hug of scent and wine and old cigars, the gentlest of kisses on the baby's head, and then they were gone, Graham's voice audible through the closing door, 'That's the most disgusting thing I've ever seen.'

Only Winifred stayed behind. 'What did I hear him call her?'

'Crystal.'

'Is that what you've decided? Have you decided already?'

Susan nodded, but it wasn't true. They'd agreed not to choose the name until after the birth, not to tempt fate by naming it in the womb. He had never mentioned Crystal; he hadn't been interested in names.

'I can't imagine what made you think of it,' said Winifred. 'It doesn't sound . . .'

Susan waited. Even Winifred would hesitate to say that the name chosen for her great-niece sounded slightly common.

'We don't know anyone called Crystal, do we?' Susan said, when they were home again at Chanting Hill.

'That's the beauty of it.' Teddy took the baby from her. 'The name is fresh. It has no strings attached, no-one to be compared with.' He smiled at the child, as gently and completely as if all he wanted in the world reposed there in his arms.

'Your aunt is disappointed.'

'Why?'

'Well, because it isn't a name anyone knows, it isn't a family name.'

'She can't have thought we'd call her Winifred?' Teddy turned to her. 'You don't want her to have such a name. You couldn't!'

He didn't hear the disappointment in her voice. 'No, but I might have liked to call her Elizabeth, after my mother. She's our only girl. People do tend to use family names.'

Teddy pressed his lips against the baby's head, as if to seal her with his will. 'Her name is Crystal. It has a ring to it. She will be the most beautiful woman on earth, and her name will express her perfection.'

Two years after her husband's death, Leonora Cohen suffered a stroke that paralysed her down one side. Teddy received a call from the hospital. Only partial recovery was expected, did anyone hold her Power of Attorney?

Teddy went to her bedside. Leonora insisted he bend down for a kiss.

'No-one but you has been to see me.'

'Surely someone has?' said Teddy. 'What about your friends and family?'

'No family left, my dear. They're all dead.' Her good hand pressed his against the bedclothes. 'I'd never stopped to count before, but do you know, I believe I am the very last.'

Teddy knew there were no Cohen children, but her will had named a number of legatees.

'They were just my friends, people who have been good to me over the years,' said Leonora. 'I have outlasted them all.'

'There must be someone,' said Teddy.

'Only Howard, and he's in Australia.'

'Who is Howard?'

'Sister-in-law's nephew by marriage.' Leonora released Teddy's hand. 'I don't expect he will fly to England to visit a remote aunt. He probably doesn't know I exist.'

Before he left the hospital, Teddy provided Leonora with a pen to sign the Power of Attorney that he had brought in his briefcase.

'Why didn't we do this before?' she cried. 'You should have taken over long ago. I know I can rely on you entirely.'

Teddy went back to the office. 'Mr Rowtham called again,'

17

said Phyllis, holding out a slip of paper. 'He wants you to ring him right away, he's on that number until four o'clock.'

Teddy took the slip into his office. Phyllis followed him. 'I asked him if I could help but he was quite abrupt.'

'Indeed,' said Teddy.

'Do I –' said Phyllis diffidently '– is his name one I should recognise?'

'He's our builder,' said Teddy shortly. 'He wants me to pay his bill.'

'Oh, I see,' said Phyllis, retreating.

'I owe him a fortune for the work on the house.'

Phyllis reached the door. 'Perhaps I'll make a cup of tea.'

'Good idea.'

She closed the door behind her. Teddy sat down and drummed his fingers on the desk. Rowtham's invoices were in the top drawer. Teddy had thrust them there when they arrived. There were other bills too: one from the garage for repairs to Susan's car that had cost more than the car was worth; another from the dentist. Susan had decided Lucian's teeth were too prominent. Someone on a village committee had told her about a man in Harley Street. Teddy could detect no change in Lucian's appearance, but the surgeon's bill could have paid for the new kitchen.

The bills would have to be paid. Rowtham's especially. If Teddy didn't pay it would be all round the village in no time. Teddy's fingers clenched on the edge of the desk. It couldn't happen. He couldn't allow it to happen. People would never say that Teddy Ransome wasn't all he was cracked up to be.

A week later Leonora Cohen was transferred to a nursing home. Acting under her Power of Attorney, Teddy instructed an agent to put her house on the market. The asking price was low enough to attract a buyer very quickly.

'What did you get for it, Teddy?' Leonora asked, offering her cheek for a kiss when he went to report the completion of the sale.

'Pots of money,' said Teddy, smiling.

'Pots of money?'

'Pots and pots,' said Teddy.

'Oh, goody.' She beamed like an elderly pixie.

'And I've got it all safe and sound in the bank.'

Leonora liked the nursing home. Teddy paid her bills direct. All her assets were in his name; the Power of Attorney enabled him to sign her cheques, to spend the proceeds of her house as he saw fit. Rowtham's bills were paid in full. And the garage and the dentist. Teddy traded in Susan's car for a brand new one, big enough to carry the baby's cot as well as the two boys. Susan was delighted.

The party that followed Crystal's baptism was the first of Teddy's great occasions, the first time they entertained at Chanting Hill as if it were their own. Caterers were hired, a marquee erected on the lawn; all the best glass and silver was used, even the 'ancestors' goblets', as the boys called the engraved glasses that filled two cabinets in the dining room. Susan felt it a little excessive, to go to such lengths for a christening party, but Teddy had no inhibitions. He wanted to show it all off, for people to see what they had. He even took her to London to choose her costume. 'It's important that you look right, Susan. It doesn't matter how much it costs.'

'It's just a christening, Teddy.'

'It's an opportunity. I've invited one or two people who will be impressed by Chanting Hill, who will expect a certain standard.'

'Such as who?'

'City people.' He waved his hand. 'You don't need to worry. Just be yourself and look as good as you possibly can.'

Winifred came up from the Lodge before the service to show Graham and Lucian how to tie their bow-ties.

'How many ancestors were there, Aunt Winnie?'

'Will we be ancestors too?'

The old lady measured her reply. 'You'll have to have some descendants first.'

Graham thought about this, submitting his shoulders to Winifred's clothes brush. 'If I am the eldest, I am the descendant. I am the inheritor.'

Again Winifred paused. 'People inherit what they deserve.'

The church of St Agnes lay in a shallow dip of land on the other side of the hill; a structure of grey stone, of spire and gargoyles, and tall narrow windows that cast a cold, white light on sparse congregations. It could be reached by a footpath from the Lodge. Every Sunday, just before eleven, on the section of the footpath visible from the kitchen of Chanting Hiil, they would see Winifred hurrying along in her blue wool coat and hat, with a coin in her pocket for the collection. Sometimes Susan went with her. She liked the old church; she sat on the parish committee that raised funds for its restoration. She would join Winifred on the footpath and walk with her, chatting about homely things, the children, the weather, droughts and showers, the aphids on the roses. 'Mr Hills would have dealt with those in no time. Mr Hills was never beaten by an aphid.' The old lady had walked the path almost every Sunday of her life, but her clearest recollection was of walking it as a child, with Hugo beside her, and Nanny at the rear, the sound of the church bells mingling with the barking of the dogs left shut in behind the tall house-gates. She showed Susan the point on the path, marked by a particular stone, when the barking and ringing were audible in equal proportions; after that stone the barking would grow faint, eclipsed by the harsh clanging that summoned them to worship.

The bells rang for Crystal's baptism. The church was packed, a squash of bright hats nodding and turning – more like a flower show than a church service. Graham and Lucian looked tidy and unfamiliar in their miniature suits, childish imitators of the lawyers and bankers and stockbrokers who filled the church. Suitably awed by the crowd, the degree of pomp that imbued the proceedings, they stood still and quiet until the service was over and the guests flowed out on to the step. Photographs were taken. Teddy had notified the local press. He had organised chauffeured limousines to lead the procession the short distance back to Chanting Hill.

Winifred refused to ride in the car. 'I am not so decrepit that I cannot walk from here to the house!'

Susan went with her, leaving Crystal with Teddy and the boys in the car that led the convoy that snaked back around Chanting

Hill.

'Crystal behaved well,' said Winifred.

Susan smiled. 'She's always good when Teddy is there.'

Winifred opened the small gate in the fence that separated the church land from the field behind the house. 'Does anyone on your side have that very dark hair and pale skin?'

'No,' said Susan. 'We're all pretty fair. I expect she'll lose it all soon.'

'Teddy is quite dark,' said Winifred.

'But not as dark as Crystal.'

'No.' They had reached the edge of the field. 'Crystal's colouring is that of her paternal grandmother.'

Susan's step slowed. 'Was Clara dark like that?'

'She certainly was,' said Winifred. 'And she had the same startlingly blue eyes.'

'But Crystal's are just baby blue. Surely they'll fade?'

'I think you'll find they don't,' said Winifred. 'It's all rather unfortunate.'

Susan took the old lady's arm. The guests' cars were parking along the drive. Doors were banged, and they could hear tyres turning on the gravel. 'Do you think that's why Teddy is so entranced with her?'

Winifred matched Susan's quickening steps. She didn't answer. They had reached the garden. Guests flowed towards the marquee on the front lawn. Assisted by a phalanx of women, Teddy was settling Crystal into a cot draped with lace. The women cooed and chirruped, as much, Susan noticed, at Teddy as at the cot.

The party lasted late into the night. When all the champagne had been drunk Teddy offered spirits and wine from the old cellar. Susan went up to the nursery to give Crystal her late feed. The nursery was in the attic, but still she could hear the hubbub of voices. Crystal tugged at her nipples. The blue eyes, which had gazed in surprise and delight at the guests who had queued to admire her, fluttered open and closed; she was almost asleep, sucking instinctively. She had barely cried at all – the merest gasp of surprise at the dousing of baptismal water, and she had seemed to enjoy her first party as much as her father, smiling

21

blissfully as she moved from arm to arm, from cooing kisses to roguish tickles, an air of satisfaction on her small features.

At ten o'clock Susan ventured out in search of the boys. The party surged around her, relentless. Music was playing and there were people dancing in the hall. She wondered which of these people Teddy was trying to impress. None probably: the people to be impressed would have gone home when the champagne was finished.

Other people's christening parties are not like this, she thought. Other people invite only family and close friends – other people's guests go home at six o'clock.

She found Lucian asleep in the larder with a basin of prawn crackers. Graham was still up, wide-eyed, watching his father playing host, sucking in the style of glad-handed bonhomie that characterised Teddy's social relations.

It was after midnight when the last car hooted off down the drive. She heard Teddy blundering about, turning off the lights, switching on the burglar alarm. He came up at last, smiling glassily, a little unsteady.

'Quite a party, eh?'

'Have they all gone?'

'Mm – most. Except Johnny – he's on the couch. And Diane might still be here – can't be sure.'

'Who is Diane?'

'The girl who came with Johnny.'

'Where is she?'

With an exaggerated gesture, Teddy put his fingers to his lips. 'Might have been a bad girl.'

'What do you mean?'

Teddy giggled. 'Can't tell,' he said, stumbling into bed.

When you come in from the snow Chanting Hill feels warm even though it isn't. It's only warmer than outside. There is a fire in the morning room and it is warm in the kitchen but everywhere else is cold. When I wake up my breath is like smoke. This morning the cocoa that was left in my cup was frozen.

Mr Hills is mending the toboggan. Winifred says we can take it out on the hill. She's cross because the people from the village have been playing up there, making marks on the snow. They're trespassing, she says. It's our land.

Why don't you tell them to go?

She wrinkled her nose at me.

I'll tell them to go, I said. I'll go and shout at them.

No dear, she said, in her I-don't-know-what-I-shall-do-with-you voice. You mustn't be so rough.

I went anyway and shouted at them all. Get off my land! Get off! Get off!

She dragged me away. It's not your land. You mustn't be so rude to people.

I had to sit in the nursery without a fire. My fingers turned blue. She never lets me have a fire. She says she and Papa played up here without one. I must get used to being in England. I have been spoiled. Branksome will cure me, she says. I will learn to be an English gentleman at Branksome.

I hate Branksome. Everyone is mean and cruel. They laugh at me because I don't know about Hospital Corners and Branksome Knots and Outdoor Shoes. They say I talk in my sleep and call out for Mama and Honey-ayah. They stole the chocolate Mama sent me. The mangoes were brown and rotten. I wish she wouldn't send treats. No-one else's mother sends treats. They call me Mango-brain. They steal my shoes.

Winifred says I am an ungrateful boy. Four generations of Ransomes have been to Branksome. I am very lucky.

I don't want to be an English gentleman. I want to go back to Pentecost. I want to be there in the morning with Sahilil and Jaleb. Sahilil comes after Jaleb. He is supposed to come first and bring up the wood for the stove but he is always late. He runs up the path and forgets about the mud. When he gets inside he scratches his ears and yawns like a dog. Jaleb laughs at him.

They put me up to sit on the table while they get the stove alight. There is the pan of black ash to be taken out and then new wood and newspapers and the matchbox from the larder. They make a lot of noise, banging the pan and sweeping and then all the chatter and laughing. They give me sweet tea to drink from a tin mug, just like theirs. No-one else gets tea like that, not even Honey-ayah. And buttered toast with sugar. The kitchen is like home to them, part of their house.

Winifred says it's vulgar to put sugar on your toast.

THREE

In the early years at Chanting Hill, Teddy had kept wine on the racks in the old cellar, taking a torch down the rickety stairs behind the door in the lobby. When the cellar was converted into a rumpus room for the boys, there was nowhere to keep the wine but in a cupboard under the stairs. As a treat for his fortieth birthday, Susan commissioned the installation of a new wine 'cellar' in a small cupboard-room off the kitchen. The new cellar was lined with a special thermal material; there was a machine to control the temperature, and sufficient racks to store nearly two thousand bottles.

Teddy was enchanted with the idea. 'My sweet Susan,' he said, bundling her into his arms. 'You've done all this without my help?'

'It's for your birthday, I wanted it to be a surprise.'

The door to the new cellar led from the kitchen and matched the units so well that Crystal, home on an exeat, was completely deceived.

'We'll have to fill it up! It's a waste of electricity to keep it half empty.'

So far, the cellar held four hundred and thirty-nine bottles. A record book hung inside the door, bottles were logged in and out, and the temperature recorded as often as anyone re-membered.

Susan had paid for the cellar with a cheque drawn on her personal account at Blairs Bank. The cheque exceeded the balance in the account but her statement showed no overdraft. This happened no matter how much she spent. Teddy had an arrangement with Blairs. She kept a record of her transactions, checked them against her monthly statements, but it was only a game. The balance on her account never altered. There was a steady feed from another account. A drip, drip by automatic transfer, compensating for every withdrawal, so the balance never dropped below a thousand pounds. It was nice. It was like having a little pot of gold and if, sometimes, it made her feel unreal, as if she were treading air, then she regarded that as her failing and no fault of his generosity.

'But what would happen if you were really ill?' she asked, one rare day when he was home in bed with influenza.

'Doesn't this 'flu count as really ill?'

'No! I mean really ill, what if you had a stroke or something, and couldn't work?'

He hushed her question aside. 'That's no way to talk to a patient!'

'I'm serious, Teddy. Would there be any money if you weren't here? What would happen to me and the children?'

'There's more than enough, my love. The bank has full instructions.'

'But the money isn't endless, surely?'

'No, it isn't endless. But there is more than enough. You mustn't worry, Susan.'

She didn't raise the subject again. He was clever and successful. They had everything they wanted and if she wasn't quite happy then that was her failing. No-one could blame Teddy.

She washed her hands under the tap and rubbed in a dab of hand lotion. Her skin was drying out like the meringues, moisture slipping away into the air, leaving only a crust, stiff and fragile. It had happened to their marriage, imperceptibly; the soft, flexible affection of so many years had begun to dry out, become stiff and arid, shored up by possessions.

Warm sunshine streamed through the wide glass doors behind the kitchen table. She slid them open and stepped out on to the terrace. The aubretia was in flower, and along the wall of the kitchen garden new bright leaves were appearing on the bald threads of creeper. The iron gate stood open. Near the far wall the boy from the village was bent over the cabbages, hoeing.

'All right, Mrs Ransome?'

'Yes, thank you.'

'Those dwarf beans you planted are coming on a treat.'

Susan bent to pull a weed from between the flagstones. The stone felt warm to the touch, and as she straightened the greenhouses bounced the bright sunlight into her eyes. She noted that the boy had opened the ventilators. Inside on the slats, orderly rows of seedlings were poking through the compost, tiny and green and fragile.

'Mother!' Crystal's voice came from the stable, high and faint. 'Mother! Phone!'

Susan hurried back through the gate. 'Who is it?'

'David Bell.' A fragment of impatience carrying across the field behind the garden wall.

'Hold on, I'll take it in the kitchen.' She hurried up the terrace steps, feeling a varicose vein throb in her leg. The kitchen phone was on the wall, green, to match the units. She waited until she heard the click as Crystal put down the stable extension.

'David?'

'How are you, Susan?'

'Well, I'm fine.' She leaned against the kitchen table.

'I've got something you must see.'

'What is it?'

'Not something you've ever thought of, but I know you'll want it.'

'Won't you tell me what it is?'

'A cellaret.'

Susan paused. 'You mean a cruet?'

'No, nothing like that. A cellaret is a kind of wine cooler. They're not very common. Do come and have a look. It won't be in the shop very long, it needs some work and I've already had someone else make an offer.'

'You old trickster, David.'

'It's no trick. This one is unusual because it's still in original

27

condition. Most of them were converted into sewing boxes. There's a pretty steady market for examples as fine as this.'

'I'll see if I can come in before lunch.'

She went upstairs to change. The clock in the hall struck eleven. She put on a clean frock and was brushing her hair when Crystal appeared in the doorway. Her sweater was speckled with sawdust. She had walked straight up from the stable.

'Don't wear your boots in the house, darling.'

Crystal sat on the bed and lifted one leg in the air. 'Will you help me pull them off?'

'This is hardly the place for it.'

'I know, but I'm here now.'

The leg waved around over the bed. Susan grabbed hold and pulled at the boot, contriving to keep the dusty foot of it away from her dress.

'Are you going out?'

'I have to do some shopping.'

'And to see David Bell?' The scorn in Crystal's voice was faint but discernible.

'He has something in the shop that he thinks we would like.'

'More stuff? God, Mother, when are you going to decide the house is full? You could open an antique shop yourself.'

'I shall go to the supermarket as well. Will you get your own lunch?'

'What about the meringues?'

'Heavens! Thank you for reminding me. I'd forgotten them.'

Crystal ducked away from her hand. 'It doesn't take much to distract you. The very thought of another antique and you're off to town like a rocket.'

'Darling, that's not true. Look, I'll bring you back one of those good pizzas you like from the deli.'

Crystal picked up Susan's brush and ran it through her glossy, almost black hair. 'It's all right Ma, I'm a big girl now, I don't need to be bribed.'

The air inside the car was hot and stale. Susan opened the windows and drove to Winton Abbas with the sunroof tilted open, letting the breeze ruffle her newly-combed hair. She hoped Crystal would remember the meringues. They'd be no good if they were too brown. She planned to serve them as a rather superior pavlova, sandwiched with layers of cream flavoured with almond liqueur and a compote of raspberries. Teddy would select a suitable wine to go with the pavlova, another for the cheese. Nothing would go wrong. Their guests would be impressed. He would smile at her across the table and raise his glass. She would be doing what he wanted her to do, being what he wanted her to be: a good wife.

It was what she had always been. It was all that, implicitly, in the twenty-three years of their marriage, he had asked her to be. No more and no less than a good wife at home, raising their children, preparing meals, smiling at him. If this was not what she wanted – not all that she wanted – if, sometimes in the night, Susan longed for more, something that was not contained in all the things they owned, in the life they led, in their strange, truncated marriage, then she could not blame Teddy. She had never tried to be anything else, had played up, always, to the role he made for her: the little woman at home, who might be cheated but whom he would indulge, spoil, stay with, in the end. Crystal played up to him too, though she was not quite old enough to exploit him, to make something, in the way her mother did, out of his emptiness; the unfilled core of him that loved no-one, that thought of happiness in terms of belongings, possessions accrued, smart dinner parties, ancestors' goblets.

The streets of Liberté were strewn with flowers. Their sweet scent gusted on the warm, salt-pungent air. The islanders saluted as Hugo strolled through the marketplace in his white uniform. Women offered him their wares: mangoes and pawpaw, handfuls of chillies and bunches of green, pungent coriander. Beyond the town the hills piled up, green and lush, studded with granite rocks as black and smooth as the skin of the market traders. England, Chanting Hill, even the War, seemed suddenly distant, faded and dreary.

'This is our feast-day,' cried a woman as he passed her stall. 'Today everyone is happy.'

Hugo had not thought of what the holy day might mean to the island that carried its name. In the flurry of work and routine that accompanied the docking of his ship, he had not thought of it as a day when the islanders would celebrate: all the colours and religions, black and brown and white, Christianity and pagan creeds coming together in a welter of flowers and music and the sway of hot Costa bodies in the beer halls. A day when white islanders celebrated at the Central Hotel, their dancing a refined echo of the joyous carnival outside; the day the matrons of Pentecost brought out their daughters, to view, to be viewed; an array of colour, the more precise for the presence of the Allies, the officers, the white uniforms that spoke of money and England.

The public rooms of the Central Hotel were decorated with streamers and painted paper lanterns. A band played on the verandah. The night was warm and humid, cigarette smoke hung in the air. All Pentecost society was there: the planters and their wives, farmers from the hills, bankers, government officers, the *notaire* from the town, doctors from the hospital – and, from the Liberté Academy, clusters of girls laughing together, nervous and innocent. The naval officers stood at the bar, slightly apart, their uniforms crisp and clean. The band played dance numbers from Europe, fast and rowdy, causing the matrons to catch their breath.

Hugo sucked the ice from his glass and let it melt on his tongue. She had been there since he came into the room, her dress the dark green of the Pentecost hills, her hair richly black, hanging smooth and straight on to her shoulders. At home, in the garden of Chanting Hill, frail, white blooms peeked up through the grass every spring, their petals as smooth and clear as anything he had ever seen. Such was this girl's skin.

He ordered another gin and sipped it, watching her. The crowds swelled around him. Young officers crossed the floor en masse, asking for dances at random. Hugo hung back.

'Come on, Ransome!'

He shook his head. Already he felt separate, apart from the rest: his longing not the kind the others felt, the simple adventure of girls and moonlight and their own brave uniforms. The girl in the green dress had been approached twice; each time she refused to dance. He watched her light a cigarette, pouting her lips around the white tip. It irritated him. He wanted her to remain as she had been, beautiful and still. He bought another round of drinks and sent a waiter with a note and a glass of white wine.

'Will you be my wife?'

She kept the note folded, anxious eyes looking for its author, the wine left untouched. As he approached she put out the cigarette. The other girls stood aside. He clicked his heels and she smiled. He led her to the dance floor and as they danced she carried the note between her fingers.

She will, he decided, closing his hands over hers, resting his face in her hair. I will have this lovely girl and I will have her island. She will bear me fine-boned, healthy children, a new line of Ransomes, vigorous and strong.

'My name is Clara,' she said simply. 'Clara Baton.'

'Where do you live, Clara?'

'At Mahana, my father has a plantation.'

Another officer lent Hugo a car so that he could drive her home. They held hands in the dark. Her home was fifteen miles along a twisting coast road. She directed him through a pair of gates and he caught a glimpse of the sign, 'Baton Estate'. He stopped in the drive, a little way from the house and she let him kiss her lips and her neck before she ran inside, his note still safe in her hand.

Hugo sat on in the darkness. The Baton Estate was all around him, acres of trees in the moonlight; the silent planter's house quaint and beautiful. He planned a letter to Winifred. Chanting Hill was to be kept for his descendants, for the children that Clara would bear him. Winifred could look after things, see that the place was kept weather-proof and the furniture dusted. One day another Ransome might live at Chanting Hill, perhaps a son or grandson who could bring it to life. Hugo had no use for it. He wanted only the brightness and colour, the vivid present of Pentecost: Hugo wanted Clara Baton.

He was still there as the first grey light crept up over the sea. The dawn brought a new edge to his plan. Daylight showed him the flaws, the grass growing high between the trees, outbuildings

31

neglected, the plantation house itself peeling, faded.

He drove away as the first thin reed of smoke rose from the chimney. A Costa passed him, heading towards the house on foot. Hugo waved a greeting and the Costa grinned back, stopping to stare at the retreating car. Outside the gates a small boy stood by the side of the road, with a barrow of coconuts. He held one out as Hugo went by. Hugo waved and the boy began to chase after the car, slashing the top of the coconut with a knife as he ran. Hugo pulled up. A small black hand came through the window. Coconut milk dripped onto his tunic. Without inhibition or pause, the boy licked his fingers and rubbed at the stain.

'Where did the coconuts come from?'

The boy gestured with his thumb. 'Is a grove by the compound'.

You live in the Baton compound?'

'My father is Sahilil. He is a servant in the house. My name is William.'

'Do you want to be a servant?'

The boy grinned at Hugo. 'I shall be a carpenter.'

'Will you indeed?'

'There is no carpenter in Mahana. The man in the next village charges too much and does bad work.'

'And where will you learn your trade?'

'My father is saving the money.'

Hugo reached in his pocket and gave the boy a handful of rupees. 'Study well, William.'

The boy gurgled with pleasure. As Hugo put the car into gear the hand came back into the car, black and pink and sturdy. 'You forgot the coconut, master.'

Hugo ate it as he drove along, crunching on the white flesh, his whole being humming with joy.

A fresh coat of paint disguised the decay of the plantation house. Waiters were hired from the Central Hotel; Jaleb and Sahilil wore red robes with gold cummerbunds. Sweeping through the guests, directing trays of glasses and canapés, Jaleb was at ease, as if he had done this all his life, as if this entertainment was a commonplace at the Baton house and not the once-in-a-lifetime bank-loan event that it was. Louis Baton banking on his new son-in-law. A band played on the lawn. Clara danced with her husband. Hugo was light-footed, elegant, sweeping her round as if she weighed nothing.

'This is the beginning of everything, Clara.'

She laughed. In the corner of her eye, behind the fence, she could see the plantation workers, silent faces watching this white man's merriment.

'We shall always be happy if we love one another like this.'

Clara saw her bridesmaids watching. Envy and thirst in the other girls' eyes. Aileen had caught the bouquet outside the church; white lilies trapped on a hoop of bougainvillea.

'Oh Clara,' she cried. 'I'm not ready to be married yet!'

Clara's answer was lost in the congratulations and confetti and the matrons of Pentecost kissing her cheek. 'Neither am I.'

The *notaire* asked her to dance. His steps were slower than Hugo's, his face beaded with sweat.

'I am very happy for this day, ma petite.' His smile was round and simple. 'For so many years I have been advising your papa, so many times in the court – one creditor and then another. Each time he has come with a sadder face, less hope in his eyes. Each time he has said to me, what about Clara? What will become of Clara? And now,' he clicked his fingers, his short fat body light-footed for a moment. 'Now all the problem is solved. Clara is saved by a shining knight. Look!' He pointed at Hugo. 'Even his uniform is correct. A knight in white uniform!'

Clara smiled, felt her lower lip curling under her teeth.

'No more creditors,' said the *notaire*, beaming. 'This is a lucky day for Batons.'

The dancing went on all afternoon. Crates of empty bottles stood in towers behind the house. As it grew dark, Louis Baton took Hugo to one side.

'She's only a girl, you know.'

Hugo smiled. 'She'll be all right with me, Mr Baton. She's a Ransome now.'

They shook hands, Louis smiling benignly, his tongue thick with gin. 'Call me Louis, old chap. Family now.'

'Louis,' said Hugo.

33

'But d'you know what I mean?'

'Yes Louis, I do.'

And she's never known anything . . .'

'Good.' Hugo changed the subject. 'Something I want to talk to you about, Louis.'

'Anything. We can talk about anything now.'

'I'll be called back to Europe soon. Everyone knows that.'

Louis nodded, belching discreetly. 'I'll look after her. Don't you worry about Clara. She'll be safe with me.'

Hugo patted the hand that clutched him for support. 'When the war's over, I'm coming back here for good.'

Louis stared up, trying to focus on the suntanned, smiling face above his. 'Not taking her to England?'

'No. We shall live here in Pentecost. Clara belongs here, it is the place that gives her her beauty.'

'What, what . . .?' Louis tried to focus on the question he wanted to ask.

'I'll buy the estate.'

'No, no. You can't do that.' Louis belched behind his hands. 'There's bugger-all left. Bankrupt, you know. All but down the plug-hole.'

'I know,' said Hugo. 'But I can make it go again.'

'No.' Louis clutched Hugo's arm. 'You'll be wasting your money.'

'I don't think so. We've got plenty of time. I'll do some research. I'm sure all it wants is a little investment.'

'How much . . . what sort of . . .?'

'Oh, I'll pay you what it's worth, Louis. You'll find we Ransomes are very fair in our dealings.'

Louis beamed. 'I think we might have a little toast on that, don't you?' He shouted for Sahilil. The houseboy weaved through the crowd, his brown feet swift and at home on the evening grass. Behind him came Clara, a little paler now that the sun was down, the lower hem of her wedding dress pattered with dust.

Hugo took her hand and kissed it. There was gin on his breath. 'Louis and I have been having a little talk.'

Clara could see the sheen of sweat on her father's face. 'Papa, you haven't been – '

'I'm going to buy the estate,' said Hugo. 'When the war is over.'

Clara looked at her father. 'But Papa – '

'It's all right,' said Louis. 'Hugo knows the place is finished. He doesn't mind a bit.'

She felt the tears pricking behind her eyes. 'Don't shame me, Papa. Not on my wedding day.'

Hugo was gathering her from behind. 'There's no shame now, my darling. We are all for each other.'

He took her up to the house. She could feel the silk clinging under her dress. Her knickers were damp with sweat. Somehow they had lost her father. Most of the guests had gone. One of the hired waiters was collecting glasses on a tray. Inside the house Hugo put his arm about her waist and covered her lips with his.

'I love you, Clara.'

She tried to smile. He kissed her again, more forcefully, and put his tongue in her mouth. The tongue was wet and tasted sour. Involuntarily, she clenched her teeth.

Hugo let out a shout. 'Bitch!'

Her face stung. There was blood on his lip. He picked her up. The world turned upside down. Her head was near the floor. She could see his shining boots. Then a closing door. He dumped her in a chair, wiped his tongue on his handkerchief.

'I'm sorry, Hugo. I didn't mean to hurt you.' The spots of blood on the white handkerchief were very small.

'Take off your clothes.'

She remained where he had put her.

'Come on. This is what we're supposed to do.'

She wanted to ask about the tongue, but something in his face prevented her. First she took off her shoes. White leather pumps stained by the dew. Then she took off her knickers and the slip under her dress. This was how they did it at school, changing for the swimming class, leaving the dress until last as a kind of modesty tent.

But there was no bathing costume to reach for. Her underwear looked limp and rude on the arm of the chair. She had not looked at Hugo, had turned her back. He made a lot of noise; she heard his shoes hit the floor one by one, and the creak of the bed as he sat on it. She kept her back to him.

'Come on, the dress too.'

The bed creaked again. He was standing behind her. 'You can't make love in your wedding dress.'

His fingers pulled at the fastenings. When they were loose she helped him lift it away from her. Something urged her to say, 'I'm sorry, Hugo. My mother died when I was little. She didn't tell me about the wedding night.'

'Your mother wouldn't have known about this.'

She was naked, still with her back to him. A voice in her head said, What about your hair? She felt her hands creep down to cover it. He moved forward behind her, slowly his hands crept round and placed themselves over her breasts. It was oddly comforting. She felt herself nuzzle into his cupped palms. Behind her he groaned.

The floor creaked. There was a ticklish sensation of his tongue on the back of her neck. Then something pressing below, like a thick hard finger pressing into the crack where her bottom began.

'Ugh!'

She pulled away but he was too quick. Now his forearm pressed her breasts until they hurt. The thing was between her legs, jabbing at her. He pushed her onto the bed and pushed her face into the pillow. 'Shut up! Shut up! Do you want them all to come and watch?'

The thing forced its way inside her. 'Jesus, you're so wet,' he whispered.

Had her body betrayed her? His hands were lifting her from the bed. She thought he would split her open. Was this it? He was thundering against her, the bed shaking as if all the rocks of Pentecost were rising up from the sea. The pain was too sharp to bear. She cried out and heard him answer; through the thunder of the bed and his body and the knife-pain between her legs, he called out to her, 'I love you, Clara.'

Five weeks after the wedding Hugo was recalled to Europe. Clara joined the other wives and girlfriends on the dock, waving her handkerchief and dabbing her eyes. He had given her what seemed a very large sum of money. When the ship was outside the harbour she walked into Liberté and ordered a new red dress, and asked the cobbler to dye her dancing pumps to match.

Mr Hills has been instructed to roll the tennis court. Aunt Winifred has decreed that I shall have some friends.

Theodore, she said at breakfast, a boy of your age should be more sociable. If you are to become a successful lawyer you must learn to mix with the right sort of people, and you must find the right sort of girl to marry.

Why should I become a lawyer?

This question, like so many of my questions, is answered obliquely.

Why should you not be?

What if I want to be a farmer?

There's no land. You know that, Theodore. The Ransome farms were sold before the war.

I could buy another.

Winifred shrugs. The law is a fine profession, one very suited to gentlemen without independent means. It is up to you to make what you can of your life. You have had more than many boys – a good education – all the benefits.

She does not specify these benefits. She does not speak of the things I do not have. We do not hear of parents who love one another, mummies and daddies who sleep in the same bed, children who are loved, not despatched like unwanted parcels.

Winifred need have no fear. I'll make what I can of it. I shall be as rich as any Ransome ever was. There will be nothing I cannot have. I will go to law school and I will join the Winton Abbas Tennis Club and there will be Afternoons at Chanting Hill.

Mr Hills says no-one has played tennis at Chanting Hill since Mr Hugo played there. I asked Aunt Win, Was Hugo any good at tennis?

Oh yes, she said. My brother was good at everything. He was a natural athlete.

Perhaps I have inherited my tennis then?

It's like stopping a jolly little train. One minute she's full of zest, pink with enthusiasm for our new sport – the next she is grey again.

It was my mistake. Easy to make. I have inherited nothing. My name may be Ransome and I live at Chanting Hill but I am not a Ransome. Not the real thing. As Auntie Win said this afternoon, Not quite.

Not quite.

FOUR

There being no winter or spring, the temperature almost constant all year, it was the coming and going of the rain that marked the seasons of Pentecost. From March to November the island was dry, rainless, the sun burning out of a cloudless sky, scorching the earth, the lush colours turning brown and grey under a coating of dust. Clara resumed the life she had known before the wedding; knitting for the Red Cross, swimming parties at Governor's Bay, curd and syrup at supper time, dances at the Central Hotel, young soldiers with adoring eyes.

Hugo's letters arrived in batches, sometimes a month or two apart. Gradually she came to dread the sight of the manila envelopes, of his steady, sloping script. They were letters from another world, letters from a stranger, addressing a wife who did not exist, a neat, pliant woman, waiting meekly at home. ('Are you still smoking, Clara. Do stop it, won't you? Try to give it up by the time I come home. Smoking is such an unattractive habit in a woman . . .')

The sailor's uniform was crisp. He smelled of leather and polish, the hard leather of his belt, of his boots under their sheen of Mahana dust, light as pollen on the shiny black.

'Salford.'

'Is it a big place?'

Johnny laughed. 'You could say that. But we're so close to Manchester, we're getting swallowed up. You have to live there to know that you're in Salford – that it's not the same.'

There were freckles all over his face, and golden hair covered his arms. His nose was peeling from long afternoons on the cricket field. Hugo's nose had never peeled, thought Clara. Hugo could play cricket all afternoon and his nose wouldn't peel.

They sat on tall stools by the bar. 'What will you do, Johnny, now the war is over?' she asked.

'I'll be staying at sea I expect. This is my job.' He pronounced it 'me' job.

'*My* job.'

'What?'

'Sorry.'

He looked at her sternly. 'I'm English too, you know. More than you are.' Suddenly he grinned. '*Ah cum from theer. This is 'ow we talk.*'

She shook her head. 'Johnny, I like it.'

'What?'

'The way you speak, everything.'

His eyes were green as a cat's. Pale in the bright sun, searching her face. 'Do you? Do you really?'

'Yes.' She could feel her face turning pink. He had taken her hand. His felt coarse and damp. 'I like you, Clara. I like you a lot.' He paused, choosing his words. 'Will you come down to the river?'

'What do you mean?'

'I know a man who can hire us a boat.'

'I don't know.' She tried to free her hand but it was held tight. 'What if it rains?'

'The boat's got a cover – like an awning. We can pull it up and be as dry as anything.'

'I still couldn't, it's too far.'

'Haven't you got a friend? It would be all right if you brought a friend.'

He pulled her closer to him. She could smell his skin, strong soap and fresh sweat.

'I'll have to see.'

As if by mutual consent, neither mentioned her father. Or

Hugo. Aileen Barrett still wore a brace on her teeth. Clara had forgotten how ugly she was, and how lonely. It was easy to be her friend again, to persuade her to cover up – pretend they were together while she went alone to the river with Johnny.

'I like you, Clara,' said Johnny, more confidently this time. He had paid off the boatman and seemed to know where to go, rowing with swift confidence between the high walls of mangrove. The day was overcast; a canopy of dark, low cloud hung over the river. Just as he had promised, the boat had a canvas shelter, like a carriage roof that could be lifted at one end. She saw him look at it from time to time as he rowed, running his tongue between his upper lip and his teeth.

The place where they stopped had been visited before. A rope lay in the water, one end tied to a thick root that projected like a gnarled finger. A sodden cigarette packet was trapped in its curve.

She spread her skirt over her knees. There was a small puddle of water in the bottom of the boat. 'I hope this water won't spoil my shoes.'

Johnny moved across the boat to sit next to her. His face flushed, he seemed more out of breath now than when he was rowing.

'I'm glad you could come, Clara. I'm ever so glad.'

She looked around. There was nothing to see but the mangroves and the grey sky over their heads. 'I can't stay long. Aileen's mother is expecting me for tea.'

'It's only two o'clock.' He put his hand on her knee. She could feel the tremor of it. 'I'm going to kiss you, Clara.'

Warm air pulsed silently around them. He wiped the sweat off his lip and put his mouth over hers. She could taste salt and saliva, then his tongue, warm and bold, pushing between her lips.

'Please don't.'

'What's wrong? Don't you know French kissing?'

'No.' She wiped her mouth with her fingers. Her lips were wet with his saliva.

'I thought you knew a bit, Clara, you being married and all.'

'I still don't like it.'

'So what do you like? What does he do that you like?'

'That's none of your business.'

'Honest though, I won't tell anyone. What does he do in bed?'

Clara looked into Johnny's eyes. There was no scorn there, only curiosity. 'We are man and wife . . .'

'Go on.'

'Well, what do you expect?'

'Do you like it?'

Clara looked away.

'Go on, you don't like it, do you? He doesn't treat you right. It don't come as no surprise to me. I've always known it was all talk with those officers.'

'He's very generous to me.'

'That's nothing to do with it. I can see by the look on your face he's never made you feel nice. He's too stuffy with his own importance.'

'A residue of loyalty to Hugo made Clara open her mouth to protest. But the word was too right, too apt, especially as Johnny pronounced it. Too *stooffeh*.

'Aye,' she said, giggling. 'Hugo can be a bit stooffeh.'

Johnny lay back and lit two cigarettes. Without asking her, he put one between her lips. 'I think it's time you had a bit of fun.'

She sucked the smoke into her lungs. 'What do you mean?'

'Wouldn't you like to know how it's meant to be?'

'Johnny!' She felt a little outrage, and then a small feeling of dismay as she saw him throw the empty cigarette packet into the water. It was the same brand as the packet that was lodged in the root.

She tried to move away but he leaned forward, taking hold of her arms. 'I won't hurt you, Clara. I'm just going to show you how nice it can be.'

The boat rocked as he pulled her towards him. The small puddle of water wet the hem of her dress. He kissed her again, and this time his tongue felt less strange. His hand was on her breast. She could feel the sly wriggle of his fingers finding their way between buttons. His tongue pushed hard against hers. His breath was rapid, rattling a little, against the wetness in his nose.

*

42

Sometimes, during long afternoons at Chanting Hill, when the boys were at school and Teddy busy in London, Winifred would come up from the Lodge to sit with Susan in the drawing room. Never idle, her large, bony hands flitted like nimble pincers over a piece of embroidery. Their talk was of small things; the garden, Winifred's scorn for the new gardener.

'He doesn't trim the edges properly, Susan. Mr Hills would turn in his grave.'

They talked of the children, the boys' progress at Branksome, Lucian wanting to be a lawyer like his father.

'But they don't teach children properly these days. Even at Branksome – ' This was one of Winifred's familiar themes. 'When my brother was there the boys were under the rod. They learned quickly and knew what was required of them. Graham and Lucian seem to just drift. All this nonsense about wanting to smoke in their rooms and include girls in the sixth form. There was nothing like that in Hugo's day. They came home twice a term and wore coat-tails every day of the week. Even when Teddy was there, one felt confident that they would teach him properly, that he would come out a gentleman, with the right morals and the right manners.'

Sometimes, Susan would gently try to turn the subject to Teddy, to draw out a fragment of the other history, her husband's story, the little boy from Pentecost.

'Was it a big change for him, going to Branksome? Did he fit in with the other boys?'

Winifred rested her needle. 'Hardly. You know, the day I first took him there, with his trunk, I was ashamed. He was so unlike the other boys, with his sunburned face, his language littered with odd words, bits of patois that he could not distinguish from the King's English.'

'But he had been to school in Pentecost?'

'Only to the local mission in Mahana.'

'Could he read and write?'

'Yes, but that was all. My dear,' Winifred leaned forward to touch Susan's arm, to impress upon her the remembered outrage, 'his playmates in Pentecost were black! Children from the compound! He ran about with no shoes on, chattering away

43

in their pidgin English. It was too dreadful.'

'So you went out there to rescue him?'

'I didn't think I would.' The old lady held her stitches closer to the light. 'I didn't want to. I was nearly forty, I had my own life. I didn't want a child to care for – particularly not the by-blow of an unsuitable wife. When Hugo wrote to me I was appalled at the idea. And the way he asked! – no please about it, just would I take this child away so that he could get on with his life! And what a life – what a waste. He should never have gone back to Pentecost after the war. There was no need. He could have bought Clara off. Even her own people would have seen the sense of it.'

Winifred paused to dab her nose with a handkerchief. 'Do you know, while he was here, convalescing from that wound, Hugo and I had the bitterest arguments of our lives – just as though we were children in the nursery again, but worse, because this time he was not hurting me deliberately. He really could not help himself. When he came here with that terrible leg I thought I had a chance. I scoured the country for meat and fresh fruit. Mr Hills worked like a demon to make the garden bloom. I would have done almost anything to persuade him to forget this fantasy he had created, forget Pentecost, above all put aside the unsuitable marriage. But he wouldn't hear of it. "She's not some native girl," he insisted. "She's as English as we are."

'It was nonsense of course, but he believed it. I said that if she was so English he could bring her home to Chanting Hill.

'But that was his point; as much as he believed himself to be in love with Clara, he was in love with Pentecost. "You are so cold and bleak in England," he would say. "In Pentecost the sun shines every day. Imagine it, every day is warm. You struggle here with the garden but the place is dead for half of every year. In Pentecost the flowers bloom all the year round, the colours would take your breath away."

'There was nothing I could do. He went back there long before his leg was properly healed. In a way I think I had made it worse. I remember pointing out how seldom she wrote to him, how her letters read like something copied from a newspaper. He became obsessed with getting back. With proving me wrong.

44

We had always been so close, and now this girl had come between us. After so much quarrelling he didn't write to me often. I heard that he was spending a great deal of money on the plantation, that he was drawing heavily on his funds.

'Once or twice there were letters asking me to get something for him – a piece of equipment, or a textbook. Then I heard that they'd had a son. I heard it from a woman in Winton Abbas whose uncle had a Government post in Liberté. Hugo had said nothing about it, I thought my informant must be mistaken. And then out of the blue, six years later, I received a letter asking me to take Theodore away, to put the boy in to Branksome, to bring him up here, in England. I was more than a little surprised, I can tell you.'

'But you did,' said Susan. 'You did go and fetch Teddy? You did as your brother asked?'

Winifred leaned back against her chair. 'I said I would go and see. I meant just that. That I would go and see what the set-up was. I didn't mean that I would take the boy; only that I would go out and see what could be done for him.'

'What made you decide?' Susan pushed the question, too interested to take care of her words. 'Surely Clara didn't want him to go?'

'I know how it looks, now. After all these years, it's easy to judge.'

'I didn't mean – '

'It was what I found that made up my mind,' Winifred interrupted. She resumed her sewing, the needle moving smoothly through the cloth. 'The Baton estate was falling apart. I hadn't seen my brother for years and I barely recognised him. There was hardly a moment when he was sober. And Clara as bad. Clara did nothing at all. A throng was living off my brother in the compound; filthy black men, feeding on the produce of the kitchen garden, the chicken run, on meat that was ordered by the cook. No-one did any work. Hugo seemed to spend all his time at the Mahana Club and Clara, when she was not also in the Club, mixing with her empty-headed friends, was drunk in the drawing room.'

'And Teddy?'

45

'Your husband was in the care of a black woman.'

'The ayah? Honey?'

'Was that her name? Perhaps it was.'

'So you brought him to England?'

'Hugo had already booked the passage. He kept telling me it would be all right. The boy could go to Branksome; I would have no trouble with him. But it wasn't easy. Clara was hysterical.'

'Do you think Hugo was right? That it was the right thing to do?'

'Right to take the child away?' Winifred barked out the question. 'How could it be? I can't tell you the dismay I felt. Clara was not to blame. The girl was simply of a different class. She was beautiful but stupid. To take her child away was cruel; the child had done no harm. Hugo should have simply left them and come home – but of course he wouldn't. He would never admit he was wrong. Even when we were children he had this notion of honour, of standing by your actions, even if those actions were stupid.

'And by then there was money involved as well as his pride. He had spent so much on that plantation, he couldn't leave it. And I think he did believe that he could repair things. That they would start anew – that without Theodore there, as a constant reminder . . .' Her needle jabbed in and out. A butterfly was materialising on the cloth, part of a set of antimacassars for the small sitting room of the Lodge.

'I put Theodore into Branksome Prep,' she said, after a silence. 'I tried to do the right things. Above all I wanted him to be a gentleman, I didn't want the Ransome name disfigured.'

'Did Teddy . . . was he homesick?'

'Oh yes. We shared a cabin, you know, on the ship coming home. I could hear him crying in the night, under the pillow of course, but still audible, even against the noise of the engines.'

My father is very tall but he falls over if he doesn't have his stick. There is a bit missing out of his leg. Like a big bite. The hole is wrinkled and purple. Winifred says he is a hero.

Winifred is very old. Her hair is curled and yellow. She has a deep voice and big hands like a man. She loves my father more than anyone. There are pictures of him in her room and a big painting in the hall which she says is him but it isn't. The man in the picture is wearing funny clothes. His face is nearly the same as the other pictures in the house. They go round and round the walls like pictures in church. Winifred says they are all Ransomes. Winifred is very proud that she is a Ransome. I asked her if there would be a painting of me one day and she said, 'Not quite' and she made a face as if she was eating a lemon. I hate that face. She wore that face when we went to the ship. I thought she was angry with me and she was, but that was later when I ran away from the cabin. I took my satchel. The sandwiches had cheese and mango jam that Jaleb made for my birthday. People ran all over the ship, calling my name. The man who found me gave me a sweet.

Oh, Theodore, she said. Never do that again. I thought you had fallen overboard.

I was waiting for the sea to be blue, I said.

What do you mean, child?

The sea at home is blue and white. This sea is grey and dirty.

That's the weather, you silly boy. It's the same sea, it just looks grey because of the clouds.

When the sea is blue I will jump into the water and swim to Mama.

She is letting me sleep on the top bed. I have to climb a ladder and there is a board to stop me falling out. She sleeps in the bed underneath. She wears a white gown up to her neck and down to the floor. In the night I pretend she is Mama but her arms are too thin and stiff.

FIVE

A cable came to the plantation house. A boy on a bicycle, his face bright with sweat.

Orders from Hugo. Clara was to meet him at the dock in a hired car. DO NOT RELY ON LOUIS OLD FORD. LEG ALMOST HEALED BUT NEED SOME HELP.

Clara did as she was bidden. She didn't wonder why help would be needed, it was too hot to think of anything unpleasant. There had been one other cable – announcing his injury. She had crumpled the paper in her hand. Turned to her father, shouted at his waiting face, 'Why couldn't he be dead?'

An injured leg meant nothing; it would just be a nuisance. She would have preferred an arm in a sling, a plaster cast perhaps. Something visible but temporary, a hero's wound.

She asked the driver to wait in the car-park, and walked alone onto the quay. The ship was already there, ahead of schedule. The quay teemed with lorries and trucks; cranes swung their great arms, like blind crabs. A small group of people disembarked, carrying luggage and cardboard boxes tied with string. Porters surged forward to assist them. There was no sign of Hugo. Twice she made enquiries, feeling like a bothersome child as she entered the office near the depot where she could see a man in uniform through the open door. Twice she was reassured. Commander Ransome was on board. They would be bringing him down as soon as there were men free to help.

The stink of diesel from the lorries made her dizzy. She sat on a bench near the Customs shed and turned her face to the breeze.

Why did he want her to hire a car? Surely the old Ford would have done? There were only three cars for hire on the island and two of those were used by the Governor's staff. Perhaps Hugo had a lot of baggage – perhaps there were presents for her? She wondered if he would like her new hair-style. It was short. Johnny said it made her look older, more sophisticated.

Johnny.

One last time before his ship sailed, they went to the river. 'We've had a good time together, eh?' he said. 'No hard feelings.'

The sea in the harbour was choppy, churned up by the movement of tugs, the coming and going of small boats, military and civilian. She watched their movements, the sway and dip of the larger vessels alongside the quay. Her stomach churned as if she herself were at sea. She could feel a rim of sweat on her forehead.

Johnny had been a mistake.

A strange assemblage was moving towards her; a muddle of arms and legs, like a monstrous spider. She stared. The spider paused. She felt dizzy again and closed her eyes. The sun beat against her face, a red fire behind her eyelids. When she opened them the spider was moving, crystallising, as it drew close, into three men, two carrying a third, in what looked like a kind of sedan chair, across the uneven, crate-littered concrete. The men on either side of the chair smiled at her. Even with their burden, staggering at the awkwardness of a weight carried sideways, she saw that they looked twice, the familiar second look that lasted longer and took in legs and breasts and the curve of her hips. The chair was lowered to the ground. Clara stood back. He had grown a moustache, sunglasses hid his eyes. His helpers brought him to his feet. He leaned with both hands on a heavy walking stick.

She stepped forward, forcing a smile. 'Hello, Hugo.'
'Clara.'

He could not take his hands from the stick to embrace her. Awkwardly she put her arms about him. 'You've lost weight.'

49

'Just a little.' He turned his face to kiss her. 'I can't tell you how happy I am to see you.'

Her laugh was shrill. 'Well, it's taken a wound to bring you back to me!'

'This is nothing, I'll be fine as soon as we're together again.'

He could scarcely stand. Sweat stood out on his forehead. Despite his new leanness, he was too heavy for her arm. The men brought a wheelchair from the First Aid post.

'Here, sir. We can use this now. It's a clear enough stretch from here to the car.'

'I tried to spare you this,' said Hugo. 'I thought that if the chaps brought me this far, I'd be able to manage. I'm sorry.'

The wheelchair needed oil. In a clumsy, squeaking procession they moved towards the car. One of the men pushed the chair while Clara walked alongside. Hugo tried to keep hold of her hand but it was too awkward. When she pulled away he didn't resist.

The process of putting him in the car and then loading his trunk in the boot seemed to take hours. She stood to one side. The world had turned cloudy, her tongue felt huge. Her fingers scrabbled for the stick of cologne in her handbag.

'Clara, what is it?'

The ratings hovered about her.

'Why didn't you tell me?'

One of the men put his hand around her waist as he helped her into the car. Automatically she smiled. Inside the car, Hugo took her hand.

'I'm sorry you've had to hang about for so long. I shouldn't have asked you to come.'

'I'm not ill, Hugo. It was just the smell of the lorries.' She cleared her throat. 'When will your leg be better?'

'Oh, in time. It's just a bit slow to heal. To tell you the truth I've come back a bit sooner than the medics advised.'

'Why?'

'What d'you mean?'

'Why did you come back before it was mended?'

'Because of you. I couldn't bear to be away any longer.'

Clara could not look at him, at the thin pale face smiling

50

round at her.

He squeezed her hand. 'You are pleased, aren't you – that I'm home?'

'Yes,' she said. 'Yes, of course.'

His luggage included bottles of gin for her father. They drank a few toasts before supper and then the men carried on afterwards, out on the verandah. Her father was telling jokes, laughing at the end of each one, whether Hugo laughed or not. Clara sat a little apart. The moonless sky was alight with stars, bright enough to pattern the garden with shadows. Beyond the drive she could see the plantation, tall trees in a little sway-dance with the breeze.

The servants had cleared the supper table. Sahilil came out to bid them goodnight, bringing with him, as he always did, the old alarm clock from the kitchen. 'For the time, master, in the morning.'

It was one of the rituals of the house. The clock was brought in to be wound up, its time aligned with that of Louis' wrist-watch which was itself solemnly adjusted each evening by reference to the BBC World Service. Clara had no doubt at all that the alarm was superfluous. The routines of the house had been unchanged for decades. The compound would be awake before dawn with the alarm clock or without it.

Her father, making a joke of his drunkenness, peered down his nose at Sahilil. 'Morning might come a bit soon, better ask Miss Clara.'

Sahilil, without any change of expression, turned and held out the clock to Clara.

Her father raised his hand. 'Second thoughts, Sahilil old boy. Better give it to the new master. Commander Ransome owns us all now, you know. New regime. New broom. Better get sweeping!'

At this, inexplicably, her father and Hugo roared with laughter. Hugo, when he tried to set the clock, was too drunk to see his own watch. The servant looked up, meeting Clara's eyes. 'It's all right, Sahilil,' she said, 'I'm sure you'll wake in the morning as usual.'

'Seriously, though,' said Hugo, when the servant had left the room, 'I'm going to make a go of it.'

'No good, old chap.' Her father's speech was slurred. 'This plantation'll never make money. Wrong soil, ground too uneven, too close to the sea.'

'I'm going to have a try.'

'Thought you'd want to go back to England, now the war's over.'

'England's finished. All the heart's gone out. Nowhere to go but downhill.'

'Not sure Pentecost isn't finished too,' said Louis. 'The Costas think they're big men now, they want to have a say.'

'They'll settle down,' said Hugo.

'You'll need money, y'know. Nothing happens here without money being spent.'

'There's enough.'

'But if you've got it, why waste it'?' Louis held out the bottle waving it over Hugo's glass.

'It won't be wasted. I shall make back twice what I put in.'

When the time came for bed, Hugo was drunk and helpless. Clara had never undressed a man before. He howled as she dragged the trousers over his injured leg.

She lay beside him in the darkness, sweat slippery on her skin. Neither the gin nor the wound had quenched his lust but his strength was gone. He gave her something to hold, a dull soft thing, pulsing. She tasted bile in her mouth.

In the morning she looked once more at the pages of her diary, weeks and weeks without a mark. Babies could be born early.

In the years after Teddy joined the partnership, the firm of Harbour Lowe & Robbins grew and changed. Five partners became nine and then twelve. Small in the context of the big law firms that dominated the City, Harbour Lowe & Robbins developed a reputation as a 'niche' practice, known for its expertise in the burgeoning field of medical negligence. Acting for a clutch of insurance companies, household names defending claims against doctors for negligence in treating their patients had become profitable. As patients became more litigious the insurers' attitudes hardened; premiums rose, as did the amounts awarded to those who sued successfully. The role of the lawyers became more important and their fees rose accordingly. The firm continued its more traditional work, residential property, modest commercial work and general litigation, but medical negligence became the focus of the practice. Seven of the partners were specialists and these became the driving force behind the firm, dominating meetings, appearing on radio programmes and writing articles for journals and newspapers to reinforce the firm's image as leader in the field.

Increasingly, as this speciality eclipsed the other strengths of the firm, Harbour Lowe & Robbins ceased to be the natural home for the private client practice that Teddy had inherited from Arthur Wright. Teddy's speciality – acting for private individuals, dealing with the estates of the deceased, the affairs of the wealthy and ailing – became remote from the mainstream business of the partnership. Teddy's clients would have been better suited to a firm in one of the Inns, or the High Street of a provincial town. They stayed with Teddy because they liked him; his fees were sizeable but not outrageous. They trusted him and, despite its new prominence, the old City name of Harbour Lowe & Robbins retained a certain cachet among the clients who paid Teddy's fees.

Years later the question would be asked: Why was it only him? How did the situation develop where Teddy Ransome was the only person who dealt with private clients of the firm? The answers were numerous and vague, but had to do with money and glamour; the greater glamour of the medical negligence work: the faint scorn that attached itself to the old-fashioned business of wills and trusts, administering the estates of the deceased.

That Teddy attained and preserved his status as a partner was due to oversight and greed rather than any considered policy. The partners permitted Teddy's presence, the anachronism he represented, not because they particularly supported (or even understood, in any meaningful way) the field of law in which he specialised, but because the partnership had become a money machine. If Teddy's practice had been unprofitable they would have shed him as easily as a snake will slough off an old skin, but the bills Teddy rendered to his clients were respectable, sometimes impressive. The people who instructed him were rich, and they always paid. And when it came to sharing profits at the end of the year, Teddy was dignified. He would shrug in a careless way and accept a gentlemen's portion, slightly less than he put in, even after taking into account the cost in square feet of the 'Ransome Suite', as his small empire at the end of the corridor was called.

Teddy's partners liked him. He was generous when it mattered, gregarious, and unfailingly courteous; if none of them could claim to know him well, it was put down to the fact that everyone worked so hard, and his practice and theirs so seldom overlapped.

The offices that the partners laughingly called the 'Ransome Suite' had once been the sanctum of Arthur Wright. Teddy took it over when Arthur retired, a suite sectioned out of what had once been a boardroom in the anonymous building of which the firm occupied the fifth floor, overlooking St Paul's. The main door bore only a small label, matching those of others on the corridor, but it led, not to an ordinary office, but to an inner reception area where Phyllis Maitland had her desk. Phyllis was utterly unlike the secretaries who worked in the rest of the firm. With her steel-grey hair, her bouclé suits and careful, short nails, Phyllis presented no distractions; she was loyal and discreet. She was, Teddy recognised, a kind of office Winifred, someone on whom he could always rely, who loved him in spite of herself, who offered him a safety net. The bonus of Phyllis, as compared with the real Winifred, was that he felt no guilt; for Phyllis there was no need to be grateful.

Her desk stood squarely in front of Teddy's door. Her telephone intercepted his calls and her presence intercepted visitors. This arrangement suited them both. Her loyalty went without question and her age, her steel-rimmed spectacles and steel-grey hair, secured him from the unwanted and the unwelcome.

To the right of Phyllis's desk, another door opened on a pair of small offices divided by a glazed partition. One of the pair was furnished entirely with filing cabinets, ranks of steel that contained all Teddy's files, neatly labelled and locked, and a large metal safe the size of a wardrobe.

The second office contained a desk, a word processor linked to the firm's computer network, and a small library of books dedicated to the fields in which Teddy operated: Inheritance Tax, Probate, Trusts and Powers of Attorney. Teddy made no use of the firm's main law library, which lined the walls of the reception area; his own collection contained all the books he needed. Phyllis kept the loose-leafs up to date, barred the door to the young secretary whose job it was to monitor the firm's books – there was no other call on Teddy's books; no-one else in the firm was interested in Teddy's subjects.

A series of young trainees had occupied this second room, taking their turn in the private client 'seat' as part of their training contract. Recently there had been questions at Partners' Meetings. The trainees who sat in Teddy's glass office had complained of lack of contact; there was plenty of reading, scouring Inland Revenue Extra-Statutory Concessions, plenty of use of the word processor, drawing on the precedent wills and settlements, or chasing external sources for stock-market reports, but very little training in the law, very little 'hands-on' experience. None of Teddy's trainees ever met a client, and any letter they might draft on Teddy's behalf was altered and corrected, not by Teddy himself, but by Phyllis. The trainees complained that her attitude was dismissive, unhelpful, that if they were not to be trained by the practitioner himself then they should not be sent to sit in the Ransome Suite.

In another firm, perhaps one not so entirely devoted to its specialist field, and to maximising its reputation and profit, such complaints might have caused an enquiry; a partner might have asked why it was that no-one but Teddy ever saw his files, why the trainees who served their time in the Ransome Suite received so little guidance. The Partners' Meetings had lengthy agendas; Teddy was always there in person, smiling, courteous, self-deprecating. The partners had no cause to quarrel with his figures. He regularly exceeded his billing target. His punctual, highly legible time-sheets invariably recorded more chargeable hours than the firm's budget required.

The solution to the trainees' complaints was a simple one. At the suggestion of another partner, and with Teddy's smiling assent, it was agreed that no more trainees would be sent to the Ransome Suite; that a private client 'seat' would no longer be offered. Gradually the empty glass office became like its neighbour, filled with locked filing cabinets. Nothing was sent to the archive. Each year when the auditors came round, carrying out random checks, Phyllis was ready for them; she took pride in the pristine folders of papers and correspondence, with colour-coded labels to indicate the contents. The absence of the trainees made Phyllis more comfortable. She could serve Mr Ransome exclusively; keep his office in the same immaculate condition as she kept her home, her clothes and her iron-grey curls. The office was the centre of her life. Keeping Mr Ransome's papers in order, his telephone answered and his diary regulated, satisfied her spirit. She congratulated herself that she could type without error, and knew the index number of every file. It wasn't necessary to understand the contents, Mr Ransome never asked her to take responsibility of that kind. All he needed was for her to look after him, to be charming to his clients and discreet to his wife. Phyllis was content.

To the south of Mahana the road petered out into a maze of alleyways drained by soft-sided mud gullies that smelled of sour water and rubbish. Here the poorer Costas lived; the servants of the town, beach sweepers, refuse collectors, their hovels built of what the town discarded. And here too, where the land was too poor to cultivate, the soil too thin over the granite crust, stood the Mahana Clinic, a long, low structure of wood and thatch shaded by a pair of leaning jacaranda trees. A wire fence and a carpet of browned blossom marked the boundary. Urchins, playing in the storm drains, stopped to stare at Clara. She was a rare sight: a white woman alone, on foot. These days the planters preferred the hospital in Liberté, or private physicians who would come to their homes.

The attendant blinked.

'I'm sorry, I didn't make an appointment.'

She was left to stand in the doorway; a glimpse of the surgery, the doctor looking out at her. There was a movement behind, the queue shuffling back as a Costa was turned out to wait. Clara barely noticed what had happened. It was part of the world she took for granted: Costas were servants and labourers; they would sit in the back pews in the church, stand in a separate queue at the post office, wait without question for a white woman to have her consultation.

The doctor wore a priest's collar under his tunic. His accent was Irish. He talked while he examined her, as if her body were another's. 'You needn't have come down here, you know. One of my colleagues has been treating Commander Ransome's leg – he could have seen you at his next visit.'

'I didn't want him to know – until it was sure . . .' Clara stumbled.

'A terrible thing, that injury to the Commander's leg. Terrible to see a good man mutilated like that.'

'Yes,' Clara repeated, gazing at the ceiling as the doctor's hands pried, cool and sure.

'But I think you have some good news for him.' The doctor smiled.

'When will it be?'

The priest-doctor smiled. 'About twenty-six weeks.'

'No more than that?'

Again he laughed, 'It'll be long enough by the time it comes!'

'You won't tell him, will you?'

'Why no, dear. It's for you to tell. And a great joy it will be.' He gave her a typed sheet. 'You must make an appointment at the hospital. It's important that you go regularly.'

He shepherded her to the door. 'Have you no car with you?'

'It isn't far.'

'Even so!' The shock in his voice carried a question. She felt his eyes searching her face, and would not look at him.

'Even so,' he said again, more gently.

She opened her bag. 'How much do I owe you?'

'I could send you an account.'

'No. I'd rather pay you now.'

The attendant was sent to fetch her change. The doctor

57

touched her shoulder. 'You go carefully now, Mrs Ransome.'

Bare-headed, her hat dangling forgotten in her hand, she walked back through Mahana and took the short-cut across the plantation. Crickets chirruped in the grass on the side of the path. There was no wind at all. The trees drooped tall and silent. Ahead of her on the path she could see Hugo and her father nearing the house. It was the end of their patrol, the end of the long slow circuit of the estate that was made every morning, her father moving as slowly as Hugo: an old man and a cripple surveying the acres of neglect.

Jaleb was preparing lunch. From the back of the house came the smell of roasting chicken and potatoes. Clara went in through the kitchen and straight to the bedroom to change her shoes before going out to the verandah. Hugo's drink was already poured. He sat slumped in an armchair, his bad leg stretched out on a stool.

He lifted a hand in greeting. 'Hello my darling. Bloody hot, eh?'

'Isn't it,' said Clara.

'Will you have a drink with me?'

Through the doors she could see her father by the sideboard, downing a short one alone before pouring another to mix with tonic. She went and took hold of his hand.

'What is it?'

She gestured for him to be quiet and pulled him away from the windows. He brought his drink with him.

'Papa, I want you to listen to me.' She led him towards the corridor.

From his chair on the verandah, Hugo heard the door bang. The sound stirred the parrots. The cages swung gently as the birds scampered about inside, squawking and tutting. After a moment one of them shouted 'Sahilil!' and the other took it up, imitating Louis' voice. 'Sahilil! Sahilil!'

The servant appeared, a brief shadow from behind the shutters tapping the cage with a broom handle. 'Hush now!' 'Hush now!' the parrots shouted. 'Sahilil! Hush now!' Sahilil went back to the kitchen.

Moments passed. Hugo drained his glass and slipped the last

sliver of ice under his tongue. He was turning to call for the servant, half raised from his chair, when Clara reappeared, pulling her father behind her.

'Clara, my darling, what is it? You look as white as a sheet.'

The parrots began to call again. Neither Clara nor Louis would look at him. Hugo felt himself subsiding back into the chair, placing the glass carefully on the table.

'Sahilil!' screamed the parrots. 'Sahilil!'

She spoke slowly. The screaming of the parrots accompanied her words; their noise, whooping around the verandah, disguised what she said so that it was as much her face, alternately fearful and defiant, as her incomplete sentences that gave him what she had to say, the impossible truth filling the air.

'Will somebody silence those parrots?' cried Louis.

Hugo was shouting too. 'What are you saying?'

She clutched her hand to her chest, as if to hold in her breath. He caught the last of her sentence. '. . . it can't be yours.'

The parrots shrieked with laughter. 'Sahilil! Sahilil! Shut up!' Louis cried. He was making for the cages, stumbling a little with the effort. Then the servant appeared, running. 'Is finished now. I will stop them now.'

And it was over. The cages swinging under drapes of green velvet, the flap of the servant's feet retreating, a sudden squall of silence.

It was Louis who answered. 'The man was a cad, Hugo.' Clara stood silent, holding the back of a chair. 'I thought it was a boating party – lots of young people, blameless.' Louis sucked on his pipe. 'This man took advantage – Clara is so young.'

Hugo started to rise, his stick clattered on the hollow verandah floor. 'Then you should have kept her at home! Why did you think I wanted her to stay with you, you old fool, but precisely because she is young? Because I would be so far away. And – ' He lurched towards them, unsteady without the stick. 'And because she is so lovely!'

Louis rose hurriedly. 'You need a bit of a refill, old man. Where's that boy got to?' He grabbed Hugo's empty glass and made towards the kitchen.

Hugo stared at Clara. 'How could you have done such a thing?

After all your promises? When I have given up so much for you.'

Clara said nothing. She could think of nothing to say. She played with the fastening of her bracelet, clicking the loop in and out of the catch.

'I wouldn't have let her go boating if I'd known,' said her father, returning with Sahilil bearing fresh glasses on a tray. 'She's only just told me herself. I thought they were always in a group. I'd no idea this Fairweather – '

'Fairweather?'

'That was his name. Apposite, isn't it?' The old man sighed. 'I am sorry, Hugo. I'm as sorry as I could be.'

Clara played with the bracelet, clicking the catch again.

'And you Clara, are you sorry?' demanded Hugo.

For a moment she hesitated. She could cut through all this, if she chose, she could puncture this great balloon of indignation that hovered between them. She could answer with the truth. No, I am not sorry. I wanted to know how it should be.

But her father turned his face, imploring her. Behind him, beyond the verandah, she could see the edge of the plantation, the long, tangled grass, the ailing trees drooping in the dust.

'Yes,' she said, 'I am truly sorry. I will do everything I can to make it up to you. I really will try, Hugo. No-one else knows. Babies often come early. We can make it our child, just as if it were really – '

'No!' Rage made Hugo stand again. 'Never.' He leaned down, scrabbling for his stick. 'It will never be my child.'

'But my dear chap . . .' Bravely her father interposed. 'It's not impossible . . .'

Hugo shook his head. For a moment she thought the truth was coming; that there could not be a child, that since he came back there had been nothing to make a child with, nothing but the soft thing like jelly in a muslin bag, that night after night she was given to hold, to pump uselessly for life.

Hugo had his stick once more. He stood erect, head up. 'The Ransomes are not cowards. We do not run from our errors.'

Clara let out her breath. 'Hugo, I promise . . .'

'You can promise me nothing! Your promises are worth no more than a whore's. It is I who will make promises. It is I who must live with this.'

He turned and hobbled from the room. She called after him. 'Hugo, you must tell me. What are you going to do?'

He didn't pause. His answer came back from the passageway, distorted by the enclosed space. 'I am going to think. Tomorrow I will give you my answer. My conditions.'

'Phyllis, would you come in?'

Teddy's voice squawked on the intercom. Phyllis picked up her notebook and went in to his office.

'Do sit down.'

He had several files open on his desk. By reading upside-down, Phyllis could see that the one on which he was working was the Willard investment file. She clicked the top of her propelling pencil, straightened her skirt and was ready to take dictation.

'A letter to Jamie Clarkson, please.'

There was no need for details. Phyllis knew that Jamie Clarkson was the stockbroker who looked after the Willard portfolio. Phyllis wrote automatically, her pencil drawing swift, precise hieroglyphics. It was one of her conceits, that she could write immaculate shorthand, as well as cope with the dictaphone. Dictaphones were considered more stylish. Phyllis suspected that Teddy used his for show as much as conveni-ence. She had seen him picking up the microphone just as someone came into the room, observed an endearing flamboy-ance in the way he clicked the recorder off and on while his visitor waited to speak.

Phyllis preferred to take shorthand. There was contact in it, a certain intimacy in sitting together, pausing while he thought for words, helping him sometimes to rephrase a sentence, to make the meaning flow. This time there was no hesitation.

'We have been considering the Willard portfolio in the light of their new circumstances,' dictated Teddy. Phyllis knew what these circumstances were, just as the stockbroker did: that the Willards were both too old to manage their affairs, would soon be selling their house in Oxfordshire to move to a serviced apartment more suited to their needs.

'We're going to need liquidity. And there will be certain expenses related to the move.' Her pencil flew over the page of her notebook.

'I enclose two certified copies of their Powers of Attorney and on their behalf, I should be grateful if you would arrange the sale of one half of all the stocks and shares. I shall ask my secretary to send you the certificates and I shall be glad if you will remit the proceeds to me.'

As Phyllis went back to her desk, Teddy rose and wandered over to the window. His office overlooked the bleak emptiness of Paternoster Square. He watched a cluster of office girls make their way across, the wind whipping their skirts.

I'm doing this for Crystal, he thought. It's just a loan. Crystal taps a store of love in me that I did not know I had. She is beautiful and clever. I can deny her nothing, let nothing spoil her chance. Graham and Lucian too, of course, but they are boys and will win through. Crystal is like her name, a clear bell as hard and fragile and beautiful as glass.

The Willards have more than they need. They hardly know how much. 'Just look after it, will you,' the old boy said. 'We're too old to be worrying about all that.'

A loan from a client is more elegant than a loan from the bank. A man in my position cannot tell his bank manager that he has no collateral. I cannot tell Cyril Towers that I do not own Chanting Hill; that I am just a bastard really, and all this grand living is a sham.

The Willards will make us a loan. There's no need to worry them with the details. I can clear the overdraft and put something towards the decorator's fees. Susan wants to revive the kitchen garden. It hasn't been touched for decades. There are walls to be rebuilt, greenhouses to be restored and paths to be relaid. There is much talk of fresh vegetables and a second big freezer for storage. We'll need a full-time man just to dig and weed. And more dinner parties to eat it all.

The Willards will make us a loan. It will be an investment.

Phyllis typed the letter and signed it on Teddy's behalf. She did this often, considered it part of her duties as a secretary to ensure that the mail was dispatched even if Teddy had to leave the office before she did.

She extracted the Willards' share certificates and the original Powers of Attorney from the safe in the adjoining office; these would have to be copied and then certified by another partner. It was a nuisance, this business of certification. She was obliged to knock on doors along the corridor, searching for a partner who was neither out nor on the telephone. Eventually she found one of the older partners, Harry Rich, in his office.

'And what have we here?'

'These are copies of two Powers of Attorney. I need to have them certified for the brokers.'

'I see,' said Harry Rich as he scribbled his signature below the stamped certification.

'They're selling their house in Oxfordshire,' Phyllis volunteered.

'And what are they going to buy?'

'One of these new apartments for the elderly – with someone to call if anything goes wrong.'

'Sounds jolly sensible,' Rich smiled.

'Teddy's hoping they'll sell the Oxfordshire house soon, so that he can re-invest the money for them.'

'And they've given him sole power to act for them?'

'Yes, that's what they wanted.'

Rich smiled again. 'I'm sure Teddy will look after them.'

Phyllis gathered the copies and went back to her room. Teddy had already gone, he was due to attend a reception in the City. There was a tang of aftershave in the air.

Phyllis filed the carbon copies, and locked the share register in the safe cabinet. The letter to Jamie Clarkson caught the last collection of post.

SIX

Clara dreamed. The sultry air under the mosquito net found its way into her sleep; Johnny Fairweather with a stain on his khaki shirt, blood puddling above the polished leather holster at his belt. Hugo carrying not his stick but a sword.

She sat up. The baby had begun to cry, a small, murmurous sound that asked for comfort as much as food. If only Honey would sleep in the house and not scuttle back to her shack in the compound every night. Honey knew what to do when he cried like this. Clara's nightdress clung, damp and creased, to her skin. Silently she left the bedroom and switched on a table light in the nursery. Teddy's cry built into a squall, his small body flailing, hot and angry below the double drape of mosquito net. With soft hushing noises she gathered him up and went out to the verandah. There was no relief from the heat. Warm, moist blackness swam in from the garden. The compound was in darkness. There were no lights, no sign of life but the huge noise of the night, of frogs and cicadas and the sharp clicking of tree squirrels. From the child in her arms came a sour smell of milk and prickly heat powder and the grease that Honey Jellawella smeared on his buttocks.

Clara wanted a drink. A cup of tea that would moisten the dry mouth of too many gins and tonic in the Mahana Club. They had spent the evening as they spent every evening: dinner in silence, Hugo scowling as he chewed, Sahilil creeping about, bowed and apologetic. They ate none of the customary food of the house.

64

Their diet was English: roast meats, lamb chops, jars of imported mint sauce. No planter food was permitted – no rice and curry, no platters of fish marinated in oil and herbs. The only concession Hugo would make was in the puddings. He ate none – 'Sugar is a woman's food' – and thus she was permitted to choose, to eat the bowls of buffalo curd and palm syrup that had been her favourite as a child.

After dinner, drawn by the promise of light and noise, they went to the Club. There they were free, there was no need to pretend. They could separate as soon as they arrived, Clara to the Lounge where she would find her friends, Hugo to the Men's Bar.

The women who drank with Clara in the Lounge Bar wore bright lipstick and tight skirts and gathered her in with their laughter. The talk was of scandals and servants and how the Costas would ruin the land when Independence came. Clara said less and drank more than the others, basking in their common discontent, measuring her own disappointment with theirs.

Hugo's evenings were less convivial. She heard that he commandeered a certain chair, a table in the corner, and drank alone, turning the pages of a book or a newspaper, tapping his pen over a crossword clue.

Late, as late as they could, they returned home, Hugo driving very fast. Through a haze of alcohol she watched the car lights swing and sweep over the road, catching the turns of the trees as they turned onto the estate.

During the day Hugo sat in his study. He was studying cultivation, estate management, accounts procedures. There was something frantic and childish in the way he worked. As if he could become an expert overnight; as if in the space of a year or two he could learn what her father had learned in a lifetime, and knew better, and that had still, in the end, not been enough to keep the plantation in profit.

Clara did not, could not, care. For as long as she could remember the plantation had been dying; each year a little more diseased, each year a little more unkempt, blown trees obstructing the aisles. Hugo had achieved a certain order. The new tractor clattered busily up and down. The labourers sweated while he watched but otherwise sat in the shade as they had always done. Clara didn't care if the crop would come. She didn't care if there would be something or nothing to show for all Hugo's efforts, all the money he had spent. It meant nothing to her. There was nothing they shared that mattered. All there was, the only thing that did matter, the centre of her life, was the child in her arms. The child of the 'Agreement' to which she had signed her name before he was born, when he was no more than a swelling, making her hot and sick in the notary's office.

The *notaire* was the same one who had advised her father in dealing with his creditors, who had danced with her on her wedding day, and called it a lucky day for Baton. He rose as they entered, shook Hugo's hand and bowed to her slightly, as slightly as politeness would allow. A clerk was summoned to show her to a separate room.

'So that you may study the document in peace.'

There was a chair and a desk, a fan stirring the humid air. Almost overnight her stomach had grown huge; she felt ungainly and helpless. The clerk brought her tea and a single sheet of thick paper to read.

'The child will bear the name Ransome. I will pay the cost of the confinement, of education and maintenance . . .'

The window looked over Central Square. Clara could see the market stalls in the centre and the grand white portals of the Central Hotel on the other side. It was market day, the pavements thronged with Costas rattling pockets of change. A chicken broke loose, running through the crowd, creating a pantomime of chaos and laughter. Its owner, when she caught it, deftly broke the chicken's neck.

The clerk came back. A Costa in a suit, one of the new breed, literate and smart. 'If you are ready, Mrs Ransome.' He showed her back into the *notaire*'s room. The air was blue with the smoke of cigars. She was handed a pen.

'Is everything clear, Mrs Ransome? Do you understand the terms of this agreement?'

Hugo's signature was neat and straight, like a teacher's

example against her unsteady, childish scrawl. The clerk stayed to witness the signing. Clara looked up into his face. 'Have you read it?' she wanted to ask. 'Do you know what it means?'

The clerk's eyes caught hers for a moment. His were full of sadness.

In the car Hugo said, 'You've done the right thing, Clara.' She said nothing. After the signing, when everyone had relaxed and the lawyer was speaking to Hugo of other things, she had tried to read the rest of the Agreement. Its language was pompous, thick with words that she had never used, for which the Liberté Academy for Young Ladies had not equipped her.

'The child, who being not of my blood but bearing my name to save the honour of my wife the child's mother, shall be maintained and educated in the parish of Mahana until he is of an age to be dispatched to England in the care of such person or persons as I shall in my absolute discretion think fit and at my expense until his education is complete whereupon all his claim or call upon me shall cease and in consideration whereof the said mother CLARA RANSOME nee Baton AGREES AND CONSENTS irrevocably and without reservation to surrender the child as hereinbefore described and not to follow the child to England but to remain with me her lawful husband for the rest of her natural life . . .'

Her copy of the Agreement lay folded in her drawer, like a secret letter, a love letter, like something warm and full and not the thing it was, a pact of hatred, a pitiless revenge for a wrong unintended, unplanned, without malice, even without pleasure.

How could I have signed it? How could I? What will happen when the day comes? Silently, at night, she asked herself the questions over and over. The answer was a mountain too high to climb, without a pass or route of relief. I signed, I agreed!

She remembered her father's face. His entreaty. 'You must do as he says, Clara. You will not get another husband. A divorce and a bastard child will be the end of you.'

'But I can't.'

'What is it that you can't?'

'I can't barter like this.'

'Think of the child. What chance will it have here with you on your own? Hugo is prepared to send it to school in England, to keep you, in spite of it. He has rescued the plantation. You ask too much that he should raise a bastard in his own house.'

Quiet at last, Teddy lay slumped over Clara's shoulder. She walked into the kitchen. The stove was cold. She had no idea how to light it. A basket of logs, fuel for the morning, lay beside the door. Three small lizards watched her from the wall. The bald gleam of an electric light (one of Hugo's innovations, light at the press of a switch) presided over her looking into the cupboards, searching for the tea caddy.

'Perhaps he will relent,' she said aloud. 'There is time yet. Perhaps when Teddy starts to talk.'

The lizards gazed at her, unblinking.

'Sometimes there are signs, sometimes he gives himself away.'

The lizards' tongues flicked.

She poured from a jug of milk into a glass. As if he could smell it, the child on her shoulder stirred. The milk was lukewarm, already slightly sour.

She put down the glass and shifted Teddy's weight on her hip. His eyes were open, as dark as the night sky, staring at her, and there seemed to be words for her there, in his stare. Wounded, accusing words: You could love me better.

Johnny Fairweather's words. You could be nice to me, Clara. If you really liked me, you would show me.

The light dimmed. Insects seethed and clicked against the bare bulb. In the morning they would be dead, killed by the light that had brought them to it.

'It is the same for me,' she said aloud. 'I was drawn to Johnny Fairweather as you are drawn to this bare bulb. It is nothing, it promises nothing, but it is here, it is light in a dark world.'

Wings flicked round her face. Teddy's eyes closed. He seemed at last to be sleeping. Clara made her way back through the dark house. From the bedroom she could hear Hugo's snore, long satisfied roars.

*

'You can have anything you want,' said Teddy.

The oysters were on a separate slip attached to the menu, the price written neatly in one corner.

'Oysters?'

'Why not?'

'It's a bit corny, isn't it? I mean . . .'

Teddy lifted an eyebrow. 'Well, then.' He smiled – a contented smile, as if he was relaxed, but his eyes were alert, watchful.

'Don't look at me like that,' she said, and straight away felt a fool, gauche.

'How would you like me to look at you?'

She shifted in her chair, sitting upright.

'Are you uncomfortable? Would you prefer me to sit next to you?'

'No!'

The look in his eyes softened his laughter.

There was a packet of breadsticks on the table. She tore it open and offered him one. He said no but when she started eating one he leaned forward and nibbled the end of it.

'Is your name really Theodore?'

'Teddy, for short.'

'That's more likely.'

'More likely?'

'Not so pompous.' She took another swallow of wine. 'You could be a bit of a cuddly teddy.'

She saw that a dozen responses hovered on his tongue but all he said was, 'And does your name suit you?'

'I don't know. It's a bit of a silly name, people tend to suppose there's nothing in my head.'

He squeezed her hand. 'I promise I'll discover exactly what is in your head, I'll find out everything you want me to know about you.'

The oysters arrived in a single bowl. With much ceremony he selected the largest and leaned across the table to slip the contents into her mouth. She swallowed, tasting little but seawater and a hint of metal, like licking the pipes of a radiator.

'Will you do the same for me?'

69

Her fingers shook as she lifted the shell and, so close to his mouth that her little finger touched his lips, scooped the oyster gently onto his waiting tongue.

It was impossible to be dainty. Their fingers collided in the bowl. When the oysters were finished he dabbed her face with his napkin. 'You have a smear on your chin, Annabelle. It's most becoming, but I fear I shall become too distracted to eat.'

She paused. Suddenly she wanted to say that he was making a mistake. At nearly thirty years old she was no bimbo. It was just the champagne that had made her giddy. Dimly she tried to calculate how much she had drunk at the reception before he had somehow lured her into his car and this exclusive, expensive restaurant.

'Why so serious all of a sudden?' Teddy asked.

Because the real Annabelle is a serious person.

The real Annabelle wants more than a quick fling with a married man.

'Well?' His face was very close, smiling, his eyes holding hers.

'I was thinking of you driving,' she lied. 'You must be over the limit.'

'I'm an astonishingly good driver.'

'Yes, but if you're caught you'll lose your licence.'

His eyes narrowed. 'I won't be caught.'

She looked at her watch. It was later than she thought. The Tube wouldn't run for much longer.

His hand came across and covered the face of her watch. 'Stop worrying about the time. I'll get you home, safe and sound.'

'But how will you get home – how far do you have to go?'

He smiled. 'My home is in Wiltshire. I don't go back during the week. I have a room in my club.'

Another course arrived. Pasta with a simple pesto sauce. When she had finished Teddy reached across and mopped the oil from her plate with a hunk of bread. He ate with an air of concentration, as if the food were important. It could have been interpreted as greed but his expression held something else, something akin to hunger, despite all that he had already eaten.

She stole another glance at her watch. Almost a quarter to one. What am I doing?

He ordered coffee for them both and the waiter brought the bill. As he completed the credit slip she studied his face. Forty-something, she decided, slivers of grey at the temples. His colouring was slightly Mediterranean, sallow skin and the darkness of his beard showing in the shadow along his jaw. His features were too irregular to be handsome, but his eyes, unexpectedly blue, caught her attention – had made her look back when he had spoken her name across the noise of people and glasses earlier in the evening.

'What do you do, Annabelle, for this august City institution?'

'I'm very lowly,' she had answered, gesturing at the throng of brokers who were the hosts of the evening. 'I work in the back office.'

'I don't know about lowly,' Teddy had said. 'You're certainly lovely.'

She had nearly walked away, scorned such a crass overture, but his smile mocked his words; a complicated smile that acknowledged the crassness but at the same time confirmed the message.

She woke the next morning with a throbbing head, the residue of too much wine lingering in the sour taste on her tongue. Unable to face getting dressed she swallowed some aspirin and telephoned the office. Her boss was in a meeting and she had to leave a message with the receptionist. 'I'm afraid I won't be coming in today. I'm not well.'

The receptionist's voice carried a sneer. 'Shall I tell them to expect you tomorrow?'

'I hope so,' she said.

A small sense of guilt added to her physical discomforts. Never again, she told herself. So much wine, such a charmer. But married, with half-grown children. What could possibly come of it but heartbreak?

But then, as if it had happened a moment ago, there was the feeling of his thumb describing a circle on the soft skin above her eyebrows; round and round with a gentle, confident pressure. She had leaned closer, felt her lips parting, something inside her shivering with delight. He continued, watching her, rolling her

71

skin under the ball of his thumb, until the waiter returned with his receipt.

As they left the restaurant he put his arm about her waist and propelled her gently towards his car.

Then there was the moment when it all evaporated. She sat in the car while he put his briefcase in the boot. She felt tired, slightly sick from the wine. Her shoes, that she had kicked off under the restaurant table, crushed her feet. She wanted nothing more than to be home, alone in her own safe bed, but as she reached for the seatbelt he was beside her, taking it from her hands. His lips were parted, she could feel his tongue, just the tip of it, finding its way between her lips.

'No, Teddy.'

'Yes.'

His breath was coming in snatches. His tongue insisted, his fingers felt for the buttons of her blouse, gently and relentlessly he found his way under the cotton lace of her bra.

'I don't want to do this.'

He teased her nipple into hardness, rubbing its tip until the blood drained from her legs. 'You really don't want to do this?'

'I really don't.'

He sat up. His hand was still on her breast. 'This part of you does.'

'Yes, maybe. But I've had too much to drink. You know I have. You're taking advantage.'

'I wouldn't do that, Annabelle.' He pulled her towards him again, but this time it was to give her a chaste kiss on the cheek. 'I wouldn't do that for the world.'

As they drove away he put her hand on the steering wheel and covered it with his own. When they arrived in Orchard Street he came round to open the car door and gave her nothing but a soft, fluttery kiss on her neck.

She felt slightly sorry, slightly guilty for letting him buy her supper and then turning him down. 'I'm sorry if I . . .'

'Shh . . .' He put a finger over her lips. 'It was an absolute pleasure.'

The porch light came on automatically as she approached the steps to the front door. She looked back. He had been standing by his car, his arm along the roof, like a man posing for a picture. He blew her a kiss.

Late in the morning she made a jug of coffee and, during a long, careful shower, rubbed conditioner onto her hair and razored the small stubble from her underarms and legs, conscious of what she was doing; conscious that, despite having pushed him away, she was preparing herself for him, wanting to be ready.

Almost noon, half a day spent waiting and then the telephone rang.

'It's me.'

She said 'hello' in the voice that she had practised.

'Can you hear me?'

The line was noisy. She had to shout. 'Yes! Where are you calling from?'

'I'm in my car. I'm breaking all the rules for you, driving with one hand.'

His voice faded and came back. 'I phoned you at work but they said you were ill. Are you all right?'

'Yes. I'm fine. It was just the wine.'

There was a pause. The phone hummed.

'. . . wanted to apologise. I was out of line last night.'

What was it she had planned to say? How to answer, how to be dignified without putting him off entirely?

'You don't need to apologise, Teddy.'

'You're not angry with me?'

'There is nothing to be angry about. I'm glad you phoned, I didn't thank for for supper.'

'I'd like to take you out properly one day, if I may?'

She swallowed; what did properly mean, exactly? She tried to think of something neutral.

'That would be nice.'

'You'll let me?'

She didn't answer, he didn't expect her to.

'I'll ring you soon and make a date.'

She said goodbye in the same light tone as he did.

Her headache came back. She took some more aspirin. This is absurd, she told herself. You can't want this man. There is

73

nothing about him that is attractive. The day before yesterday you wouldn't have given him a passing thought.

But then there was that feeling of the blood draining from her legs.

Three days of silence. It was the weekend. On Sunday morning she painted a picture for herself: Teddy in a dressing gown – elegant, silk with a plush collar. For some reason, though it was early April and the days overcast and cold, she pictured breakfast on a patio, a white cloth and glasses of orange juice. The picture was trite, like an advertisement for the good life, but it was what she saw. His was the good life. His car, the monogrammed shirt – everything pointed to a life of ease.

Yesterday we blocked up the stream at the bottom of the garden. Bubi had a wheelbarrow full of stones. He pushed it all the way from the road. Bubi is bigger than me. Honey says I should stay away from him; she says the children from the village are too rough. But I like Bubi. We put all the stones in the stream to make a dam. The water ran sideways and everywhere. There was a lot of shouting. The chicken lady chased Bubi with a stick. The water went into the chicken runs and all over the compound. The latrines don't have flush pulls. When the water went in it came out again with heaps of Big Jobs and pieces of newspaper. Honey smacked my legs. The men from the compound had to take out the stones. Mama didn't come to see. Honey said I was lucky that Papa had gone to Liberté. No-one will tell Papa about the water. They all hate him. Even Mama.

'Jamie Clarkson did what?'

Teddy's voice was mild, but there was a gleam of annoyance in his eyes.

'He telephoned the Willards,' said Phyllis. 'He said he wanted to check with them about selling their shares.'

'But I have their Power of Attorney! He has no business to question my instructions.'

'He said he just wanted to check – as the sales were substantial.'

'And what did Mr Willard tell him?'

'It was he who told me Mr Clarkson had rung.'

'And?' By this time Teddy had taken off his coat and was halfway into his office.

'Mr Willard said he told Mr Clarkson to do exactly as you say. That he had absolute faith in you and that was why he and Mrs Willard had given you their Power of Attorney.'

'Hmmph!'

Later, Teddy called her for dictation. 'I'm going to write to Clarkson and tell him the Willards will take their business elsewhere.'

Phyllis took down the letter and typed it. Teddy transferred the care of the Willards' portfolio to his own favourite stockbroker, Elystan Jones, a half-commission man with one of the lesser-known firms. 'Elystan won't give me all this grief,' said Teddy, as he signed the letter.

SEVEN

Teddy took a box of cakes to the Mahana Parish School. 'Happy Birthday, Theodore' was written on the blackboard in yellow chalk.

The class sang for him. Teddy stood up, feeling the pink smile on his cheeks. The little class gathered around the box: children from the compound, big-eyed at the brightly-coloured icing. There were no plates, no forks – sponge and icing were stuffed into open, laughing mouths. Teddy felt a big, happy love for them all. When class was finished Bubi raced him down to the beach; there were crabs to be tormented: small sand crabs and the bigger ones in the rock pools, monsters with hard green shells, and tiny fish and crunchy things with a hundred legs to chase over the rocks.

Honey was waiting for him at the beach. She was there when he arrived, but not as she usually was, sitting under a shady tree. Honey stood in the full sun, watching him, frowning, and even as he played he knew the afternoon was not as it should be, that she would call him soon, long before the sun went down, that his being seven was not a birthday such as his other birthdays had been. Teddy knew, without thinking of it, that there was a connection between his birthday and his mother's tears, the shouting at breakfast and the visitor from England.

His father's voice from behind a newspaper: 'What you want has nothing to do with it.'

His mother's high, sharp giggle.

So few explanations; so little warning.

Jaleb had put the iced cakes in the tin. 'Who is she, this Winifred?' Teddy asked.

The servants shrugged their shoulders. 'We do not know of this lady.'

'Is Aunt Winifred like Honey? Is she like Honey?'

His father answered. 'No, Theodore. Winifred is my sister. She is a lady, not a servant.'

Honey held his hand as they walked home from the beach. 'Why couldn't we stay, Honey? Why couldn't we stay on the beach?'

'It is time to come home.'

'But it's my birthday. We always go to the beach on my birthday.'

'Aunt Winifred is come.'

And the words that meant nothing, just a person arriving, a grown-up like any other, carried a portent, a weight that the cries of the shopkeepers, the lazy waves of greeting from the workers walking home from the estate, could not dispel.

Jaleb came round from the kitchen. In his hand was a parcel of sandwiches wrapped in waxed paper. 'You will be hungry on the big ship.'

Teddy put the parcel in his satchel and shook Jaleb's hand, the tall cook bending steeply to the small, solemn face of the white boy.

'You will come again, Teddy-master. We will wait for you.'

Jaleb's brother was to drive the car. Elias was one of the new men, back from the short-lived wealth of war. He had come to the verandah one New Year's morning, holding out his driver's licence, had waited hours, Jaleb hovering, anxious. Elias had a scrap of paper in his breast pocket, faded ink, a reference from a building contractor who had prospered in wartime. Hugo laughed aloud. 'Have you done nothing since the War?'

But he gave Elias a job. Jaleb's brother was to be a mechanic, to maintain the plantation machinery, to make such spare parts as were needed out of the hulks of old Baton plant that rusted at the back of the compound. This recycling was the first sign of economy, the first sign that the money from England would not last forever.

With his driver's licence and his peaked cap, Elias was also the chauffeur, the one who drove the car for Clara and collected the shopping from the store at Mahana; the one who had met Hugo's sister, Winifred, off the boat, brought her to Mahana; the one who would take her back, accompanied now, to the dock, the ship, the place where Clara would say goodbye to her son.

Elias arrived as Teddy's trunk was being carried from the house. Full of self-importance, his short fat legs squeezed into a pair of black trousers for the occasion, he supervised Sahilil in storing the luggage in the boot, huffing and muttering until it was done to his satisfaction.

All the staff, the people from the compound as well as the house servants, had turned out to see the departure. Clara saw in their faces their puzzlement at the savage habits of the whites, sending a small boy so far from home.

Hugo stayed in his study, out of sight. The room was falsely named these days. No studying was done there any more. Hugo had long ago devoured all the books he had been able to buy; he knew all that could be learned from the study of books. If the estate was not prospering it was not for lack of study, but lack of experience; the arrogant belief that he could succeed where her father, after forty years, had failed. These days the study was simply the place where Hugo counted bills and wrote letters to the bank, drawing money from England.

Winifred sat in the front seat of the car, tucking her skirt against her legs, as if to define the small space that would separate her from Elias. She spoke to Teddy through the open window.

'You're not to get into the car until you have said goodbye to your father.'

Clara said, 'Hugo hasn't bothered to come out, Winifred. I don't see why – '

'I won't hear of it.' Winifred had not raised her voice but the effect was as if she had shouted. 'Theodore, go to the study and tell your father you are ready to leave.'

'I don't think he wants to see me,' said Teddy in a small voice.

'Nonsense. He will want to see that you are properly prepared for the journey.'

Teddy moved from one foot to the other, his legs like sticks beneath the unfamiliar grey flannel shorts.

'Go on, Theodore.'

'He prefers to be called Teddy,' said Clara.

'Teddy is a childish name. He must get used to being correctly addressed.'

Clara was ready with a rejoinder, ready, in her helplessness against the greater anguish, to fight this small detail. 'You must at least call him what he is used to, he's too little for you to change everything at once. If he wakes up in the night and you don't even call him Teddy he'll – '

She did not finish her sentence. Teddy had pulled himself away, his satchel tossed onto the drive, running back to the house, up the steps and round the verandah, his feet loud on the boards. Honey ran after him, and Jaleb and Sahilil, all the house-servants darting up after the child.

The sound would be with Clara forever, an indelible echo on the verandah floor, the clapping sound of Teddy's feet, with Honey Jellawella running behind, with her lighter step and her skirt lifted as they ran past the kitchen, smells drifting through the fly screen, coffee beans and boiled milk, calling after him, 'Teddy-master, Teddy-master, stop now!'

But it was not Honey who stopped him, not Jaleb. It was not Sahilil who stopped him, coming behind Jaleb, letting go with his tongue a bubbling speech like a river in torrent, high and meaningless but for the warning it gave of danger, alarm, like the chickens that squawked in the coop by the kitchen path and, louder than Honey's cry, 'Teddy-master, Teddy-master, you mustn't run now. It is not the time for running.'

None of these stopped the boy, stopped his running feet or his high, wet-faced shrieking. It was the stick. Stuck through the double doors. Hugo would not come out. Not as a father might, to gather the child in his arms. It was the stick that came out, cutting across Teddy's shins, bringing him down with a thud, bruising his knees and his chin on the hard plank floor.

Jaleb was there first. Hard brown arms and the smell of

starched cotton. And then Honey, the soft folds of her skirt and the oiled smoothness of her hair.

Clara fought her way through. 'You bastard, Hugo. You cold, heartless bastard!'

Hugo went back behind his desk. 'Be careful whom you call a bastard, Clara.'

Clara carried Teddy back to the car, rage like an ague shaking her limbs. The compound people shied away, hesitated by the gate, forgetting to wave as the car roared out onto the Liberté road.

Clara watched the back of Winifred's head. All through the commotion Hugo's sister had remained in the car, her prim, pork-pie hat pinned to her yellow-white hair. She wore a linen suit, a string of pearls. The hands resting in her slightly crumpled lap had trimmed, unvarnished nails. She wore no rings. Winifred's hands, like the rest of her, were large and angular and hard. Clara's heart turned as she thought of the little boy at this woman's side, travelling aross the sea with only this ugly spinster to comfort him.

As if he had shared her thoughts Teddy nudged closer to her, but he kept his head turned away, watching the donkey carts that wandered beside them, moving at the same pace as the car. They passed a team of oxen, hauling a load for the market, the car squeezing past, with much use of the horn, a wall of brown, heaving flanks by the windows, loose-fitting hides flapping like ancient empty breasts on the great beasts' legs. One defecated as they passed, a belch of steaming brown splashing the side of the car. Winifred wound up the window. Nothing would persuade her to open it again. Inside the car the stale air swirled between them, warm and sweltering.

Clara put Teddy's hand on her knee and smoothed his fingers. His hands were sunburned, like his face, the colour of warm tea.

He smiled at her, weakly. 'Will I like boarding school, Mama?'

'Of course you will. Boarding school is very exciting. You'll have lots of other boys to play with.'

If he heard the tremor in her voice he gave no sign of it. His face was turned back to the window.

81

They reached the outskirts of Liberté. Strings of open-fronted shacks lined the road. Heaps of smooth orange coconuts were for sale, trays of mangoes and cassava, pawpaw and breadfruit. Cows grazed on small corners of grass; at the junction of the Mahana Road, a pitiful collection of shacks clustered round a stand-pipe, a dog drank mud-coloured water from an open drain. Winifred put her handkerchief over her nose as they drove past, 'Really, what can they be thinking of?'

Teddy's hand curved around Clara's knee. His fingernails were scrubbed pink and shiny for the journey. Winifred had seen to it. She had seen to everything.

As they approached the docks, cranes and masts in a grey, spiky pattern on sky, Clara had a sense of dislocation, of time and events passing, and yet not passing at all, as if every sensation she had ever known, every moment of fear and anguish, was gathered in the scene before her. She could see again the wheelchair, the husband too lame to stand and hold her in his arms; she could see herself alongside the creaking chair, feel again the unbearable burdens of falsehood and dread. Now she could hardly look at the place. As they drove inside the perimeter fence, two white women with a small boy and a servant at the wheel, they merited barely a glance from the sentry at the gate. The white bulk of the *Europa* loomed beside them. Porters ran alongside the car, shouting for work. Winifred got out, clutching her hat against her head, as if to hold herself aloof from the swell of brown humanity that surrounded them. A dark sweat-stain marked the armpit of her linen suit. The trunk had Teddy's name painted in white letters on its side. Labels had been sewn into every garment, onto a corner of every sheet and towel, even his sponge bag was labelled. Winifred had seen to everything.

Clara imagined how it must have been in the nursery at Chanting Hill. Winifred and Hugo, the brother and sister, close in age and alike in appearance. Clara had never seen Chanting Hill, the house that Hugo had left behind for Pentecost, for her. Winifred had spoken of the views from the windows, oak and elder shading the long drive, the privacy and quality of a country house in England. A place where a young boy would learn the manners of a gentleman; where he might learn those things that his parentage denied him.

They were to say goodbye on the quay. Winifred had decreed that she would take Teddy to their cabin herself, that Clara should not come aboard. 'We don't want the child to be unsettled.'

Clara took off her gloves. Teddy's face was very white. He was saying something to her, tugging at her hand, but she could barely hear him. Shock or grief filled her ears with noise.

'Mama, I want to stay with you.'

She bent down. 'No, darling, you musn't say that. You must be brave.'

'But I don't want to go without you.'

His fingers squeezed hers so hard it hurt. His face turned red, changing in a flash from white to scarlet, his eyes brimming with tears.

'You'll be all right, my darling. You'll see. I'll be thinking of you every single day.'

It was too much. She could not keep the words straight. She pressed the little boy into her arms.

He had played the adultery game before. They met in a wine bar, a place she had never heard of. He told her exactly where to stand, and when he arrived, a little late, he didn't answer her wave but came slowly through the room, studying all the faces in the crowd before coming to sit with her.

'You're quite the spy,' she said.

He answered her seriously, 'We can't be too careful.'

They spent a day in the country, she playing hooky from her job, he pretending a visit to a client. They drove deep into Kent and stopped for lunch at a pub surrounded by fields of hops. He held her hand across the table while they talked, he kissed her neck at the end of the day, his hand taking hers once more in the car, turning in her lap as if to measure the width of her thigh.

She wanted to say, yes. Yes, you can – we can go back to where we were that first night.

Instead, all the way back to London, he talked about his family. At great length he described Chanting Hill, his sons,

Lucian and Graham, who were almost grown up, his daughter Crystal, for whom he had bought a pony, who was bright and clever and affectionate and (quite patently) spoiled. 'I wish you could come to Chanting Hill,' said Teddy. 'You could meet Crystal, I know you'd like her. She's such a wonderful girl.'

Speaking of Crystal produced a change in his face, in the tone of his voice, put a light in his eyes that was otherwise absent. When, in moments of affection, he called Annabelle 'my poppet' she wondered if he also called Crystal his poppet, and if in some way she was his Crystal made whole, the woman his daughter could not be for him.

She let the thought pass. It didn't matter. The affair, liaison – whatever it was – couldn't last. They shared only the small, easy things – food, bottles of wine, Mozart. The only cause for dismay was that she liked him so much. Sexual attraction, a kind of crush, these were the ordinary ingredients of an affair, the seeds of its ending. You could pretend to share love of a sort, but only of a frivolous kind. To like each other was a different thing, far more dangerous. Annabelle did not want to like Teddy too much. She did not want any deceit; she did not want this slow creep of affection that might be so hard to undo. But the truth – like the dripping of a tap, persistent, not to be escaped from – the truth was that she liked him and she wanted him, as completely as she had ever wanted anyone; she wanted his hands on her breasts, his body pushing apart her thighs; she wanted all the time they could have, no matter how little it might be, how soon he might go.

It became their habit to meet for lunch on Mondays at a little place south of the river; he would choose the wine and she would choose their food. Asparagus, or a salad to start. And then fish, a steak of halibut perhaps, buttered and grilled. They never had pudding. She read somewhere that people who drink a lot of wine lose their desire for sweet things, that the sugar in the wine makes salty cheese more attractive. He liked to choose the cheese for her, wielding a knife over the board to select a morsel for her plate. Squares of strong, exotic saltiness were popped into her mouth, followed by a grape or a slice of apple, to clear her tongue.

The bills for these meals were huge. He paid them un-blinkingly, still talking, even holding one hand, as he signed the slips for his credit card.

'Are you really such a rich man?'

'It is my clients who are rich.'

Later, when there was time to reflect, time to wonder how much he had deceived her, if he had deceived her more or less than all the rest, she remembered these words. It was, she came to believe, the closest he ever came to the truth. He followed the words with a clasp of her hand, an expression on his face that contained, as well as the obvious things – lust, hunger – a kind of plea, a search for something. Was it approval? Collusion?

The first time he came to supper at her tiny flat in Orchard Street, she laid a white cloth on the table, and tall red candles. As he parked the car she put on a tape of Schubert's String Quintet. He carried a bundle of roses, yellow, rather than red, and held them out to her, hesitating on the doorstep, as if he were shy.

She took the flowers out of his hands. Briefly, before they went inside, he held her, his arms hard, pressing her against him as if he feared she would slip away. And then it was past, he walked ahead into her sitting room.

'Something smells good.'

'It's just pasta.'

'Ah, but the sauce!' He followed her into the kitchen, lifted lids while she put the roses in a vase. 'So many talents!' he grinned.

She was going to say, 'You haven't tried it yet,' but he was admiring her dress.

'You look so good in bright colours.'

'But you,' she said, 'you're wearing a black tie.'

He touched his neck. 'Sorry, I meant to change.'

'Have you been to a funeral?'

'Yes.' He undid the knot.

'Whose? Someone close?'

'He was a client.'

'Even so, you must feel a little bit sad.'

Teddy shrugged. 'Death is bread and butter when you're in my trade.'

85

'You sound like an undertaker!'

'Perhaps that's what I am, in a way. I undertake certain tasks.'

'But what happens when they die – you've lost a client?'

'Not exactly, and they don't all die at once. This one has left a widow and adult chidlren. The widow will need me even more now that her husband is gone – to protect her from her greedy daughter.'

They ate the pasta, drank the wine. She made a jug of coffee and put it by the fireplace. The music swam around them, gilding the air. Everything was right, the setting of a thousand love scenes, but Teddy's thoughts were of his day, and the sharp, unpleasant voice of Isabel Willard.

'I've been looking through my father's papers.'

'Oh yes?' Teddy had said, pleasantly.

'There are one or two things I should like to discuss with you.'

'Certainly.' Teddy helped himself to a small square of crushed olives from the tray of canapés that Isabel held in her hand. The event was more like a cocktail party than a wake, he thought, looking around.

Willard's daughter showed no trace of grief, of the solemn, protracted funeral service with which the afternoon had begun. 'I was surprised to find that Daddy had changed his stock-broker.'

'Yes,' said Teddy.

'Jamie Clarkson has been their broker for years.'

'Yes I know,' said Teddy. 'But there have been a lot of changes in the City. You may have heard of Big Bang.'

Isabel put down the tray. 'Big Bang was in 1986, if I remember rightly. You changed my father's brokers only recently.'

'It took some time for the changes to take effect. One of the effects has been that there are fewer and fewer stockbrokers who are still willing to deal with the small investor.'

'My father was hardly a small investor.' Isabel was still smiling but there was an edge to her voice.

'It's all a matter of degree,' said Teddy, smiling too. 'I'm glad to say your father sold at just the right time. Overall the portfolio has done rather well.'

'Has it?' She picked up the tray of canapés. 'It's not for me, you understand, though I believe he did leave me a small legacy. My main concern is for my mother.'

'Of course,' said Teddy, smiling again and reaching for another square of crushed olives. 'Fortunately, the portfolio is quite liquid at the moment.'

'You mean there's cash?'

'Oh, quite a lot,' said Teddy. 'So we'll be able to pay all the legacies just as soon as we get the grant of probate.'

'So there's enough – for my mother?'

'There are ample funds.'

'You and mother are the Executors of the will?'

'Yes.'

'But you will keep me informed, I mean – ' Another funeral guest distracted her attention before she could finish her sentence. She said hurriedly, 'You've always been very kind to my parents. I wouldn't want you to think – '

Teddy swallowed a mouthful and put his finger to his lips. 'Not at all. Only too glad to help.'

He crossed the room to where Mrs Willard was sitting, as if on a throne, surrounded by mourners who were chatting animatedly with each other, oblivious of the elderly widow in their midst.

Teddy took her hand.

'Oh, Mr Ransome.'

'You must call me Teddy.'

'I shall try to remember.' A small handkerchief was crumpled in her fist. 'Do you know, it's one of the hardest things, trying to remember everything.'

'You mustn't worry,' said Teddy. His voice was warm and sympathetic, intimate in the hubbub of the crowd. 'You have lots of people to help you.'

'Do I?' The old lady looked questioning.

'Your children. I've just been speaking to Isabel.'

'She's too busy,' said Mrs Willard. 'And my son's the same. They're here now, of course, but they're too busy with their own lives. They'll keep coming for a bit, but in month or so it'll just be phone calls.'

'I'm sure they'll do more than phone you,' said Teddy.

Still holding his hand, she pulled him close. 'I'm so glad I have you to look after me,' she whispered. 'I know I can rely on you completely.'

'Of course you can.'

'You'll look after the money, won't you? Isabel has been asking so many questions – I can't remember the answers . . .'

'I shall look after everything,' said Teddy.

'She wants to know what there is – what happened to the money from the house.'

'The money is safe,' said Teddy. 'You really mustn't worry.'

Winifred is taking me on holiday. We are to stay in Bournemouth for two weeks in a hotel. An hotel, Winifred calls it. Special clothes have been bought for me. A straw hat which I shall not wear and white trousers and a blazer. And shorts. Even W. must know that only prep-school boys wear shorts.

She says Bournemouth will be crowded and there may be Common People there. If I meet any, I may not speak to them. How will I know they are Common?

Because they will be dressed incorrectly.

You mean I may only speak to men in straw hats?

You know exactly what I mean, Theodore.

She is a daft old brush.

The weather is hot. Even Chanting Hill is quite warm. She has moved my bed out of the nursery. I have the Green Room now. Not Hugo's room. That would be a sacrilege. The Green Room was used for the guests who used to come to Chanting Hill when Hugo and Winifred were children. The window-sills are big enough to sit on. I read there sometimes at night when the moon is very full. She does make me go to bed so early.

Nine o'clock news and then off you go, she says. Early to bed and early to rise, makes a man . . . blah, blah, blah. She likes these little sayings. As though they can make things true, like prayers. Winifred doesn't pray. We go to St Agnes' church every Sunday but I have never seen her pray. She only opens her mouth to sing. Afterwards she waits in the churchyard to speak to her bridge friends. They collect like sparrows and talk and talk. I could go home and come back again in the time she spends talking in the graveyard. Not to just anyone of course. Mr Hills the gardener can go by, doffing his cap, and she doesn't say a word. Not in the graveyard with her bridge friends – though she'll talk to him no end in the garden about her fuchsias. She has great tubs of them on the drive, and more in the beds at the back.

My mother sent me to England when I was seven years old. I cannot remember her face.

Winifred has been going on about the ancestors. They are not my ancestors, she says. 'But you will marry a nice girl one day.'

'How will we know she is nice?'

'Well,' Winifred flutters, pushing the pins into her hair. They do no

good those pins, it all creeps out again. Like a dead bush. 'Well,' she says, 'a good wife and children are what you need.'

So the question is unanswered. I must marry a good girl and have good children. They may somehow excuse me, my coming into the world slightly flawed.

I cannot remember Mama.

It says in a book in the library that after five years there is only bone and hair and dampness in the ground. Especially in hot climates, like Pentecost. The worms and scuttlers do their work more quickly in the heat. Fuchsias are girls with rude red lips.

EIGHT

A wind had come up, a prelude to rain. Clara remained on the dock, watching the tug, bouncing a little on the swell, hauling the mass of the *Europa* behind it. Long blasts filled the air. There were other people waving, calling final, unheard farewells. If they recognised Clara they gave no sign. She did not see them. All her heart and life was in the huge, clumsy liner being towed out to the swelling grey sea.

Two or three times Jaleb's brother came to fetch her to the car. Each time she said, 'Wait, Elias, just a little longer.'

'We must go, Madame. The rain is coming, and darkness also. It is not wise on the road after dark.'

At last she got into the car and they sped away, Elias keeping his hand on the horn, scattering children and stray cattle. They were well out of town when the downpour began, a sudden wall of grey. Muttering, Elias slowed the car, tapping ineffectually on a stick attached to the steering column. It was no good; the wiper worked only on one side.

Clara could see nothing at all beyond the glass. She sat alone on the rear seat, surrounded by the pummelling rain. The noise of it freed her; she let herself cry out, great tearing sobs. Elias shook his head, the car swerving as he turned to look at her. 'Is a bad day, Madame.'

The journey seemed endless but as they drew close to Mahana she asked him to turn back, to make a detour, anything to defer arrival. She dreaded the sight of the house, the stillness that would greet her: no Teddy, no scamper of footsteps.

'It is not safe, madame.' Elias hunched his shoulders over the wheel.

'We won't come to any harm,' cried Clara.

'It is the master's wish.'

Clara sank back in the seat. 'Oh.'

Elias's eyes were in the rear-view mirror. 'It is not Elias who makes this rule.'

'No.'

'It is late already now. Already there will be trouble.'

'I'm sorry, Elias,' said Clara. 'I didn't mean to get you into trouble.'

The driver shook his head and once more tapped the wiper switch. 'Is a very bad day, Madame.'

The rain that drowned Clara's weeping, that slowed their journey back from the dock, the same rain had fallen all afternoon on Mahana, flooding the compound. Mud washed in through the doors of the workers' hovels, trickled down the bare concrete walls. Jaleb's house was drier than the others, having a concrete floor, raised a foot or so above the ground, and a roof of red tiles instead of the usual corrugated iron. His wife could be seen in the doorway, seated on a chair with their youngest child on her lap, her knees splayed wide. The other houses were less watertight, Hugo's proud improvements already patched with plastic and thatch – poor defence against the monsoon. Dripping water made indentations in the floors, mixed with the mud to form a wet, inescapable sludge. Women held their skirts high, men hitched up their sarongs, mothers held their infants up to the warm rain, allowing the downpour to rinse the mud away.

Sahilil's wife, Justine, had come over to Jaleb's house when the rain began. She was short, very dark-skinned. In the compound they called her the chicken lady, for she was in charge of the master's chickens – not a job as such, but one of the myriad tasks for which a small payment could be secured. She wore a yellow dress, one of the mistress's cast-offs, with a black sash for a belt. She had worn it today to mark the little master's going, with her dry, crinkly hair tied in a knot low on the back of her neck. Sore, red-stained gums showed when she smiled.

'Look after Mary,' Teddy-master had said, speaking to her in the servant patois that was forbidden in the house but was spoken freely in the compound, and around the coops; and, on this day of parting, on the steps of the house.

'I will look after all the chickens.'

'But especially Mary. She is my friend.'

Jaleb was home, sent from the house by the master, long before dinner-time. Seeing the women in the doorway he went off though the rain, darting from tree to tree across the plantation, heading in this zig-zag fashion for the shelter of the bar down by the beach wall; there would be others there, bottles of beer to be drunk, and talk, gossip, wonderment at the strange ways of the Englishman.

Justine sat with Jaleb's wife in her doorway, watching the rain that fell straight and steady through the windless afternoon. They waited – all the compound waited – for the return of Elias, for the story he would tell, the great perplexity of this journey to Liberté, the giving of the child to the great ship, to the master's sister, the walnut, as they called her, for the dry hardness of her face and the shrunken, withered thing her womb would be within. They watched and chattered and from time to time were silent. The car had been gone a long time, longer than the time needed for the journey to the dock and back. The two women sat on in the doorway, their chatter dying away as the grey, pink-tinged light of the monsoon day slipped into a brief, blurred twilight.

On the far side of the estate, in the shelter of a stand of cashew trees, Honey Jellawella was busy. It was Honey's task, hers by common consent, to tend the shrine that stood there, cased in glass against the elements. The task was hers because she made it so, a monthly ritual, cleaning the shrine, whispering prayers for the dead, for her husband buried there seven years since, and the older graves, crossed with white stones, where lay the bones of the old plantation slaves.

The shrine was smeared, the statue of Our Lady dusty and speckled with insects. With reverent care Honey cleaned the painted clay and polished the glass. The vinegar she used came from Clara's kitchen – not stolen, asked for. Clara waving her hand, too distracted. 'Take it, take it. I can't get drunk on vinegar.'

The ground around the shrine, sheltered by the cashew trees, was almost dry. When her task was complete, Our Lady clean, restored to her shrine with fresh flowers and a new candle, Honey stayed on as she always did, kneeling before the statue, turning the beads of her rosary, '. . . Blessed art thou among women and blessed is the fruit of thy womb . . .'

The daylight slipped away. '. . . Holy Mary, mother of God, be there now and at the hour of our death . . .' Her prayers were for the soul of Jellawella, buried here beside the old slave bones, for the little master Teddy, lonely with the English aunt on the great sea, for Clara whose tears would be flowing now like the rain. Prayers, too, for herself, for what would become of her now there was no child to be nursed?

'You shall stay with us, Honey,' Clara had cried, as if the question were nothing. 'We need you to look after us just as much as Teddy!' And she had laughed her high shrill laugh that gave away her suffering.

Elias drove the car as close to the verandah as possible, but still on the walk up to the door Clara was soaked, the new, white shoes she had worn for this day of parting stained with mud. She took them off on the verandah. Her feet left a trail on the polished floor of the hall. In the sitting room a single light had been turned on. The mosquito blinds were down but, even so, there was a gathering round the bulb, moths and flying ants, flicking and colliding inside the shade.

She went to the sideboard, poured half a tumbler of gin and tried to drink it down neat. It was too bitter. Gagging a little, she stumbled towards the kitchen. Sahilil was dozing on a chair. The noise of the rain had drowned the sound of the returning car. At the sight of her he jumped up, hastily fastening his tunic.

'Madame is wet.'

'It's only rain.'

'There is no cooking. The master has sent Jaleb home. He says no cooking tonight. Only Sahilil for sandwiches.'

'I don't want anything to eat, Sahilil.'

'Honey Jellawella has prepared the curd for you.' Sahilil opened the larder. Inside, under beaded cloths, was a bowl of curd and a jug of palm syrup. 'She says I must serve you this for your strength.'

'I don't want anything at all, Sahilil. I just want a bottle of tonic.'

He darted to another cupboard and brought out two bottles, opened one and put it on a small tray. Ignoring the tray, she took the bottle and poured the contents over her gin. The mixture clouded and fizzed. She drank it as fast as she could.

Sahilil followed her back to the sitting room, bearing the second bottle on the tray.

'Where is the master?' said Clara.

'He is in the study.'

Clara felt the gin taking effect, a lifting of weight from her shoulders. She smiled at Sahilil. 'I don't suppose he's doing much studying in there.'

'He has been there all day, Madame.'

Sahilil hovered, poured her a second drink, and then a third. 'You needn't stay, Sahilil. There's nothing more for you to do tonight. You get on home, Justine will be waiting.'

'The rain is stopping soon, Madame.'

'Good.'

The servant still hovered. 'Sahilil spoke a question today, Madame.'

Clara turned her head. 'What?'

'Sahilil has asked the master for something.'

'What did you ask him?'

'To pay for the apprenticeship. For William to go to apprentice school.'

'You asked him that today?'

'William gave him a coconut.' The servant stepped forward, smiling. 'A time ago, when he was the same age as the little master, William gave the master a coconut.'

Clara swallowed her drink and closed her eyes.

Sahilil went on. 'I told of the apprentice school for carpenters and the master said he would pay.'

'I'm very glad,' said Clara. 'Now, go on home.'

'Is not all badness today, Madame.'

Clara said nothing. Sahilil lingered. She opened her eyes. He was holding out the alarm clock. 'For the time in the morning, Madame.'

Clara waved the clock away. 'We needn't pretend any more, Sahilil. You can come any time you like.'

When he had gone the house seemed very still, as if the little man's activities had somehow kept its emptiness at bay. Twice Clara forgot herself, rose to go to the nursery, to check on Teddy. Twice her whole being lurched with pain. He was not there. The nursery was empty. The whole house was empty, nothing but the creak of the timbers, the drip and purl of emptying gutters. Shadows in a damp cave, she and Hugo were all that was left.

Out on the verandah a legion of toads deafened the night, drowned the creaking of the floor as she walked to the end and turned the corner. Lights shone from Hugo's study, illuminating a section of the verandah, casting a silhouette on the rain-sodden lawn of the pillars and the valance of fretwork that hung from the roof. A pair of china lamps stood at the sides of his desk. They had come from England, as had the books that lined the walls, leather bindings rotting in the damp air.

Making no attempt to hide herself, Clara stood in front of the french windows and looked in at her husband. The desk lamps were tall and their shades very closely woven, so that light travelled upwards and downwards, but little passed through. The result was two circles of light on the ceiling, illluminating the uneven plaster, criss-crossed with insects that flicked and cracked in the brightness, and two pools of light on the desk, not quite meeting, so that the centre,where Hugo was sitting, was comparatively dark, the papers in shadow.

Reflected light from the ceiling made the top of his head glow, and light from the desk lit the under-part of his chin. The rest of his face, the space between eyebrows and lips, was dark. She couldn't tell if he was looking at her. There was an empty bottle on the desk, another on the cupboard behind him.

Had he been there the whole day, sitting at the desk with his bottle? Had he been thus when Teddy ran round the verandah?

Had he heard the small feet running and stood in wait with his stick?

Hugo tilted his head. The movement was slight but enough for the light to catch his eyes, staring at her.

'Well, Clara?'

She took a step inside. After the coolness of the verandah, the air in the study smelled leathery and stale. A moth followed her in and headed straight for one of the lamps. It dashed itself against the shade and fell stunned to the desk, close to Hugo's hand.

'Did the ship go safely?'

Clara nodded. 'It was a bit rough outside the harbour, the waves looked huge.' She paused, remembering the sight of the great white ship ploughing out into the open sea. 'The Europa was so big, I don't suppose they felt it on board.'

'And Teddy behaved himself?'

'He didn't make a scene, if that's what you mean.'

'He has learned something, then.' Hugo rose from his chair, yawned and stretched. It was as if they were discussing something remote, a matter of indifference. 'It will help him at school if he can control himself.'

'And does your sister always control herself? Will Winifred allow herself to show him any affection at all?'

'He will have to learn to be self-reliant.'

'But he's seven years old!'

Hugo put up his hand. 'Don't shout, Clara. Theodore is no longer a subject for discussion.

Clara ignored him. 'I thought I should die when he walked up the gangway. Winifred held his hand as if she were taking him to a punishment. He looked so little, even his trunk is bigger than he is!'

'He will outgrow his trunk.'

'But will he ever outgrow this – this abandonment?'

'He will learn that love is a precarious thing. Not to be trusted. It might save him a great deal of pain later on.' Hugo's eyes grew large. He had moved around the desk and stood now, close enough to touch her. She could not read his expression.

'Clara, it is for the best. You agreed yourself, that he should go.'

'I had not borne him then. I had not held him in my arms.'

'No, and because of that you were able to see clearly the wrong you had done. It is behind us now.' He held out his hand. 'I've waited all this time, Clara. I am willing to make a new beginning. Now that he's gone we can forget what you did. We can live as if all that had never been.'

Clara brushed his hand aside and reached for the empty bottle on his desk. 'Is this what you mean? That we can be drunk together for the rest of our lives, drown ourselves in bottles of gin?'

'The gin won't be necessary any more. We'll sleep in peace, without a constant reminder – without that bastard of yours screaming all night.'

She could not have said, afterwards, how it happened, the exact sequence of events that followed. She would have agreed that the bottle was still in her hand. That she had raised it as one might raise any convenient thing to make a point, to make a stand. She did not remember raising it to hit him, or even to threaten the violence that he answered with. She could re-member only Hugo lunging around the desk, clinging to it for support until he hurled himself at her, whether simply to knock the bottle from her hand, or already intent upon the assault which followed, she could not tell. She could hear herself screaming, howling and yelping like a puppy caught underfoot. She heard the sound of her new white dress tearing from the neck to the hem and felt the harshness of the carpet against her skin and heard the hard thump of her body on the hollow floor. His face was blue and purple above her, eyes like huge gleaming spheres, angry and hungry. Her arms were pinned to the floor, his knees pressed against hers until she felt they would break. Tearing against her skin, he forced his way into her, pushing and thumping until she thought her insides would be torn apart.

Honey heard the return of the car, the slamming of doors, the old saloon brought up close to the dry verandah. She heard Elias go down the drive when he had finished parking the car, whistling a defiant song of freedom that was played in the beer halls and could be heard sometimes on a Saturday night, carried on the wind from the beach. From her seat under the cashew trees, through the whisper of her prayers, through the drip and gurgle of the storm drains, over the croaking of toads, she heard Clara's first cry. And then another, a scream. Honey stood up. She heard the master's voice, roaring. These were sounds that had been heard before; anger and shouting were part of the pattern of life in the Baton house, but never had Clara's answers sounded so anguished, so fierce and defiant and afraid. It was a distance to the house; Honey lifted her skirts, her bare feet stumbled over hidden roots, water from the puddles splashed high on her legs. Her feet made no sound but it mattered little, such were the screams that ruptured the darkness. She reached the back steps, thundered on the hollow wooden floor of the verandah, round to the study doors. Clara screamed still. There were red welts on her cheeks, blood on her lips. The master's bare bottom pumped up and down, his shirt open, his mouth open, his face without dignity or shame. Honey had seen it all, covered her own mouth in dismay, before she noticed the others who watched with her: Jaleb's wife, and Justine, and some of the labourers from the compound; Sahilil too, with Elias, their eyes wide and glittering.

Honey pushed them all away and closed the study doors.

There were messages on his desk. Teddy pushed them aside and picked up his calculator. It was three years since the proceeds of the Willards' house had been paid into the firm's Client Account. He had intended, at the beginning, to invest the money for them, to replace the holdings he had sold when they gave him Power of Attorney. Then the market rose rather sharply and he had decided to wait. There was no point in buying shares while prices were high. He would keep the cash on the Client Account until the moment was right. Interest rates were good and the Willards had enough income to go on with. Rowtham was pressing him to pay for the extra bathrooms that had been installed at Chanting Hill. Teddy drew a cheque in his favour from the Willard Client Account. The transaction was simple. A separate ledger was maintained for each client. Money could be drawn off on the signature of one partner.

The Willards' money had also paid off the debt he incurred when the stable was built for Crystal's pony. The transactions on the ledger print-out represented a kind of diary. He could see precisely the point at which falling interest rates had forced him to start supplementing the Willards' interest with payments from their capital. He could see when the funds he held for Mrs Cohen, the proceeds of sale of her properties and investments, had declined to the point where there was no longer enough to pay the nursing home and he started to draw on the Willards' funds for her too.

The figures were surprising. How easily Leonora Cohen's money had gone. And now the Willards'. It was so simple to do, he hardly considered the risk. When the bills came in he simply requisitioned a cheque from the Client Account and gave it to Phyllis to deal with. Phyllis had no reason to question any transaction, and he was careful to choose only those clients who would never question their own affairs, who relied upon him completely.

George Willard's death was unexpected and inconvenient. Action was needed if the daughter was going to ask questions. Telling her there was lots of cash had been a good move. The gleam in her eye was unmistakable. Cash was something she understood.

Only Teddy and Mrs Willard would have to swear the probate papers. 'I'd like to appoint my children, you know,' Teddy recalled his client's words, 'but they're so busy with themselves. Everyone is in such a rush all the time. I know you'll do a good job, Ransome. You'll take care of my wife if it's me that goes first.'

Nevertheless, the value of the estate would be published when probate was granted. He would have to make it look convincing. Taking the keys from his drawer he unlocked the door to the filing room and stood for a moment in front of the cabinet, his finger on the list of files within. An old one caught his eye. 'Miss Winifred Ransome – Will and Personal Affairs.' The file was old enough to be the buff, treasury-tag style that the firm had long since abandoned in favour of bright- coloured binders. Winifred's will was the most precious of all the papers his safe contained. From time to time, though he knew its contents by heart, Teddy would take out the will and read it, renewing the comfort it gave him.

Sometimes he feared the will bothered Winifred, nagged her, that even now she feared Hugo's wrath. There were days when he was conscious of her watching him, as if to reassure herself that she had done the right thing, that he was all the things he seemed.

Teddy dropped Winifred's file back into its sling. Precious as her will might be, it could not help him soon enough. The Willard problem needed a solution now. He opened another drawer and ran his fingers along the labels. There was really only one possibility left, one account unplundered.

'Mrs Kathleen Holland,' he said aloud. 'You can help me out of this little difficulty, can't you?'

He lifted a file out of the drawer. Kathleen Holland had been dead for nearly two years. She had never been Teddy's client while she was alive. Her will had been drafted years before she died, and appointed as her Executors her brother and her husband, John Holland. It was on a technicality that Teddy became involved. The Hollands had no children of their own and Kathleen, who was wealthier than her husband, didn't approve of John Holland's family. Her will provided that John would receive the income of her estate while he lived but after his death it would all be paid to the National Bird Watchers Association.

Kathleen's brother died before she did but the will was never updated. In view of the continuing trust, John Holland could not prove the will alone. He was required to nominate a second person to act jointly with him. His great friend, George Willard, recommended Teddy.

The irony is, thought Teddy as he turned the pages of the file, that Mrs Holland's estate is one I thought I never would touch. I wouldn't have dared. John Holland was a details man, he'd have noticed if I'd slipped by so much as a pound.

John Holland's death, just eighteen months after Kathleen's, was a windfall. Cash from both their estates was sitting in an account at Blairs Bank. Teddy laid his calculator on top of the cabinet and did some rough calculations. To use the Holland money involved a considerable risk. The National Association of Bird Watchers already knew the value of Kathleen's estate. Sooner or later, Teddy would have to account for it, but John's death was a complication, and complications equalled delay. John's personal estate would be charged to Inheritance Tax, and, though Kathleen's would pass free to the charity there would still be Revenue forms to complete, clearance certificates to be obtained. Kathleen's money could provide a temporary safety net. He could reimburse the Willard account and keep the nosy daughter at bay.

It wasn't a solution but it would do for the time being. 'You have the luck of the devil,' said Teddy, his voice bouncing dry and clear from the walls of glass.

It was one of life's pleasures, one of Susan's consolations, to go past David's window in the High Street, to feel her heart beating a little faster when she was beckoned inside. Neither the restrained window display nor the showroom within exhibited any prices, but David knew his market. Sometimes, like today, he had something to show her, in this case the cellaret that he had bought at auction with Chanting Hill in mind, or a piece that he had bought for the showroom but knew she would want – such as the little writing table that looked so pretty in the sitting room, and the eighteenth-century French mantel clock in the library.

It was from David that Susan had learned to recognise what was good, to sort out the Ransome furniture that was valuable and worth preserving from what David called 'brown furniture' – plain wardrobes and chests of drawers that David said were solid enough but dull, 'utterly brown'.

It was David who had arranged for the good things to be restored, sent the portraits – the Dead Uncles, as the children called them – to London to be cleaned; the rugs and carpets he sent to a restorer in Bath and the upholstery to a specialist in Cheltenham. When Teddy said, as he often did, 'you must do exactly what you want, Susan. You have the Ransome taste,' he could have been speaking of David Bell.

The shop in Winton Abbas had an old-fashioned bell that pinged as she walked in. David closed the door behind her.

'I just know you'll love this, Susan.' He took her arm to guide her through the showroom, between the tables and dressers and chests of drawers, their surfaces scattered with vases and silverware and delicate porcelain figures. 'Here.' He opened the lid of what looked like a large sewing-box on delicately tapered legs. 'You see, it's lined with lead, to keep the wine at the right temperature.'

'I thought a cellaret was something to do with salt and pepper.'

'No, it's a kind of portable wine cellar, to hold the bottles to be drunk during a meal.'

Susan stepped forward. The interior was divided into compartments, each large enough to hold a bottle upright. She ran her finger over the polished surface of the lid. 'I don't think I've ever seen one before.'

'There aren't very many left as untouched as this. Practically nothing has been done. The veneer needs work,' he closed the lid, 'but look at that inlay. Isn't it fine?'

'It would certainly look good in the dining room.'

David smiled. 'Just the finishing touch, I think.'

'We're having people to dinner on Friday . . .' Susan hesitated.

'I'm afraid it will be a few weeks before it's ready but if you want it you should say so right away.' Again he touched her arm. 'Why don't I put the kettle on while you phone Teddy?'

Susan looked at her watch. The time was important – David knew that as well as she did. About now, in the early afternoon, was often the best time. Teddy would be back from lunch, mellowed by wine and cigars. It was important not to call too late, not to catch him in the last rush for the evening post, or on his way to one of the meetings that so often began at six. In this part of the afternoon he would be warm, expansive, ask her to hold on while he shut the door to his office so that they could talk in peace.

103

'Well, my love,' he said, his voice warm and indulgent in her ear. His answer to her question was the same as always, the same words that he always used. 'We shall have to see what we can do.'

David poured a glass of wine from the little fridge that was set discreetly in a cabinet at the back of his showroom. Later, when she had gone, David would ring Teddy and they would haggle a little over the price. The ritual was well-established. She never knew, in the end, how much was paid.

The first such purchases had been exciting: the delivery van in the drive, men in overalls holding their treasure aloft. They called her 'Ma'am,' and she tipped them generously and David Bell stayed to advise on where the new piece should go. Recently, the excitement had changed. No longer awed by the extravagance, it was the admiration Susan craved. The admiration of her friends, mixed with a little envy. 'Oh Susan, you've made it all so beautiful. You are lucky.' She wanted that most of all, for people to know how lucky they were.

David Bell was the greatest admirer of all. Though much of what they had achieved at Chanting Hill was due to his expertise, his appreciation knew no bounds. Sometimes, when he had no assistant in the shop, he closed it up in order to come and see her. And there were occasions when he had missed an important auction or a fair, just because of something she wanted. It had happened over the vases on the half-landing. She had wanted a particular shade of blue to match the stained glass in the windows. David had thrown himself into the search, made countless telephone calls, contacted almost every dealer in the land, it seemed, until at last the right ones were found, the colour a perfect match. The vases themselves cost practicallly nothing, a few pounds for the pair, so there was no profit in it for David. Susan realised that he had done it simply to please her.

The knowledge of this, of David's mute worship, lay with her untouched, like the knowledge of a nest-egg or a box of chocolates. Something good that she could have if she wanted it, if she ever needed it.

Eventually, when the house was practically full, almost every piece of furniture had been restored or replaced, David suggested a change of decor. He knew someone who could help. For an enormous fee an interior designer exchanged expensive wallpaper for stencils and clever paint finishes. Layers of bright fabric, blinds and swags and pelmets, gathered around the tall windows like wedding gowns. It was Teddy's joke, one for their dinner parties, that they could have built another house for what it cost to dab a wall with an old sponge. But her extravagance seemed to please him, it became a token of their relationship. He made people laugh. 'Susan is having another window treatment,' he would say, as if she were to be cured of some gentle malaise. 'Susan is practising her overdraft.'

Leaving David Bell's, Susan went to the delicatessen and bought one of the large flat pizzas that were Crystal's favourite. She had said she didn't need to be bribed, but despite the small anger that the remark had stirred, Susan bought the pizza. It was necessary to please her daughter; it was necessary to overcome the tension that existed between them.

She carried the shopping in by the back door. The meringues had been taken out of the oven and there was evidence on the counter of a sandwich having been made; crumbs, a trace of mayonnaise, and in the fridge a half empty can of tuna.

She put the meringues into a tin and went out to the hall. 'Crystal?' There was no reply. Susan remembered that Crystal had said she would be going out for a ride.

She cleared the kitchen counter, made herself a salad with the rest of the tuna and took it out onto the terrace. The sun beat hot and white on the flagstones. If it stayed like this they could have a barbecue at the weekend.

The barbecue was special, unique because they had built it themselves, during the summer when Crystal was nine. Teddy was home for a fortnight – at least, he was home if you discounted the daily disappearances to the library, the ringing of the phone, Phyllis with her messages, others wanting things, questions, chatter.

The sun had shone, the children fooled around the pool. One morning, as Teddy emerged from his study Crystal wrapped herself around him, wet and skinny in her costume.

'Papa, can we have a barbecue?'

105

Susan remembered his look, the pleasure in his face as he lifted Crystal into his arms. 'Is that what you'd like?'

'We could have sausages.'

'Beefburgers!' shouted Graham.

'Baked potatoes!'

'We'll have to build it first.'

Crystal wriggled out of Teddy's arms. 'But you can, can't you? You can build it?'

'Of course he can!' Graham towered over his sister. His white, bony shoulders were dabbed with pimples.

Lucian, who until then had been lying on a sun-bed beside Susan, stood up and put his feet into flip-flops. 'Let's do it ourselves, Pa? Let's not get builders in again.'

'We could do it now,' said Graham. 'We could use the bricks left over from the stables.'

'There's only one condition,' said Crystal.

Teddy turned, reaching for her. 'There's a condition, is there? You'll let us build you a barbecue but there's a condition?'

'The condition is that you don't answer the phone and you don't go back to the library today.'

'Not once?'

'Not once 'til it's finished. You can go back when we start cooking.'

He bowed his head, smiling. 'You're very generous, ma'am.'

Crystal took her father's hand and pulled him to the place where a barbecue could be built, beside the wall of the vegetable garden. 'Here.'

'Right here?'

'And you're not to do any other work until it's finished.'

Teddy went indoors and re-emerged in a pair of denim jeans that no-one had seen for years. The bottoms were slightly flared, slightly too short. Lucian and Graham shrieked and teased. The building of the barbecue proceeded with a great deal of laughter. Teddy dug out a foundation and the boys chased Crystal with trowels of soft mud, ignoring her cries of 'pax' as she skittered and tumbled, barefoot on the grass.

'Are we going to design this thing?' Teddy shouted, taking off his sunglasses to wipe the sweat from his brow.

'Now?' cried Susan. 'But you've already started it, you can't start designing when you've already begun!'

'My Papa can do anything in the world,' cried Crystal.

Suddenly the project became serious. Sheets of paper were spread across the picnic table, anchored with stones. Plans were drawn, with talk of updraughts and angles, and competition in the matter of laying a straight course of bricks. The construction took two days and the result was large enough to roast a sheep.

Unanimously they voted it the best barbecue in Wiltshire. It was used, despite Teddy's protests, as soon as the cement was dry. Graham and Lucian helped to carry firewood, split logs from the cellar and kindling from the copse in the garden of the Lodge. Briquets were scorned, it had to be a proper wood fire with real logs and smoke. There was plenty of smoke – the summer night was almost dark before there was heat enough for the cooking to begin. Teddy opened a bottle of wine and took it upstairs to his bath. He emerged just as the sausages were browning, the jacket potatoes cooked inside their envelopes of foil. That night, that whole summer fortnight, he was the person he could sometimes be, as charming and affectionate and funny a man as you could wish for. The tubs of flowers glowed in the twilight, geraniums and lobelia, trailing down the shallow steps from the kitchen.

So serious Crystal had been, when the cooking was done, holding the tongs with both hands, her smudged face pink in the firelight, placing hot charred sausages into folds of pitta bread stuffed with salad and chutney. Graham complained that his sausages were burned but ate them just the same. Someone knocked a bottle of ketchup onto the flagstones. The boys scrapped over who should clean it up. Teddy took Crystal on his knee, in the way he had with her, so marvellously loving and gentle. She sat like a little princess and let him butter her bread. They ate together, sharing the food. Teddy kissed her cheeks and called her his poppet, his favourite little cook. Crystal seemed to glow, as if she were lit from within, and not all the teasing of the boys or the sudden flames as a forgotten slice of bacon caught fire on the rack, could part them.

107

Susan smiled at the memory; and felt the familiar tugging at her heart, the unacknowledged envy, the wish she had, and hated herself for having, that Teddy would give to her some of the adoring affection that he gave so freely to his daughter.

Winifred had put her finger on it. 'That child has an unfortunate likeness.'

'What do you mean?'

'It was there when she was born. Now it is even stronger.'

'You mean she looks like Teddy's mother?'

'She is the image of Clara.'

The words lingered in Susan's thoughts, no matter how she tried to forget them; they coloured her love for Crystal, fuelled the small jealousy that she tried to suppress.

The bedclothes were on the floor, underwear scattered about the room. Their bodies were damp with sweat. Teddy had gone on for hours, stroking and licking, thrusting and smoothing without any sign of tiredness. There was a sensuality in the man, a kind of languor that kept him from over-heating. Annabelle had felt herself giving way, surrendering to him in a way that was as dangerous and satisfying as a plunge into cool water on a warm summer's day.

She plumped the pillows behind his head and lay in the crook of his arm. He had spoken hardly at all, only murmured endearments, meaningless phrases, nothing real, nothing that she would remember. Despite the intimacy, they had managed to keep themselves intact; their separateness surviving.

He stared at the ceiling.

'Teddy?'

'Mmm . . .?'

'Tell me about your childhood. About Pentecost.'

'That's very old history.'

'There must be something to tell.'

'Pentecost is very beautiful, you'd love the beaches.'

'Were you happy there?'

'Sometimes.'

She turned to look at him. The room was almost dark. She asked nothing more, but after a minute or two he began to speak.

'My mother's parents were fourth-generation white settlers. They came from France originally. The plantation was never very successful. By the time the war came it was nearly bankrupt. Hugo Ransome was an English naval officer, he spent a few months in Pentecost during the war. He met my mother at a dance, they were married nine weeks later, and then he was recalled to Europe where he remained for the rest of the war. He was wounded in the leg. When, eventually, he went back to Pentecost, things weren't quite how he expected them to be.'

'Your mother had met someone else?'

'She hadn't just met someone else. She was pregnant with me.'

'So, who was your real father?'

'I know nothing about him.'

'What did Hugo do? Did they divorce?'

Teddy stirred, easing the weight of her head on his arm. 'The Ransomes are very strong on honour. Hugo behaved towards my mother in a way that he thought was honourable.'

Annabelle waited, and when he said no more, asked another question. 'Are they still out there?'

'Hugo is there. My mother is dead.'

'You don't visit him?'

'No.'

'Never?'

'It was what my mother agreed. I would have his name and he would pay for my upbringing, but as soon as I was old enough I was sent to school in England and he would have nothing further to do with me.'

'How old were you, when you came here?'

'I was seven.'

'And did she come too, your mother?'

'No.'

'But surely . . .?'

'The normal rules didn't apply. Part of the agreement was that she would remain in Pentecost.'

'How could she agree to that?'

'She had little choice. Hugo had the money. He had rescued

her father from bankruptcy.'

'It must have been terrible for her, sending her child to another country.'

He shrugged. 'I don't know whether she suffered. I didn't see her again. All I received were parcels of food. She'd got hold of a catalogue from Fortnum & Mason. She used to order hampers. Things she thought I would remember from home. Rotting mangoes.'

Annabelle could think of nothing to say. His voice was strangely high and cracked. She rather doubted that Fortnum & Mason would send rotting mangoes, but he spoke the words as if the hampers had contained something far more appalling than over-ripe fruit.

After a while he sat up and switched on the light. 'Will you make some tea?'

The kitchen was still cluttered with the debris of their supper. At the sight of the cheese-board she felt hungry but didn't want to go back and suggest they eat. She wanted to hear the rest of the story. She wanted him to stay with her, not to go off to his club when he was finished with her, but to be there in the morning, to put his arms round her at the beginning of the day.

She cleared away the supper things and carried two mugs of tea into the bedroom. He made room for her, patted the pillows.

'Tell me about Winifred,' she said. 'What was it like, coming to England and growing up at Chanting Hill?'

'To begin with I hated her. The day she came to Mahana she shouted at Elias, demanded that he carry her bags into the house. She couldn't see that it was not for Elias to carry the bags. Sahilil was there to do that.'

'Who were these people?' Annabelle started to say, but he held up his hand, imitating a voice from that other country, decades ago.

'Are you Winifred?'

'"*Aunt* Winifred," Honey said. "You must call the lady, 'Aunt'".'

'Who was Honey – ?' Annabelle interrupted, but Teddy hardly seemed to notice.

'"Mama calls her Winifred",' I said.

'"That is of no concern."'

'This new aunt was bending down, kissing my cheek. She smelled of soap and peppermints. "I shall be taking you to school in England."'

Teddy stopped the mimicry, the little play he had begun. When he spoke again his voice was flat and humourless. 'I learned, eventually, that Winifred's wish for me to call her "Aunt" was a privilege. I was to be *allowed* to call her Aunt.

'She stayed in Mahana for a fortnight. There weren't enough bedrooms. I couldn't remember Mama and Papa ever sharing a room before. There was shouting. A mirror was broken. Bottles at the bedside. And bruises on her face.

'"It's your Papa, darling," she would say. "Papa is making me ill."

'In that one fortnight, everything changed. The process began on the first morning. Instead of Jaleb and Sahilil and the early morning ritual of the high stool by the window, sugared toast and sweet tea while they coaxed the stove into life – instead of that delicious, safe routine, Winifred was there, shouting at Jaleb to wash his hands, to hold them out for inspection. As if he were a compound boy. She didn't understand who ruled, that in the kitchen, Jaleb was king.'

Teddy paused, absently stirring the spoon in his mug. Annabelle hardly dared to breathe; she had the feeling he had forgotten she was there, as if he was remembering it himself, for himself, things he had never told anyone, hadn't thought of for years.

Teddy went on. 'Winifred had been very close to her brother. They had grown up together at Chanting Hill and she couldn't forgive him for abandoning it. She thought Hugo had married beneath himself and at the same time she was jealous of my mother, of Pentecost, of the things that had taken her brother away. In a way, she was even jealous of me.'

'Has she ever been back to Pentecost?'

'No. She swears she never will. She says it's the poverty she cannot bear, but really it's a colour thing. She can't stand the thought of black people preparing her food.'

'Where does she live?'

'At the Lodge.'

'Where's that?'

'Just at the end of the drive to Chanting Hill.' Teddy smiled. 'Everything has a price.'

'Do you get on with her?'

'Of course. She's part of my life. If it wasn't for her we wouldn't be at Chanting Hill. It was she who wanted us there. She loves us now. Forgives me for being "not quite".'

Cautiously Annabelle voiced another question. 'What about your mother?'

Teddy put down his mug carefully. 'After my second term at Branksome, one day just after Easter, Winifred took me into the library at Chanting Hill and told me that my mother was dead. She said it might be for the best. That some people make such a muddle of their lives, it's best not to go on.'

He took another sip of tea. 'I didn't ask her what happened. What a relief that must have been. She must have wondered how she was going to answer my questions. The truth is I didn't think of asking. The library was so dark, so cold, I could only think of getting away.'

'What did happen?'

'Hugo killed her.'

Annabelle felt her mouth go slack. Teddy planted a kiss on her neck. 'It's all right, my love, it wasn't like that. I don't mean that he got up and killed her with an axe.'

'What, then?'

He pulled down the sheet that had been covering her breasts. 'An accident. A kind of accident.' He kissed one nipple and then the other. 'All over and done with long ago.'

Winifred and I have been having a Serious Talk. I could tell it was going to be serious because she asked Mr Hills to light a fire in the library. Mr Hills is even more ancient than she is. I found him carrying the logs up from the store two at a time and worrying at the doormat each time in case Winifred shouted at him about the mud on the runners in the hall.

All this so that we could sit on those awful old library chairs. My bottom slid about on the hard leather and the smoke from the fire made my eyes water. She behaved as if nothing was wrong. There was a file on the table.

'I want you to know exactly how things stand, Theodore,' she said. The logs spat in the fireplace and I had to keep one eye out for the sparks on the rug.

'I'm not young and it's important that you should know exactly what is yours.'

I thought we were going into the old 'not quite' routine – my being 'not quite' when it came to matters of Ransome blood and Ransome talent and history and tradition and all those things that I don't quite measure up to. But no, the old bird was warming herself up to talk about something even dirtier than my being 'not quite'.

There was a document of some sort on the table. Lots of typing and the words 'completed copy' written in large letters at the top.

'Before I say anything else,' she said, 'I want you to understand one thing.' She started to smooth the paper, as if it did not lie flat enough on the table for her liking. 'I want you to know that I bear no grudge. Your mother was not intentionally bad, it was Hugo's mistake in marrying her. I see that now.'

My feet were turning to lumps of ice. Up there by the table it was just as if there was no fire burning at all. She was cold too, you could see the gooseflesh on her neck.

'Couldn't we talk about this in the kitchen?'

She raised her voice then, such a deep, mannish voice. It used to frighten me years ago.

'Theodore, you are eighteen years old. It's time you learned that there is a proper place for everything.'

'I just thought the kitchen would be warmer, that's all.'

'The kitchen is for cooking. When you are an adult there are times when it is necessary to have a conversation in private.'

'But there's no-one else here, Aunt Win. There aren't any servants in the kitchen to eavesdrop!'

She wouldn't move. We soldiered through our Serious Talk and when it was done she let me pour us both a malt whisky and we drank it in the kitchen by the Aga.

'Did you understand what we talked about, Theodore? I'm sorry the library was cold. Those logs weren't properly seasoned. I shall have to speak to Hills.'

'Don't worry poor old Mr Hills about it, Auntie Win,' I said. 'He's too old to be humping firewood anyway. I'll do it from now on.'

'You are a good boy, Theodore.' She leaned across and patted my knee and you could see the effect of the whisky in her eyes. 'You really are.'

It's a good thing she thinks so. If I understood her right, she's going to leave Chanting Hill to me when she dies.

'It's not yours of right,' she said, while she smoothed the paper on the table. It was some sort of agreement. A copy of something her brother had drawn up in Pentecost. She said, 'My brother gave the house to me when I came to fetch you from Pentecost. To be honest with you,' and she paused here to blow her nose, 'it was a kind of bribe. He gave me the house because he wanted to stay in Pentecost and he wanted me to bring you back here.'

I wanted to ask her why. Why did Hugo want to get rid of me so badly? I know about the sailor, that I'm not his son and all that, but why take it out on me? Anyway it didn't seem like the right moment to ask. The main thing she wanted to talk about was what I will get when I'm twenty-one and what I will get when she dies.

The answer to what I will get when I'm twenty-one seems to be nothing. The Agreement says I will be housed and fed and educated until my twenty-first birthday and after that I can go to hell. That wasn't quite what it said and it wasn't quite what she said but the gist of it all (and she made quite a little speech of it) is that I should be grateful that Hugo has paid for my education and I should work very hard and make sure I get a good job because there'll be no money at all once I'm twenty-one.

Until she's dead, that is. There was a long rigmarole about annuities and how she doesn't have enough to pay for me herself but she does (courtesy of Hugo's little bribe) own the house and all the land and the garden and everything and she has left me these in her will.

Imagine! I can't have it now because the old bastard in Pentecost wants to punish me – and not me either, really, but some sailor he never met who fucked my mother while he was off getting a hole in his leg in the war. I can't have anything because I am 'not quite' but when Winifred dies I will get the lot.

Did you ever hear of anything so absurd?

I don't want to wait until Winifred is dead. She's a hundred years old now and there's no sign of her dying. It'll be another hundred years before she finally goes.

And then there is the thought of it. Winifred not being here. It has taken me so long to learn to be fond of her, how can I think of her dying?

NINE

Elias was waiting by the car. Hugo Ransome moved slowly down the verandah steps. The chauffeur had grown fat, his belly strained the buttons of his shirt. He wore his sleeves rolled and the frayed hems of his trousers hung over a pair of tattered training shoes.

Hugo made no comment. The chauffeur's attire was no more a subject for comment than the new shacks that clustered at the edge of the plantation, or the young bullock that was tethered to a tree by the drive, or the bar of the Mahana club full of black faces, the sons of house servants drinking whisky and soda, a black District Commissioner in the Lounge every day, taking advantage of the free newspapers.

Hugo climbed wheezily into the front passenger seat. Honey Jellawella called from the verandah. 'You bring him back for lunch, Elias. He is not to linger in that club and miss the lunch that Jaleb is preparing for him.'

Elias raised a hand in acknowledgement. An airy gesture, one custodian to another. As if Hugo were a charge, or a piece of luggage, or a vagrant child.

Hugo looked back at Honey, standing on the steps while the car rumbled down the drive. She had overstepped herself. Years ago she had overstepped herself. Hugo did not acknowledge her wave. The ayah had appointed herself housekeeper, and then nurse. And now warden – there every hour of the day, fussing, waiting in the hall when Hugo came out of his room, her brown eyes bright with alarm.

'We hear you coughing all the time, Mr Ransome.'

'It's nothing.'

'But it gets worse.'

She bullied him to the clinic in Mahana. And then the hospital at Liberté. The journey was no distance at all now; lorries rattled up and down the newly surfaced road, raising the dust on the bends. Tourists in air-conditioned coaches parked by the gate. The Baton Estate had become a stopping place. The guide books included a colour photograph of the house. The caption stated that this was one of the few planter houses to survive unaltered. According to the guides, 'The Batons were one of the great planter families. Generations lived and died at Mahana. At one time the family owned land from here to the river.'

Tourists stared through their tinted glass at the bullock in the drive, paint peeling in the harsh sun, the patches on the roof and the fretwork on the verandah rotted through.

'You should seek treatment in Europe,' said the Costa consultant at Liberté Hospital. 'You expatriates who have the money – there is no need for you to be ill.'

The diagnosis was written on a paper that Hugo did not read. It was how things were done now, in independent Pentecost. A letter from the hospital, a prescription for medicine from America.

Hugo did not want to be called an expatriate.

Jellawella patted his back. 'You must not shout like this. No-one wants you to go away, but there is no treatment in Pentecost for this illness.'

At night, Jellawella stood in the passage while he coughed. 'I am writing to your English house.'

Long arguments. Honey would not shout. No-one but Hugo had shouted in the house for years. The Costa woman's ways were more subtle, persistent. At last he gave her the address of Chanting Hill.

'You will get no response,' he said.

'Mr Teddy Ransome will answer.'

Hugo shook his head. The action made him cough again, a

long heaving spasm.

Jaleb brought infusions of herbs from the compound. The path to the kitchen door was shorter these days. Over the years, imperceptibly, the compound had crept towards the house. There was no longer a fence to mark the boundary. In the years after Clara's death Hugo had surrendered to the new bureaucracy, the new despots of Independence, requisitioning white men's land. Hugo had kept only the house and the garden. The estate had gone for a pittance, all the equipment included, but the Mahana Co-operative made no more profit than decades of Batons. Their tractors stalled in the muddle of grass and potholes that clogged the way between the trees, the estate workers still idled the afternoons in the shade, just as they had for hundreds of years.

Hugo watched from the verandah. The failure of the co-operative was a kind of comfort, a grim solace for his tired, lonely days. His world had shrunk to the spaces of the house and the garden, to his chair in the club and the uncertain progress of the car with Elias at the wheel; to the nagging of Honey Jellawella, the complaints of Jaleb, the shortage of buckets for the leaking roof, and the old houseboy's carpenter son coming up to patch the place and swagger about his business and how he could make the verandah floor sound if only Hugo would pay his outrageous price. And the parrots, second or third descendants of the birds who had first mocked him, who had shrieked and hooted at Clara's betrayal, still mocking him, repeating Honey's scolds, echoing his cough, the long raw hacks towards death.

'I have written to your English house,' Honey called from the passage. 'They will come now to take you home.'

In the garden of Chanting Hill a soft, summer rain had brought down a scatter of yellow leaves. The grass that had been parched and brown was greening once more. Water gathered in small dimples in the drive. Branches of oak and elder bowed low, weighed down with wet foliage.

From his desk in the library, Teddy could see the trees, the surfaces of puddles that sparkled, disturbed by intermittent

118

dripping, leaves fluttering down to lie like green and yellow paw prints on the mud. From somewhere in the house came the sound of music, a heavy rhythm accompanying a plaintive clarinet.

He could see Graham's car in the drive, shiny with rain. The kind of car Teddy would have for himself were it not for the fear of looking a fool, squeezing his spreading middle age into a bucket seat. His own car, sleek and expensive as it was, looked staid and responsible beside his son's.

Susan and Crystal were at a Show. He'd watched them pile the pony tackle into the back of the Range Rover, and put the picnic bag on the back seat, heavy with bottles of lemonade and cheese rolls and the First Aid kit. Crystal had looked back to wave goodbye, sleek and graceful in her riding gear.

Teddy muttered a note into his dictaphone, a reminder to check when the car insurance was due for renewal. Phyllis would pick it up between the business letters. The leather chair creaked as he shifted his weight. The library at Chanting Hill was no longer the bleak place of his childhood, the place where in a cold twilight, smoke from the chimney seeping into the room, he had listened to Winifred's vague little speech about muddled lives, read the terms of Hugo's Agreement, cutting him out, as cleanly and coldly as one would excise a polyp or a tumour. The hard, cold chairs from which he had shrunk on that day had been recovered in a soft tapestry weave, and the desk chair, in which he now sat, was re-upholstered in leather that was soft, almost fluid to the touch. On the wall, in place of the old Ransome ancestors, there hung a single pastel portrait of Susan, drawn soon after they moved to Chanting Hill.

Teddy smiled. Susan had the Ransome style. All of them seemed to have it, the boys, Crystal. They lived in Chanting Hill as if it were truly theirs. Susan, more than any of them, had taken to the life as if born to it. She had shown herself an expert in the matter of identifying what was good and recoverable from the great mass of old furniture that cluttered the house. She had the eye of an artist for placing the pieces as they came back from the restorer's, and for seeing where there was a gap, where some fresh item would complete a setting. It was she who had

119

given the house its new life, revived the dark interior, banished its solemnity, the gloom that had hung over his childhood.

Behind him, in the recesses of the house, the music changed its rhythm, clarinet giving way to a male voice, high and harsh. A door slammed and the sound receded, muted by heavy oak and thick carpets.

It was so nearly all that he had wanted. All so nearly done.

Teddy lifted his briefcase onto the desk and unlocked it. Inside were the files he had intended to deal with on the train, that he had left untouched on his lap while he stared through the window, watching London curl away, fields of housing estates giving way to sheep and cows, stands of trees and ribbons of fence and ditch. The views were familiar enough. He had often stared thus, watching the landscape twist and unfold, but no pleasant reflections had coloured this journey home. His briefcase had rested unopened on his lap, he could neither sleep nor read. Instead of the newspaper and a long soothing daydream to bridge the space between London and home, his thoughts had chattered at him like a brash magpie, darting and hopping, taking flight and landing, apparently free, apparently as free as the wind and yet confined, contained, drawn inside a definable space, a territory with clear if invisible boundaries. Fenced in by unease.

Unease. It was unease that had rendered the journey home tedious, prolonged. When at last he had opened his briefcase it was to take out his calculator, rather than a newspaper, to sit, tapping at the tiny keys – as if the numbers held a secret, a way out of the web. So absorbed had he been, the station came upon him unexpectedly, catching him with the briefcase still resting on his lap, with papers and the calculator to be gathered up in haste, stuffed anyhow inside, the weekend bag to be snatched off the shelf with his umbrella and the door kicked open just as the guard blew his whistle.

And the car was not where it should be. The whole week had begun badly, starting with Monday morning when he had found his usual parking space at Winton Abbas occupied by a strange car. He was forced to park near the track, where the surface was potholed and greasy. The place where casual passengers tended to park, ignorant of the damage done by cinders flung out by passing trains.

The dent in the nearside door that awaited his return was expected, inevitable. He could see it now through the library window. A small enough thing – it could be repaired, the paintwork restored – but an omen, nevertheless. The car would never be quite the same. The knowledge of the damage would be there, like the knowledge he carried now, the notes in his briefcase, the intimations of betrayal, of impending calamity.

A letter from Blairs Bank. 'Leonora Cohen's account is now overdrawn.'

It was a measure of the way things were slipping. He had let the Cohen account become overdrawn. Mrs Willard had decided to go on a cruise with her daughter. They wanted several thousand pounds at short notice. The balance on the Willard client account had been insufficient. He'd had to sell the last of the Holland stocks and send the proceeds to the Willards. Then there were Leonora's fees to be paid. There was nothing for it but to draw a cheque on her account, knowing it would go overdrawn.

The letter from Blairs Bank was signed by one Gerald Nisner, Assistant Manager. Who the hell is Gerald Nisner? Silently Teddy asked the question. Why am I getting letters from an Assistant Manager?

He picked up the dictaphone.

'Phyllis, I want you to make an appointment for me to see Cyril Towers at Blairs. Tell him I want to see him right away. And book a table at Giordani's – I'll take him to lunch after the meeting.'

Cyril would apologise for this letter from Nisner. The bank manager valued Teddy's custom and would accept his explanations. Cyril would see that an unsecured overdraft on the account of a client for whom Teddy held Power of Attorney was nothing at all when set against the business that Teddy had brought to Blairs over the years.

But why a letter from Nisner? Has there been some change at the bank? Was Cyril Towers no longer in control?

Teddy spread the papers from his briefcase across the desk,

sorted and then re-stacked them. Nothing changed. Nothing could alter the facts. The facts were that the Cohen account was overdrawn and he had no means, no source of funds, with which to repay it.

And, as if the letter from Nisner wasn't enough, fluttering into his in-tray on a Friday morning, enough to spoil a journey, a weekend, a night's sleep; as if that were not sufficient, the second post had brought a notice from the National Bird Watchers Association – they would wait no longer for the money that was due to them from the estate of Mrs Holland.

It was not their first complaint. The Association had written numerous letters, progressively less polite. At first they had simply enquired, then the enquiries became demands. There should be an interim distribution; the estate was exempt from Inheritance Tax, he could make a substantial payment without waiting for Revenue clearance. Recently they had demanded not only a distribution but an Estate Account, interest calculations, income tax certificates.

The latest complaint stated that a notice had been sent to the Senior Partner of Harbour Lowe & Robbins.

Teddy covered his face with his hands. If the partners decided to make enquiries, he was doomed. Phyllis would be no match for them. The carefully constructed files which he kept ready for the auditors' clerks each year would not stand the scrutiny of a serious investigator. One question would lead to another, and another, and it would be the whole structure of his practice – of his life – that came apart.

The figures on his calculator stared coldly back at him. He thought of Leonora Cohen, of the thousands and thousands of pounds that had been paid to the nursing home. She was the start of it all, the first temptation, whose money had been the candy in a baby's hand, too easy, too necessary to ignore. The woman was gaga, useless. She should have been dead years ago, would have wanted to be dead, if she'd known it would be like this, nurses feeding her, changing her nappies – and the cost of it all, the staggering cost of a pointless life.

But it was too late. Even if she died now, it would solve nothing. Her estate was virtually nil. To be freed from the burden of her nursing fees would not produce the money that was missing from the Holland account, or the money he would have to find before Mrs Willard died. And then there were all the other clients, the great tangle of smaller debts and loans that stretched so far back and were so convoluted, Teddy didn't believe he could ever unravel them, let alone find a way to put the money where it belonged.

With a shiver of anxiety he took the Littleford file out of his briefcase. 'Barbara,' he said aloud, 'I am counting on you.'

The wizened face of the Yorkshirewoman swam before his eyes. She liked to call Teddy 'my little Ransome'; she laughed every time she said it. Once a month he visited her for afternoon tea, like an obedient son, his eyes roving over the pictures and furniture and carpets that cluttered the house in Eaton Square. As good as anything at Chanting Hill. Just a few sales, and the problem of Kathleen Holland and the bird-watchers would be solved.

'You should sell up, Barbara.' Many times he had said it. 'Before you get too uncomfortable. Some of these sheltered flats are very luxurious.'

'But I don't want to leave my house. I'm perfectly comfortable here.'

'But you're vulnerable, Barbara. What if something happened to you? There's so much crime . . .'

'But what would I do with all this?'

Teddy brought his fingertips together; it was a trick he had learned, to take people's eyes away from his face. 'We could put some of it into store,' he said, 'and perhaps you'd let me help you to sell a few things.'

Barbara Littleford laughed. 'You sound like the people from Sotheby's! They come round here every year to talk me into selling something. You'll have to wait until I'm dead, I tell them!'

A sound in the drive distracted his attention. The Range Rover appeared, nosing between dripping hydrangeas. He could see Susan behind the wheel, made ghostly by the tinted glass. Beside her was Crystal. She jumped out as soon as they stopped, still wearing her riding hat. Seeing him in the window she waved and held up a rosette. 'We came second!'

Susan opened the back and took out the picnic bag. It was lighter now, the picnic eaten, the lemonade all gone. The tack would be in the stable already, the pony, Mercury, still to come, sharing a box that belonged to a neighbour. Crystal took the bag from her mother. They approached the house together, Crystal leaning over so that the long-handled bag would not trail in the wet. She was chattering, her free hand gesturing with the rosette.

A better pedigree than Susan's, Teddy observed to himself, watching the two of them. Crystal had nothing of Susan's light colouring; Crystal's hair was glossy and dark, her skin pale and lustrous.

A clatter of boots in the hall, a knock on the door.

'Am I disturbing you? Can I come in?'

'Yes to both,' said Teddy.

Crystal's hair was still in a tight plait and her chin bore the faint mark of a chin-strap. She sat on the edge of his desk, untied her ribbon and shook loose her hair. 'Mercury was really good today. I think we could win next time if he keeps this up.'

Teddy leaned back in his chair. Paying little attention to her words he watched her face, her fine eyes smiling at him.

'And Ma says would you like a cup of tea?'

'I'll come and join you in a minute,' said Teddy. 'And tell your mother I'd like one of those chocolate cookies I saw her making this morning.'

'There aren't any left. We took them to the Show.'

'You ate them all?'

'We handed them round. Everyone thinks Ma is a wonderful cook.'

'And so she is, but not when she gives away all the cookies.'

'You shouldn't eat them anyway. They'll make you even fatter.'

'Cheeky monkey!' Teddy reached across the desk but she darted away.

'And you'll have to have skimmed milk in your tea!'

'Skimmed milk!'

'We're all drinking it now.'

'Who is all?'

124

'The whole family. Ma isn't going to buy anything else from now on.'

'Why? You're not fat. The boys aren't fat – '

'We're doing it to encourage our tubby parents.'

Teddy grabbed his paperweight but she was gone, the door swinging gaily behind her.

The sun emerged, throwing a wash of light over the rug in front of the desk. It shouldn't be there, he thought, irrelevantly. Bright light would do the rug no good at all. He turned the paperweight in his hand, comforted by the solid form, the fine outline of the Ransome Crest under his fingers.

There would be a way out. There had always been a way out.

From the end of the hall he heard Winifred's voice. 'I've brought you some scones. I made them for the Bring-and-Buy but we didn't sell them all.'

Teddy went to the door. 'Hello, Winnie.'

'Locked in the library as usual?'

'I was just coming out to have some tea.' He kissed her cheek.

'What have I done to deserve a kiss?' Her shrewd eyes scanned his face. 'You have a guilty look, Theodore Ransome!'

'I'm thinking of eating your scones,' said Teddy, as lightly as he could.

'You look a bit peaky to me. What do you think, Susan? Don't you think he looks a bit off colour?' Winifred preceded them into the drawing room. For once all the family was present. Susan poured the tea and Crystal gave her father a look as he reached for a scone.

'I – I – ' Teddy stopped, trying to quell the stammer. 'I – I'll just have the one.'

Susan looked up. 'Why are you stammering?'

'He knows he shouldn't eat scones,' said Crystal, gleefully.

'You never used to stammer,' said Susan. 'I can't remember you stammering.'

'Do I do it often?'

'You've done it twice this weekend. This morning you called me m-my l-love.' Her voice was teasing, showing the kindly concern that had replaced the love in their marriage. 'You've been working too hard, Teddy. You're tired. You're stuttering

125

because you're tired.'

She has part of the truth, thought Teddy. I am utterly tired of trying to keep track. I used to keep a kind of tally, a mental reckoning of what will have to be put right, but it has slipped away, just as the possibility of putting things right has slipped away. This has all become too big, too well hidden and forgotten to be undone. It hangs in my head like those great spiders' webs we used to find in the trees at Mahana, vast and intricate and subtle – invisible until the sun shone.

He took a bite of the scone, letting the yeasty dryness fill his mouth. Perhaps, he thought, the stammer is a screen, a way of pausing for thought, before the wrong answer slips out.

Do I stammer to Annabelle?

Probably not. I am honest with Annabelle; as honest as our dishonest situation allows. It is part of what draws me to her – that we already share some guilt.

Once she asked me if lying to Susan is a burden, if I suffer from it. 'I know I'm not the first,' she said, 'but still you must feel something?'

'Of course. Of course I feel something.'

I did not say the rest, thought Teddy, finishing the scone. That the lies I tell Susan are mere trifles, *sliptongues* as they are called in Pentecost. Compared with the big deceits, being warmed by another woman is a sliptongue.

The meeting with Cyril Towers went badly. Another payment had gone to the nursing home. Nisner sat with Towers throughout the meeting. Teddy had brooded on Nisner – a thirty-five-year-old goon wearing a double-breasted suit that was too short in the arms, who whined his 'i's and never used two words where ten would do.

How is it, Teddy questioned, that banks, even smart expensive banks like Blairs, promote such people to positions of authority?

It was Nisner who led the discussion. 'We're so glad to have this opportunity, Mr Ransome. One or two of your clients' accounts have been concerning us for some time.' His voice was like a dentist's drill. When Teddy said there was a problem of liquidity, his skinny hands jumped out across the table.

'We're looking for some security for these overdrafts, Mr Ransome.'

Cyril Towers said almost nothing. Several times Teddy caught him staring into space, as if he wished he were somewhere else. Teddy regretted having asked him to lunch. Nisner hovered around when the meeting was over. It was impossible not to include him in the invitation, but Giordani's was full, they had trouble switching the table for a threesome. They ended up with a table near the doors to the kitchen. Giordani himself came to apologise.

Nisner didn't even look up, Teddy reflected. He eats everything with a fork. I can forgive my sons when they gobble – it is a side-effect of boarding school. Winifred used to chastise me for the same thing. They will grow out of it as I did. But Nisner is fully grown. What is the bank thinking of? Blairs will be undone by this new breed of mannerless bureaucrats.

No business was conducted over lunch. There was talk of the economy, the prospects for interest rates. Cyril mentioned Susan's housekeeping account, and they talked in a general way of the extravagance of women, the marvellous sums that Susan spent on her clothes. Then Cyril mentioned a new investment scheme that Blairs had introduced.

There was no life in it, thought Teddy. Over pudding we talked about schools and school-fees – almost deliberately, it seemed, because we knew Nisner could not contribute. He has no children – I certainly hope he has none. The children of such men will ruin the world.

In Teddy's eyes the whole morning and lunch had been a waste of time – and the day was not improved by the messages Phyllis was holding when he returned to the office. Fourteen telephone calls. Two from Susan – something she has seen in Winton Abbas. The Bird men wanted him to ring back (again). Two new clients wanting appointments (both recommended by other clients). Annabelle called (no comment from Phyllis, but no surname; it was her only concession to the frequency of Annabelle's calls, that she no longer took down the surname). And Howard Campbell waiting to see Teddy.

127

Howard Campbell. Leonora's only living relative – the Australian he had dismissed as untraceable!

Teddy looked through the one-way glass. Meek enough; denim jeans and a leather jacket. Phyllis had given him a cup of tea. He had the cup and saucer on his knee, which gave Teddy an advantage as he bounded in to shake the man's hand.

'I'm so sorry you've been kept waiting. Unfortunately I have to rush to another appointment. Could you fix another day with Phyllis? It's really impossible for me to see people without appointment these days.'

'I want to talk to you about Aunt Leonora.'

'Yes, of course. What a remarkable woman.'

'I am her only kin.'

'Are you? I hadn't realised.' Teddy shook his hand again. The cup and saucer were all over the place. 'I'm sorry I can't see you now.'

'I'm only in London for a week.'

'I see. Well, perhaps I'll see you next time you're here.'

He went back into his office and phoned Chanting Hill. Instead of Susan it was Crystal who answered. How clear her voice is, thought Teddy. They talked about her pony, and the kittens in the barn. Then Susan came on.

'David Bell has a very good piece for sale. A cellaret. Regency. It would look wonderful in the dining room. I think you should have a word with David right away. He'll hold it for us but it needs to go to the restorer and he does have someone else who is interested.'

Teddy agreed to talk to the dealer. Susan hadn't even thought about the money – she never did – but that was how it should be. He wanted Susan to be happy – to be perhaps the first person who had been happy in Chanting Hill for decades. It suits her, he thought, this role of the chatelaine; it makes her content. After all I have done, Susan at least must be content.

The noise of the traffic in Eaton Square muffled Barbara Littleford's voice on the intercom.

'Is that you, Teddy?'

'I'm a little bit early. Shall I go away and come back?'

'Don't be so silly. Imelda is coming down now.'

The intercom went silent. Teddy waited on the step. The houses on either side had been repainted. Between them, Barbara's portico looked slightly faded, the surfaces of the pillars less than perfect.

After a moment of rattling chains and sliding bolts the door opened.

'How are you, Imelda?'

The maid smiled, and answered in her thick Philippino accent, 'I am fine but Mrs Littleford is not so good.'

'I'm very sorry to hear that.' Teddy stepped into the hall and handed Imelda his raincoat. 'Shall I go straight up?'

'Please.' Though he knew his way blindfold, so often had he paid these visits, Imelda gestured to the stairs.

All the houses in the Square were the same, built upwards, the high-ceilinged hall leading to a curving staircase and the sitting room, which occupied the whole of the first floor; tall windows with a view of the Square, leafy trees hiding the traffic.

His client was in her customary chair, her stick hooked over the arm and the telephone on the table beside her. 'Well, my boy. This is a pleasure.'

'I was due to come anyway, Barbara,' Teddy took her hand, noticing the smear of blood bruises across her wrists, 'but Phyllis said you wanted to see me straight away.'

'I do, Teddy. I need your good advice.'

Teddy settled himself at the end of the sofa, leaning forward so as to catch the old lady's words. 'I've had a fall.'

'A fall? Are you injured?'

'I'm all right, but I've hurt my leg and I gave Imelda a terrible fright.'

'When did it happen?'

'A night or two ago. I got up to spend a penny. I often do, you don't sleep so soundly when you're my age. I don't know quite what happened. Imelda thinks I fainted but that's nonsense, of course.'

'Did she fetch the doctor?'

'Well that was the trouble, her room is too far away. She didn't hear me call. I couldn't lift myself up and I couldn't get to the bell. She found me in the morning, as stiff as a corpse with cold.'

'Oh, my dear!' Teddy rose from his chair.

'To tell you the truth, I've been in bed ever since. You're my first visitor.'

'You shouldn't have got up for me.'

The old lady cackled a little. 'I may be old, but I haven't reached the stage where I want handsome young men to see me looking a fright in bed. In any case, I've got my accountant coming in after you. He wants to talk about my tax.' She leaned forward and with stiff movments lifted some papers on to her lap. 'I've been thinking about what you said last time, Teddy. You've given me a lot of good advice in the past and I've usually followed it to my advantage.'

Teddy smiled. 'I do try – '

Barbara Littleford waved his words aside. 'But sometimes I've been very stubborn.'

Teddy could see that the papers on her lap included his last letter, in which he had suggested, not for the first time, that she should give him Enduring Power of Attorney.

Barbara continued. 'At first I was rather put off by the thought of it. You seemed to be saying that I should sign this because I'm likely to go gaga.'

'Not at all, Barbara. I recommend all my clients to give Power of Attorney to someone they trust. None of us knows what is round the corner, and if for some reason a person – and it can be anyone, young or old – becomes incapable of conducting their own affairs, it leaves a very tricky situation if there is no-one authorised to deal with things on their behalf.'

'What happens without such an authority? What would have happened if I'd been in a coma after my fall?'

'We'd have had to apply to the Court of Protection. If your disability looked to be long-term, the Court would make you a Patient.'

'And what does that mean?'

'The Court appoints a Receiver. It's quite a tedious business. All your assets have to be transferred to the Receiver and he or she can only take limited action without permission of the Court.'

'And who would they appoint as Receiver?'

'Usually it's someone who knows your affairs. Your solicitor or your accountant. The real problem – ' Teddy slowed his pace, to make sure she heard exactly what he said – 'the real disadvantage is that it is very expensive. The Court charges substantial fees for its services and it requires detailed accounts, and then the Receiver will have his professional fees on top. It can amount to quite a substantial expense.'

Barbara's eyes narrowed. 'And what will it cost if I appoint you as my Attorney?'

'For the present, no more than my usual fee. If something did happen and I had to manage your affairs, I would charge for the time spent, of course, but it would be a great deal less expensive than the Court of Protection.'

The old lady pursed her lips. 'Have you brought the form, then?'

'As a matter of fact I have.' Teddy opened his briefcase. 'I thought I should have it ready, just in case.'

'Call Imelda, will you? She can be my witness and then we shall have a cup of tea.'

131

TEN

Phyllis brought in her notebook. She had written the message down, as if it were just like any other telephone message. Teddy rose slightly, as he always did. She sat down in the little leather chair in front of his desk, as if to take dictation. But he had not summoned her, and it was not her practice to sit down when delivering a message.

Teddy put his hands on the desk, to steady himself against the ill omen she carried in her face. She is to show me another crack in the facade, he thought, another place where the truth is leaking out.

'Mrs Ransome called. You were on the other line. She asked me to tell you. It's very bad news, I'm afraid.'

'Crystal? Has something happened to Crystal?'

'No.' Phyllis shook her head. His question confused her, interrupted what she had come in to say. 'It's your aunt. I'm afraid she had a stroke. They found her – it was some hours before . . .'

'Winifred?' said Teddy, as if there were some other aunt, someone else, the question disguising his relief. 'Are you sure?'

Phyllis started to weep. 'I'm sorry, Mr Ransome; I hardly knew her, but I'm always upset by a death.'

Absently, Teddy handed her his handkerchief. He turned to the window, looking blindly out across the rooftops, the ugly forests of lift towers and air-conditioning units and a glint of gold from the top of St Paul's. It was as if someone had opened a window, let a draught of cool air into an overheated room, like taking off a heavy overcoat on a warm day. The feeling of relief, release, deliverance, was physical. He wanted to jump up, to telephone Annabelle, though she would understand none of it, to phone her and say 'It's all right. Everything will be all right.'

Phyllis was waiting, anxious to tell him the rest. 'She was found in the Lodge. She was at the bottom of the stairs. Crystal found her.'

Teddy felt his heart lurch. 'My little girl?'

'Mrs Ransome said she was very adult about it. She called an ambulance and waited with – her – the body.'

'But Crystal is only sixteen.'

Phyllis sucked her teeth. 'Sixteen can be quite grown up these days.'

'Even so.' Teddy straightened the papers on his desk. He wanted Phyllis to go; he wanted time to think.

Teddy rose. 'Thank you, Phyllis.' Briefly, he put out his hand to help her up. 'I'm sorry you had the rotten job of telling me this.'

Her eyes were on him, searching for some sign of feeling, shock or grief. He felt nothing, could summon no tears.

She hovered, her hand on the doorknob. 'Shall I cancel your appointments?'

'Yes, yes,' said Teddy, relieved that she should think of something to be done. 'Cancel them all.' And then, as she was going out: 'And bring me Aunt Winifred's file.'

Phyllis brought the file. And a copy of Winifred's will from the safe.

Teddy knew the contents. Had known for years. But nonetheless it was important to read it again. To know the old luck had held good.

The Lodge would fetch a tidy sum. More, with planning permission for the garden. Room for eight or nine houses and no damage to the view from Chanting Hill. If he could only tie the ends together there would be enough to pay off the Bird Men and put a convincing amount in Leonora Cohen's account. Enough to make Howard Campbell back off.

And then there was Chanting Hill itself. What would Susan

say to a sale of the house?

A row about that, perhaps – and then the question of all their things, all her treasures. If they didn't have Chanting Hill, where would they put it all?

Details. Just details. The main point was that there was a way out. He wanted to cry for relief.

He flicked the pages of the file. A receipt for an insurance premium caught his attention. He'd arranged cover for all the Ransome property through a broker who owed him a favour. The premium was hugely discounted. The receipt reminded him of the jewellery at the bank, Ransome heirlooms. Winifred wore jewellery so seldom he'd almost forgotten it was there, but he remembered going with her to the bank when it was valued. He remembered a diamond ring, a big, old-fashioned solitaire.

'I don't exactly feel sad,' said Crystal folding tea-towels into a packing case. She had spent some time in silence, trying to give the thing a shape, trying to pinch herself, mentally, to see if she could make the death hurt. But there was no pain, only a kind of bewilderment. 'I just can't grasp that she's not here any more.'

'She was a dear old thing,' said Susan, pulling out a drawer in Winifred's bedroom. 'I think we'll miss her more than we realise.'

The drawer was packed with old linen, heavy sheets with the Ransome crest embroidered in the corners. 'Some of this stuff must have belonged to her parents. You can see where she even darned the holes.'

'She always liked things to be preserved,' Crystal observed. 'In a way she was a bit like you. It pleased her no end when you had all the old stuff restored. You and she cared about it much more than Papa.'

Susan's grief was more real. She had loved the old lady; was already missing her, the figure on the path on Sunday morning, the batches of cakes and common sense. Packing up her belongings, emptying the Lodge, Susan felt a twinge of fear. Like all things lost, they could not measure Winifred's value until she was gone. They had needed Teddy's aunt (who was no aunt, but allowed the imprecision) more than they admitted to one another. With her sense of history, her Ransome name, the old lady had drawn them together; her sharp, bracing wisdom had served as a kind of coagulant, binding the family to Chanting Hill. It was she, with her unsentimental affection for them all, who had made their living there real. Without Winifred there would be nothing to pretend for; without her they would be exposed, the cracks and falsehoods of their lives clear to see.

They gathered in St Agnes'. All the family together in the front pew; Phyllis behind with Winifred's friends from the bridge club. And David Bell.

Teddy was late. The mourners whispered together in the pews. He was to have preceded the pall-bearers, led the coffin into the church. They did it without him, while the organ played softly and rain pattered on the stained glass. Susan huddled inside her black coat, glad she had decided to wear a hat after all. The bridge-club women wore hats, small, fitted styles that reminded Susan of the screw-tops of thermos flasks. Crystal wore no hat, but a twist of ribbon as black as her hair.

At last the diesel rattle of a taxi told them he had come; heavy feet on the path, the change in his pocket clinking as he ran. The church door banged. The bridge women turned, scowling their composite of interest and disapproval. The service began. Teddy read the lesson in his best voice, filling the church with rich, fluid assurance, seducing them all with dignity, and sincerity and a measured trace of grief.

The bridge women came back along the footpath to drink sherry at Chanting Hill. They smiled at Susan. Her Madeira cake was very light. Winifred's recipe.

Graham and Lucian stood around with trays of cheese puffs and vol-au-vents. Susan watched them, proud and at the same time dismayed. Their ties were loose, Graham had a streak of ink on his cuff, but they smiled at the bridge ladies, managed not to eat all the food and retired to the kitchen to smoke their cigarettes.

Like the boys, Teddy showed no hint of grief. Even as the bridge ladies drank their sherries, he was taking a couple of surveyors around the Lodge.

'What are they doing here?' she hissed, catching him as he

135

followed them out.

'I just want them to take a look. Now is as good a time as any.' She heard him talking as he hurried after them. About the garden of the Lodge, fifteen executive plots.

Would no-one mourn for Winifred?

Crystal stood by the window in the drawing room. Like most of the clothes she wore these days, her frock was a rag from a junk shop, black velvet falling in loose folds. The too-large bodice was gathered in the crook of her breasts with a fake cameo brooch. She looked astonishingly beautiful. Teddy returned with the surveyors. Susan saw him stop as he came through the door, to stare at his daughter, wonder breaking through the mask.

Crystal seemed unaware. She stayed in the corner by the window, a streak of cloud-grey light falling across her hair. The surveyors clustered around her like hungry puppies.

The doorbell rang. Teddy was in the dining room, busy with the guests. Through the hall window Susan could see a motorcycle, the shape of a crash helmet through the glass in the front door.

The courier asked her to sign for the letter.

'But it's only come from Winton Abbas.'

The motor-cyclist said something in reply, but as he hadn't taken off his helmet, Susan didn't hear him.

The letter was addressed to Mr & Mrs T Ransome. She went upstairs. The telephone was ringing in the bedroom. A woman's voice asked for Teddy, but rang off when she heard Susan answer.

Leaving the bedroom door open, Susan sat on the bed to read the letter. The paper carried the name of a firm of solicitors in Winton Abbas.

David Bell was coming up the stairs.

'Susan, are you all right? I saw you dashing up here . . .'

'Yes.'

'You look as if you've had a fright.' He reached the top of the stairs.

'It's just funerals,' said Susan. 'They get to me.'

David put out his hand. 'I hope –' He paused. Though she did not take his hand, he continued to hold it out to her. 'I hope you would tell me if there was something – if you needed me as a friend.'

She didn't answer. Down in the hall, the bridge ladies were putting on their coats.

'I must go down, I must say goodbye.'

Later, when all the mourners were gone, she found Teddy in the kitchen, sitting alone at the table. The boys had left a smell of stale cigarette smoke. She switched on the extractor. He'd opened a bottle of red wine. She watched as he drank off a glass and poured another. When he looked up, raising his head between hunched shoulders, his eyes were shining, as if there were tears there, unshed.

'She used to hold my hand in the street. She would crush my fingers as if she were afraid I would escape – or that she might. That we might, she poor dear spinster and I, that we might find our wish to escape from one another overwhelming.

'There was a shop in the High Street. I used to stand and watch the grinder turning. There were women with aprons and trays of cakes and the smell of fresh-ground coffee spilled out into the street. I always wanted to linger there, to breathe in that smell.

'I used to ask if we could go inside. Couldn't we go inside and have some coffee? She always said, "One day, perhaps".'

Susan walked across the kitchen. 'Teddy –'

'She said one day we would, but only if I was very, very good. We never did. Perhaps I never was. Never quite good enough.' Teddy swallowed the wine as if it had no taste. 'Perhaps she knew, all along.'

He gulped again at the wine. 'It's her hair I remember. It was always that colour, even at the beginning. Always that thick, greyish-white with streaks of yellow. Always coming loose, bits escaping. She would tuck them back, impatiently. That is the image I have of her, stooping slightly, with her arm raised, her fingers pushing at her hair.'

'Teddy, someone called.'

'All her dresses were the same. Always with collars, fastened to the top, her neck always skinny and red. Like Mary's. That was my first thought of her, all those years ago in Mahana. Aunt Winifred looks like Mary the rooster.'

'Teddy! We've had a letter from a solicitor in Winton Abbas. It came by hand. He didn't know before today that Winifred was dead.'

Teddy looked up. 'Who didn't know she was dead?'

'This man.' Susan waved the letter that the courier had brought. 'The solicitor says Winifred came to see him shortly before she died. He saw the death notice in *The Times*. He's sorry he didn't make it to the funeral.'

'So?' Teddy held out his hand. 'What of it?'

'He says she made another will. He's sent us a copy.'

'Give that to me!'

Susan caught her breath. Teddy's words roared out. His eyes were alight, coming at her across the kitchen table to grab the papers from her hand.

'It's all right, Teddy. She's left Chanting Hill to the children. We have a life interest, that's all. I'm sure it won't make any real difference – '

Susan stopped speaking. Teddy was staring at the document. 'This is a fake!'

'I don't see how it can be,' said Susan. 'The date is only a few weeks ago.' She broke off. 'Teddy, what is it?'

Teddy stared at the photocopy. He was more distraught than she had ever seen him.

'Why are you so upset?'

Teddy waved the paper. 'She's even made this damned man her Executor. She must have been off her rocker. She must have been under his influence!'

'I hardly think so. Winifred was entirely lucid.'

'Then why did she do this to me? Why did she want to destroy me?'

'We're not destroyed. What are you talking about?'

'Don't you see? If we only have a life interest we can't sell anything.'

'Why on earth should we want to sell anything?' Susan walked around the table. She wished she hadn't mentioned the letter. Had left it until the morning.

'If you read the letter you'll see he says she had a change of heart. There's quite a lot of detail, really. She wanted to be sure that Chanting Hill would be kept for succeeding generations. She thought you didn't care enough for the house, that because of what her brother had done, you would want to break free of it.'

'That's rubbish!' cried Teddy. 'It wasn't because of Hugo! It was because she knew. She always could see through me! She knew!'

Susan put her hand on the table. 'Knew what, Teddy?'

The message was tucked under her keyboard. 'Mr Monday called. Please ring him back.'

Mr Monday was a joke, a code. She had called him that when he was too busy to see her, when clients and family took him away from her, stealing the precious weekdays. The joke was to prevent a quarrel, to prevent the intrusion of his other, 'real' life from making them unhappy. She made light of his going. But you will come back? And the answer was always yes. And when he sent her messages, they came from Mr Monday.

And today was Monday. Annabelle phoned him, endured his secretary's false courtesy.

He came on immediately. 'Can you get away tomorrow?'

She hesitated. No greeting. Nothing gentle said.

'Be quick, I don't have any time.'

'You have to tell me, Teddy. You have to tell me why it's a week since you rang.'

'Winifred died.'

'Oh.' It was all she could say. She couldn't think how he might feel. He had always spoken of his aunt with a kind of satire, the sort of lop-sided, sloping affection that can hide passion as much as indifference.

Teddy hurried on. 'There's a place I'd like to take you. We can have lunch.'

In the morning she telephoned her excuse to the office – a sick father, needing her care. Another deceit. Layer upon layer of it: his deceit, her deceit – their joint deceit. Were they deceiving each other as well?

He picked her up at midday, kissed her briefly as she climbed into the car. They sped out of London, Teddy driving as he always did, hard and impatient through the traffic. They didn't talk. The tape was playing, loud urgent strings, the sound scattering about their ears like new leaves in a brisk wind.

'What is it?'

'Corelli. Concerti Grossi.'

He said no more until the hotel was in sight, a fine structure of red brick with tall chimneys and finely decorated gables, spoiled by a modern conservatory that was bolted to its side like a huge glass handbag.

They sat with their backs to the bar, looking out over the sweep of the North Downs, swathes of grass striated by strips of bald white chalk. The summer day was fine and clear, but from that distance the chalk looked like slopes of fresh snow.

The sofa they shared was uncomfortably deep. Teddy sat out of it, his thighs spread wide against the cushioned frame. His suit looked new: dark grey with a fine burgundy stripe and wide lapels that lay crisp and flat against his shoulders. On the table in front of them was a bottle of Chablis, a bowl of olives.

'Is it cold enough for you?'

'Yes,' she smiled and took another sip of wine, as if to demonstrate her agreement.

'There's something I want to give you.'

He reached for her hand, took a fold of white tissue from his pocket and placed it in her palm. She could feel the weight inside. His face was very serious.

'Will you unwrap it for me?'

She kept her palm stretched open as he unfolded the tissue. Inside was a pouch of frayed blue velvet. Before he lifted it, he looked up.

'I want you to know something. I want this to tell you something; I want you to keep it so that you will always know, always remember.'

He turned the fold of velvet. A ring lay, glittering, against the cloth. Dark-yellow gold with silver claws that held secure a diamond, a disc of brilliance inside a circle of tiny sapphires.

He slipped the ring onto her finger. It was the right size. She held it out to the sunlight; the diamond winked and sparkled.

'Teddy, I don't know what to say.'

What was he doing? They had been so careful up till now; deliberately, consciously, they had made no promises, no commitments. Alone, sometimes she fantasised, dreamed of a life with him, uninterrupted. But it was always just a fantasy. The affair would end with nothing. One day he would go away for good; back to Susan, to Chanting Hill. Back, most of all, to his daughter. Annabelle knew this; had steeled herself to it. It was part of the truth of having an affair.

And a dimaond ring had no part in it.

She was able to produce tears. She had practised the art as a child, holding her breath and focussing so hard on a single point that tears would form. She did it now, in the hotel conservatory, feeling the weighted tissue in the palm of her hand, afraid to show any true response, afraid of what he might say next. She stared at the ring until her eyes blurred.

Teddy took her in his arms. 'My poppet, there's no need to cry.' He put his hands over hers, his palm over the diamond. 'Let's go upstairs.'

He continued holding her hand as they went across the lobby and up the stairs. The hotel was quiet, a strand of recorded music drifting in the corridors. Teddy unlocked the door and led her inside. There were wide windows by the bed, draped with nets and curtains that matched the bedspread. Between a pair of armchairs was a small table bearing a basket of fruit and a printed card of welcome from the management.

He took off his jacket and put it on a chair.

Annabelle wanted to sit down. She had breathed so little as they came up that she felt slightly weak, as if her false tears might give way to the real thing.

He came towards her. His embrace was tight, imprisoning. He thrust his hand inside the waistband of her skirt, forcing his way down, thrusting between her legs. She tore at his shirt buttons, wanting to bite him, eat him. The ring turned on her finger and she drew her hand down his back, dragging the diamond across his skin.

Phyllis was putting on her coat. The office was clear, the outgoing mail ready in the messenger's tray. She had caught up with the filing and tidied up the papers on Teddy's desk. The telephone messages lay square along the edge of his blotter. She'd given him the blotter as a Christmas present, the same year that he had presented her with the gilt-framed mirror at which she looked as she put on her headscarf and buttoned her raincoat.

With luck she'd catch the early train and get in to Marks and Spencer on the way home. Supper would be salmon en croute from the chill cabinet. Just for a treat.

'Oh, Mr Drayton! You surprised me!' Alexander Drayton, the senior partner, had entered without knocking. Behind him was a young man from Cashiers whose name she couldn't remember.

'Is Ransome here?'

'No,' said Phyllis. 'He's been out all day. Can I help you?'

ELEVEN

'Where is he now?' Drayton turned to look at his colleagues. 'Did anyone see him today?'

'It seems he went to visit a client – a whole day's outing. Phyllis was cagey.'

It was after nine o'clock. The offices of Harbour Lowe & Robbins had been closed for hours. Most of the building was in darkness, but the lights from the fifth floor blazed out into the September evening. The senior partner had called the meeting at five, summoning all the partners and the Chief Cashier.

Before them, spread on the table, and on the floor by the window, were the contents of two of Teddy's filing cabinets, carried from the Ransome Suite by the partners themselves, the locks twisted open.

'Our first problem is Howard Campbell,' said Alexander Drayton. 'He is an Australian, a nephew of Leonora Cohen, a client of Teddy's who has been in a nursing home for many years. He complained initially that Teddy had refused to have a meeting with him. Since then he has been making enquiries about a number of properties that she used to own. It appears that the properties have been sold. Likewise she had a portfolio of investments, and these too have been sold. There is almost nothing left: no properties, no investments. Ransome has had her Power of Attorney for some years, and Campbell wants to know what happened to all the assets. He reckons even the colossal nursing-home fees couldn't have exhausted her wealth.

He has been making enquiries at Blairs and somehow – apparently the Assistant Manager was less than discreet – he has discovered that the Cohen account is quite heavily overdrawn.'

The junior partner put up his hand. 'If she has been incapacitated since before 1986, she can't have given him Enduring Power of Attorney. An ordinary Power of Attorney would no longer be valid.'

'Howard Campbell has picked that up, too. He says he is going to see the Court of Protection.'

'Has anyone spoken to Teddy?'

Alexander Drayton shook his head. 'We would have done, but for this.' He held up a letter. 'This is another matter where there seems to be a problem.' The letterhead was printed in yellow, with a bird motif in one corner. 'The estate of Kathleen Holland, deceased. The terms of the will are that, following the death of the husband, the whole of the residue passes to the National Bird Watchers Association.' At a prompt from Drayton, the youngest partner passed photocopies of the letter around the table.

'This is their third formal complaint. The first two I simply referred to Ransome.'

'You did nothing more than that?'

'You know as well as I do that we get complaints from time to time. It's almost inevitable in a firm as busy as we are. Often as not it's a storm in a teacup.'

'But these people complained twice?'

'Well,' the senior partner cleared his throat. 'The truth is there wasn't a lot I could do. As you know, Teddy's practice is pretty unique in this firm. It's so long since any of us has done private client work, I couldn't begin to tell him how he should operate.'

'So what did you do?'

'I sent him a note.'

John Railton leaned forward. 'Did you keep a copy?'

'Of course – and I have a copy of Teddy's reply. Courteous as always, he apologised that I'd been troubled and said he would arrange a distribution to the National Bird Watchers Association within the week.'

'And did he?'

144

Alexander Drayton turned to the Chief Cashier. 'I think you can take it from here.'

The Chief Cashier spoke hesitantly. 'He wasn't able to. According to the Bird Watchers they are due to receive a further distribution of about three hundred thousand pounds. The Holland account doesn't have anything like that amount in cash and, judging by the files we have looked at, no investments or anything else.'

'So what has Ransome done?'

'He seems to be trying to gather the money from elsewhere. So far we have traced transfers of cash from five other client files, mostly fairly small sums. The most suspicious transaction is the appearance of one hundred and ten thousand pounds just this week. It looks as though it belongs in the account for Mrs Barbara Littleford.'

'How has he managed to do that?'

'It seems from the file that she decided – or was persuaded – to sell some of her pictures at auction.'

'But the auctioneers wouldn't just give the money to Ransome . . .' he paused. 'Unless – '

Alexander Drayton nodded. 'It appears that Mrs Littleford has been unwell. Teddy has her Power of Attorney also. He used the power to instruct the auctioneers to pay the money to our client account.'

'And put a hundred and ten thousand of it into the account for Leonora Cohen,' added the Finance Director.

'Could it have been a mistake?'

'I thought it was, at first.' The Cashier measured his words. 'But I asked my assistant to check the other recent transfers on Teddy's client accounts. I wasn't thinking of fraud – I just thought he'd got into a muddle. Then we discovered all these other transactions. One thing just seemed to lead to another. God knows how many accounts are involved.' He drew a list from his breast pocket. 'Over the last few years there have been a great many transfers to and from Mr Ransome's clients' accounts. There are also transfers to an account at Blairs Bank which I cannot identify, but which may be in Teddy's own name.'

'Thank you.' The senior partner tapped a sheaf of papers in front of him. 'It appears, from our preliminary investigation, that the fraud is spread throughout his practice. It's extraordinary that he hasn't been caught before this.'

'I believe our auditors will have a case to answer.'

'Shouldn't they have queried these transactions?'

'Yes,' said the Chief Cashier. 'But they only make random checks and their main source of verification is the files. Teddy's files look very good and, on the face of it, the transactions tie up with the correspondence. It is only if you look at them all that you start to see a pattern.'

'Surely the auditors picked up something?'

'So far, I have traced only two occasions when they might have been alerted. The first was when Teddy had 'flu. The auditors asked Phyllis to get them a file as part of their random check on client transactions. She couldn't find the file and Teddy was too ill to comment. On the second occasion Phyllis was on holiday and a file couldn't be found. Teddy claimed she had sent it to store but the archivist could find no trace of it. Both times the auditors were scheduled to follow up the missing files but, either through Teddy fobbing them off or inertia on their part, the enquiries were not pursued.'

'But how did he hope to get away with it?' Railton interrupted.

'The only answer I can give is the one he probably gives himself: that he *has* done, he *has* got away with it, for years. There are dozens of cases where he has been sole executor of an estate, or held Power of Attorney for vulnerable old clients. Ransome had a way with the elderly – particularly women. It is clear from the files that they admired him and depended on him.'

'What about his secretary? Is she an accomplice?'

'Very hard to think of dear old Phyllis doing anything shady.'

'She wasn't exactly forthcoming as to his whereabouts. When we asked to see his diary – without telling her why, of course – she didn't want to show it to us. I had the impression she knew something she didn't want to tell us – but not this.'

'Another woman?'

'Probably. You can't blame her for wanting to be discreet.'

'Thank God for loyal secretaries.'

A moment's laughter was cut short by Alexander Drayton rising from his chair.

'In short, gentlemen, it seems that one of our partners may be a clever, we hope solitary, thief.'

'For how long has this been going on?'

'We simply don't know. It will take a considerable time to untangle.'

The junior partner spoke up. 'What has Howard Campbell been told?'

'Only that accounts of his aunt's affairs are being prepared as a matter of urgency.'

'And the Bird Watchers?'

'Unfortunately they have already contacted the Solicitors Complaints Bureau.'

'Have *we* notified the Law Society?'

'We've just given them the facts – that we'll be making a report.'

'Will they be sending someone in?'

'Yes, tomorrow.'

'Have we reported this to the police?'

'Not yet.' Alexander Drayton opened a window. 'The fact is, gentlemen, that unless the clients do so, it is up to us to inform the police.'

'And the police will want to see every last thing the firm has ever done.'

'Not quite, but the investigation is bound to affect us all.'

'Not to mention our clients.'

'Exactly. It'll be very unpleasant.'

'Have the press got hold of it?'

'Not yet.'

John Railton stubbed out his cigarette. 'The fraud itself will be small by media standards. It will only attract attention because of the name of the firm.'

Harry Rich spoke for the first time. His face was red, and his hands shook as he spoke. 'I should like to say how much I detest all this. We have been betrayed by our colleague – some of us have known him for twenty years. I knew him before he was qualified. I've always liked him. Most of us did. To learn that he has been cheating us, and cheating his clients, is very hard to bear. Stealing from one's clients, from people who trust you, is the worst crime of all.'

'I can't understand why he did it,' said Railton. 'The Ransomes are an old family. They have that huge house in Wiltshire. All the children have been to public school. There must be pots of money there.'

'Obviously it wasn't enough.'

'It's his family I'm sorry for. I fear for his sons. They will be tarred with this all their lives.'

'What happens next?'

'That depends partly on him, on how much he is prepared to co-operate.'

'Do you think he will?'

'We'll find that out when we interview him.'

'When will that be?'

'We've asked for him to be available in the morning.'

'I want you to go home.'

Graham Ransome fingered the label on his tie. His hands had stopped shaking. For a while he had thought they never would, since that first phone-call, his father's voice, almost unrecognisable: 'I've let you down.'

Phyllis was staring at Teddy. A sprig of her hair had come adrift, a loop above one eye, a signal of the disorder within.

'I want you to go home,' said Teddy again. 'I don't want you here this morning.'

Graham turned to the window, seeing nothing, hearing only the appalled quiet that had settled on the room. Phyllis moved slowly round her desk, hand over hand, as if she needed support. 'What do you mean? What are you saying?'

Teddy shook his head. 'I don't want you to be here this morning.' Leaning his bulk against the arm of the chair, he fished in his trouser pocket for a handkerchief. It was crumpled, less than white. Phyllis had never seen him with such a thing. With anything which was less than perfectly ironed, cared for.

'Something has gone wrong, Phyllis.'

148

'Oh!' For a moment Phyllis relaxed. 'You mean the girl? For a moment I thought you meant something else.'

Teddy buried his face in the handkerchief. It was Graham who spoke. 'We are not talking about some woman. My father is accused of fraud.'

Teddy waved the handkerchief, cutting Graham's words. 'There are difficulties with the client account.'

'Difficulties?' In her agitation, Phyllis picked up one of the coloured-paper pads that were used to request transactions on the client account. 'But we always fill these in correctly. They're never returned, the cashiers have never complained.' She waved the pad in the air, her voice rising with agitation. 'It's only the computer that goes wrong.' She put the pad down and tried to set it straight on the desk beside the others. 'That's all it is. You know nothing's been right since they installed the computer – I don't know why we can't go back to the old ledger system, it was so much easier to understand.'

'It wasn't the computer that caught me out,' said Teddy quietly. 'I didn't think of the nephew. I thought it would be those bird men – '

'But you've paid the bird men,' Phyllis cried.

'No, they are owed a great deal more than I have paid them.'

'But you sent them that huge cheque, only yesterday.'

'The cheque was stopped.'

'Stopped? Why? Who by?'

'By our senior partner.'

'Why did he do that?'

'The cheque was drawn on the wrong account.'

'What do you mean? It came out of the client account for Mrs Holland's estate! I sent the letter myself.'

'No, the money for the bird men came from Mrs Littleford.'

'How could it have done? It was Mrs Holland who left money to the National Bird Watchers Association.'

'Mrs Holland's estate is all gone. There's nothing left.'

'But I don't understand. How can it have nothing left? There was lots of money.'

'Phyllis my dear, I have let you down.'

Phyllis's hand slapped the desk. 'Nonsense. I've worked for

149

you for twenty years. I know exactly what has happened, you've just got yourself into a muddle. We can sort it out.' She turned her face away and headed towards the filing room.

'My partners have called in the police and – '

'The police!'

' – the Law Society have been informed. They'll be here soon.'

'It can't be true. It can't be.' Phyllis's voice rose, fear rising in her throat.

'Phyllis – I didn't want you to be here.'

'What will happen to you?'

'I'll be asked to make a statement. Then, or perhaps later, they will arrest me.'

'You must tell them it's a mistake, Teddy. They'll realise it is when they see the files. You've just made a mistake.'

'No. There's no mistake.'

'But what do you mean?'

'I've been borrowing money . . .'

'Then you must pay it back at once. How much do you owe? Surely it's only a little – '

Teddy held up his hand. 'I cannot pay them back, Phyllis. I do not know how much I owe, but it is more than I have. This didn't start yesterday. I've been doing it for years. It was as easy as anything – and impossible to stop, once I had begun.'

'Was it someone else, Teddy? Are you covering for someone?'

'No. There's no-one else. I just don't know how much is gone. At first I knew, and then I lost count.'

'I can't believe it,' said Phyllis. 'I'm going to make a cup of tea.'

Graham started to speak. 'Pa – '

Teddy interrupted. 'I tried to telephone her. I didn't want her to be here.'

Graham shook his head. 'She's been your secretary for years. She has to be told – she deserves to hear it from you.'

'I want her to go home.'

'You can't send her away. She'll be interviewed. They'll think she was part of it.'

'No!'

'Of course they will. And not just Phyllis. They'll suspect us all. They'll never believe we didn't know, that Ma didn't know,

150

what you were up to.'

'Your mother's entirely innocent. She has always been.'

'I know that, but no-one will believe it. All of us will be tarred with it.' Graham's voice rose. 'Didn't you think of that? Didn't you ever bloody think of the rest of us?'

'I thought of nothing else. I did it for you.'

'But you didn't need to.'

'You've no idea how expensive it all is, your schooling, keeping the house going, the pony . . .'

Graham jeered, 'And women?'

Teddy's head shot up. 'You're not to say that to your mother.'

Graham moved towards him. 'It won't matter to her now. You being a criminal is far worse than that. You've just wrecked her whole world.'

'It was your mother who wanted to live at Chanting Hill, to be the grand lady. She never wondered where the money came from. She never hesitated to spend it.'

'That's what women do,' Graham shouted. 'A wife shouldn't have to worry where the money is coming from, she shouldn't have to sit and wonder whether her husband is a thief. We had Chanting Hill, the place is so stuffed with antiques you could open a shop. Of course she didn't worry about money. We're Ransomes!'

'Not quite.'

'What do you mean?'

'There's no Ransome money. There never has been – not for me, anyway. We lived in the house because Winifred let us. No money came with it. I haven't had a penny of Ransome money since I was twenty-one.'

'But why?'

Teddy gave a short, bitter laugh. Before he answered Phyllis came back in to the room. She was carrying a pot of tea. 'Please, Teddy, tell me what's happening.'

She got no answer either. There were voices outside, a tap on the door. Alexander Drayton entered, followed by a man carrying a large briefcase. They had a glimpse of the corridor, shocked faces looking in.

Teddy stood up, putting away his handkerchief. Auto-

151

matically he held out his hand to the stranger. 'Theodore Ransome.'

'Richard Jacob, Law Society Complaints Bureau.' The newcomer held out his business card and, as no-one took it, put it on the desk. 'We are here to investigate certain matters.' He turned to a woman behind him. 'This is Pauline Jenkins, our Fraud Officer.'

She had dry, reddish hair and wore a plain black suit. Uninvited they settled themselves in, setting down briefcases, hanging up their raincoats. Jacob cleared his throat.

'We are empowered under section . . .' The man spoke softly, as if he held his own words in a certain awe. '. . . may suspend your Practising Certificate . . . further investigations . . .'

Phyllis was pouring tea, fetching extra cups with a grim air of busy-ness. 'Milk, sugar?'

'I'd prefer coffee,' said the redhead.

'What is your position here?' The man's voice had sharpened. Phyllis paused. She had been heading for the door. 'We will want to question you. Please remain in the room.'

'You're not the police.'

'This investigation is being made at the request of the partners of Harbour Lowe & Robbins. The police will be making their own enquiries.'

With a wooden feeling in her legs, Phyllis went to her desk. It was real then, she wasn't dreaming. She looked across at Teddy. He was rubbing the bridge of his nose.

The redhead tried the door to the filing room. It was locked. 'Could I have the key to this room, please?'

'That room is private,' said Phyllis.

The redhead continued to hold out her hand. 'Please give me the key. We have authority to examine the files.'

Phyllis looked at Teddy.

'Give her the keys.' It was Graham who gave the instruction. 'And show her your files.'

'But this is your father's practice!' cried Phyllis.

Graham's face was very white. 'I know that,' he said. His voice, which had been so calm all morning, suddenly gave way and she could hear the tears behind it, the bewilderment. 'This is as difficult for me as it is for you.'

Richard Jacob put down his cup. 'You will find that the cabinets containing files relating to Cohen, Holland and Willard have already been removed.'

'What do you mean, removed?' snapped Phyllis.

Jacob ignored the question. 'When you have shown Mrs Jenkins the other files you may go home.'

'I can't go home,' Phyllis cried. 'It's ten o'clock in the morning. I have letters to type. No-one is going through those files without me. They are my responsibility.'

Jacob's voice rose above hers. 'You would do better to co-operate, madam. Whatever you may have to hide.'

Her mouth dropped open. She looked at Teddy but he did not raise his eyes. 'Surely you'll tell them, Teddy. Surely you know I couldn't do anything like – '

Unable to finish her sentence, Phyllis took the keys from her desk and opened the door to the filing room. The redhead followed her inside. Those remaining in the office sat in silence. They could hear the metal filing drawers being dragged open, Phyllis blowing her nose, letting out small yelps.

The florist had called. Susan had just signed for the delivery when the telephone rang. She put the flowers down on the rug and went into the kitchen to answer it.

'I've let you down.'

'What?'

'Susan, I've let you down.'

She hardly recognised his voice. He was husky and squeaky all at once, as if he had been shedding tears.

'Are you hurt? Has there been an accident?'

'I've let you down. It's all falling apart.'

'What is? What's happening?'

She heard the words 'fraud' and 'arrested'; felt herself clinging to the rounded edge of the counter.

'Surely it's a mistake?'

'Yes. I've made a terrible mistake. I've been making it for years. I didn't mean it to get like this. I didn't want to have any gaps, I didn't want him to win . . .'

There was time to be impatient. This news, that was old news for him, a tale, it seemed, that he had carried in his head for years, was so old and shocking that he could not tell it coherently; her astonishment and his urgency made the words unintelligible.

'Are you coming home?'

'We have to wait for the police.'

'Who?'

'The people here. I am to be arrested.'

And then gone. The message left half delivered. What in God's name had he done? She heard herself crying, whooping into the telephone.

She called Graham's number but no-one answered the phone. She sat on the kitchen floor, clutching the receiver against her sweater, until the recorded voice of British Telecom whined at her to put it down.

It rang at once.

'Teddy?'

'Susan, it's me, David Bell.'

'Oh.'

'The cellaret is in the van. The restorer has done a good job – I'm only sorry it has taken so long. Shall I bring it out to you now?'

'No!' She pulled herself straight. As if he could see her. 'Yes – I mean – '

'Susan, are you all right?'

The same voice he had used at Winifred's funeral, when he found her alone upstairs. Burning to be needed, anxious, full of desire. She had brushed him off then.

'Susan? Are you there?'

'Yes.' She paused. Blew her nose. 'David, something awful has happened.'

'What is it? Is there something I can do to help?'

'Teddy phoned me a little while ago and told me he's going to be arrested.'

'Whatever for?'

'I'm not sure. He's done something wrong – something to do with clients' money.'

154

There was a moment's silence and then David Bell said, 'Are you alone? Shall I come round?'

'Please come. Teddy won't be here for hours. He said he would come home on the train when they've finished with him. He doesn't think they will detain him . . .' Suddenly, as the meaning of her own words came to her, Susan felt overwhelmed. 'Oh God, David, what is happening? I can't get an answer from Graham. Lucian doesn't have a phone at his digs – and in any case, what could I say to him?'

'Don't say another word, Susan. I'm going to shut the shop and come round right now.'

She went out to the hall. The flowers were still on the mat where she had put them when the phone rang. Peach and white roses for the hall. White lilies for the mantelpiece. She gathered them up, armfuls of cellophane and dripping stalks. The flower scissors were in the kitchen drawer. The round copper bowl had a wedge of usable oasis in the base. She stripped the leaves from the roses and cut two inches off each stalk. The work steadied her hands. She felt very cold. In spite of the sunshine she put on the jacket that hung by the back door. When David Bell arrived the flower arrangement for the hall was complete, a soft, fragrant mass of peach and white.

He held out his hands as he came through the door.

TWELVE

From the window of the train, Teddy could see a small park, a patch of green below the railway line. A couple were crossing the grass arm in arm. The grass petered out under a flyover. Beyond the flyover, filling the horizon, was the London of nightmares; acres of flats, towers of concrete and glass, graffiti on the walkways, high on the walls, bold and artistic and ominous.

The traffic on the flyover stood bumper to bumper, a faint haze of fumes hanging above it in the late summer air. The supporting pillars cast loops of shadow on the grass. Seagulls squatted in the sun, white, wind-blown hankies. The couple in the park reached a wooden bench and sat down very close to one another. Teddy could see that the woman was laughing. For them, for that anonymous couple sitting on a bench, it was an ordinary day, in an ordinary, safe world. His throat constricted as the train smoothly gathered speed, leaving them behind.

At Winton Abbas the porter was whistling. 'Hello, Mr Ransome. Funny seeing you here at this time of day.' Teddy nodded, smiling automatically.

The dent in the car door was still there. He put his bag on the passenger seat and started the engine. The journey to the house was short. He drove slowly, taking extra care at the crossing, pausing to let a class from the riding school go first.

A white van stood in the drive. Unmarked. Were they here already? So soon? More policemen with bulging pockets and incessantly crackling radios; inquisitors with red hair and unintelligent faces? Would there be no pause, no respite from strangers poking into things, scurrying through their lives?

He got out of the car. The front door was unlocked, it swung open at his touch. The hall looked as it always did, polished and sparkling. On the table stood a great bowl of flowers. Voices in the drawing room. He felt the urge to walk past, to go quietly into the library and shut them out. Instead he walked towards them. The talking stopped as he opened the door. Four white faces turned to look at him. Susan and Lucian and Crystal, and of all people, the antiques dealer, David Bell. No-one spoke. The clock in the hall began to strike, a whirring sound, followed by the low muffled gong. It was half-past four.

David Bell moved first, holding out his hand.

Susan collected herself. 'No, David,' she said, 'there's no need to pretend.'

Teddy looked at David Bell. The dealer's eyes were dark and excited.

'Nothing is for sale. They'll be coming to make an assessment. Nothing is to be moved.'

'I'm not a vulture,' said Bell. 'I'm not here to buy.'

'Then why – '

Susan answered without looking at Teddy. 'He brought the cellaret.' She gestured to the corner. The cellaret stood on a piece of cardboard, as if only recently released from its packaging, a square of mahogany, inlaid with boxwood, standing open to reveal its lead lining. Susan stared at the floor; her expression was utterly unfamiliar, as if a stranger had taken control of her features.

Lucian fiddled with something on the mantelpiece. From outside came the drone of a light plane passing overhead. For some reason Crystal was in her dressing gown. The tie hung loose; Teddy could see a trail of lace where the robe fell open. He moved towards her.

'Crystal, my poppet.'

'Fuck you!'

Teddy stopped, stepped back as if she had hit him.

'Bastard! Bloody, fucking, sodding, shitty, fucking, shitty,

157

shitty . . .' Running out of words, she darted from the room and up the stairs and then, as if freshly inspired, hung over the banister to finish her sentence, her dark hair in dishevelled curtains about her face, 'Fucking monster!'

Teddy turned away, avoiding the ring of shocked faces. He felt his bag in his hand. 'I'll just put this away.'

He made his way across the hall. His feet were unsteady. His bag knocked against his legs and rattled the tall blue-and-white vase beside the library door that served as an umbrella stand. The room looked undisturbed. He checked the drawers of the desk. They were still locked.

The last of the sun lay in a long, low sweep across the floor. The rug was pushed up at one end, its silk tassels turned in. He moved across to flatten it out and found himself looking at his shoe, shiny black, the hem of his trouser-leg lying at precisely the right height against the laced arch. And there was the pattern of the rug in the sunlight, spiral-haired maidens dancing in awkward twist-legged steps around the border. He remembered that the rug belonged to Winifred, would form part of her bequest to the children.

'At least,' he said aloud, 'at least the rug is safe.'

'Safe from what?' Lucian was in the doorway.

'From – ' Teddy paused, stammered. 'F-from the people who will want to take everything away.'

'And who will do it, Papa? Who will take things away from us?'

'Surely you know?' Teddy hung on to the desk.

'Try me.'

'About the . . . that I've been interviewed by the police.'

'Ma said you'd been arrested.'

'That's not quite right. I've only been interviewed so far.'

'Jesus, Pa!' Lucian's cool manner was wafer-thin. 'Is it true?'

'Yes.'

'Jesus!'

'You are less articulate than your sister.'

A series of expressions crossed Lucian's face. 'When Graham rang me I didn't believe it. You're my Pa. I can't have a crook for a Pa.'

'I'm afraid you have.' Teddy's voice shook as he spoke but the words came out easily. He had the feeling there was a torrent to come, that this sudden freedom would be unstoppable.

'You've ruined my life.'

'What?' Teddy laughed. '*Your* life? Is that all you can think of?'

'What else should I think of? I'm training to be a solicitor, for Christ's sake. That's what you wanted me to do. Now I discover you're bent. How is that going to help my career?' He ran his hands through his hair. 'Jesus, what were you thinking of, Pa – when you went out there ripping off old ladies or whatever it is that you did? Did you give any thought to us, to what it would do to us?'

'It was you I was thinking of. You and Graham and Crystal, and your mother and – '

'That's just crap. Absolute crap.'

'However you describe it, it is the truth.'

'Truth? Don't talk to me about truth.'

'You are lapsing into clichés, Lucian.'

Lucian gaped, astonished, as astonished as Teddy felt himself. This was not the conversation he had practised on the train (though it was Crystal, or possibly Susan, with whom he had imagined it). He had planned humility, sorrow, contrition. Instead there was this chill, chiding his son for speaking in clichés, no hint of repentance.

Abruptly Lucian turned and left the room, slamming the door so hard the books shuddered on the shelves. Then he opened it again, and shouted the single word, 'Bastard!'

Teddy laughed.

The door slammed again. He was alone. His thoughts resumed the course they had followed before Lucian's interruption. He flattened the corner of the rug with his shoe. They would not be able to take the rug. None of the Ransome chattels would be forfeit. He could provide an inventory of Ransome property, the pictures and furniture, even the house itself, that belonged to the estate of Winifred Ransome.

Teddy laughed again. 'Well, Hugo,' he said, speaking aloud to the empty room, 'you were right in the end. You can tell the world, if there is anyone who will listen, you can say that I was

159

no Ransome, that it was my bad, bastard blood that showed through.'

He moved over to the window. The hydrangeas were starting to turn, losing their bright summer colours. Amazing how they came back each year. It used to be Mr Hills who pruned them, cut the heads off at the end of winter. It was a sign of spring, Mr Hills moving among the beds with his secateurs, the wheelbarrow piled high with brown heads like permed old ladies, fluttering light as air.

Someone else did it now. Susan perhaps, or one of the men from the village who came down from time to time. Teddy remembered something about money. If you put a coin in the soil the pink flowers would turn blue – or vice versa. He put his face against the glass. There might be something there, if things got very bad. Hundreds of years of coins keeping the hydrangeas blue. He would dig them up for Susan. The flowers would turn pink.

The things that mattered – the things that would begin to matter.

Sounds in the hall made him turn. He could hear Susan, and the cool voice of David Bell. Susan was saying goodbye. Teddy caught the words: 'I'll do it tonight.'

For the first time since he had come home he felt alarmed. What would she do tonight? He waited until he heard a car and then opened the door.

'Susan?'

She paused, facing away from him.

'Susan?'

She didn't move.

'We must talk.'

For a moment he thought she was going to shake her head, walk away. She started to, then seemed to change her mind. She moved slowly towards him, her hands clasped at her waist, the knuckles visible, like the pink bones of a chicken. He stepped back, but she didn't enter the room.

'I'd prefer to talk out here.'

'As you wish.' Teddy stepped out into the hall.

She waited. He waited. 'Well?'

160

'Surely there is something to say,' Teddy began.

'I think it is you who has something to say.'

He could think of nothing, no way to start. 'All this b-business,' he stammered; paused. She offered him no help, nothing but her pale empty stare.

Teddy moved on, driven by the questions in his head. 'What has Crystal said – apart from just now? Has she . . .?'

'Crystal!' Susan bellowed. 'Is it only she who is on your mind? Only Crystal?'

'Of course, I am thinking of you all – I just wondered . . .'

'You may be sure your daughter is as appalled, stunned, as the rest of us. You heard her – the language she used. I don't know where she learned such words. But you see what she is really, your precious Crystal? You heard the words on her tongue.'

Susan stopped speaking. She looked over Teddy's shoulder and he knew at once that Crystal was behind him.

He turned. She came down the stairs, one step at a time.

'I've sold Mercury.'

'What?'

'I've sold him to the riding school. They've given me a cheque.'

'You've sold your pony?' Teddy was incredulous.

'And I've put up a notice about the tack. Someone wants to come and see it tomorrow.'

'But why? You've just won a prize with him. I thought you loved Mercury.'

'I do!' Crystal's voice was hoarse, her eyes full of tears.

'But then why, my poppet? Why did you sell him?'

'I didn't want him any more. I don't want anything of yours!'

'But that's silly. Look, we'll go over there. I'm sure the school will understand. We'll tell them you made a mistake.'

'It wasn't a mistake! I don't want anything that's come from stolen money. I don't want to be contaminated!'

'But sweetheart, the pony is yours. It belongs to no-one but you.'

Crystal's eyes glittered. 'You bought it!' She hissed at him. 'You stole money to buy it.'

'That's not entirely true. I've been working all my life – there have been honest profits, too. It hasn't all been . . .'

'And the rest! How can I go back to school? What can I say to my friends? I've always told them how marvellous you are. Everyone talks about Chanting Hill, how we have everything. And now it turns out you were cooking the books. My father is a thief. It's unbelievable. I hate you completely.'

Teddy looked back at his wife. In her face was a kind of horrified glee, a savage elation at Crystal's rejection of him.

LONDON SOLICITOR, THEODORE RANSOME, ARRESTED, SUSPECTED FRAUD.

Annabelle stared at the string of letters travelling across the Infotex screen, yellow on red. The flash was repeated three times and then there were others: an election in Greece, riots in India – all in the same yellow-on-red tape, ticketing across the screen. Annabelle found herself holding her breath, waiting for the flash to return. It could not be true. And then it came again.

'Bloody solicitors.'

One of the dealers was looking over her shoulder. She managed to ask a question, her voice high and piping to her ears. 'Have you seen anything else about this?'

'Nothing. Why, do you know him?'

'No!' She jolted and then recovered herself. She turned back to the screen. Impatiently she tapped the keys, calling up the reports from the other channels. There was nothing further about Teddy. She kept her face towards the screen. Fear clutched her like a cold hand on the back of her neck. Sweat made her fingers slip.

What did it mean? Who could she ask? How could she find out what this monstrous announcement meant?

Hastily, conscious of the eyes of the dealer on her back, she dialled Teddy's direct line. The call was answered almost immediately. A strange voice, not Teddy, not Phyllis. Annabelle put down the phone.

Numbly she stared at the screen. There was nothing she could do. She mustn't ask questions. If it was a mistake he would let her know – wouldn't he? If it was some mistake he would phone

162

her and laugh about it.

But it was too big to be a mistake, too dreadful. Ignoring the rest of the office, she walked down the backstairs and out into the street.

The crowds on the pavements were slow-moving, indifferent. She pushed her way through. There was nowhere to go. She didn't want to go home. She couldn't say what she wanted, except to keep moving, to get away from the screen, the yellow-on-red print with its evil tidings. She felt muddled, frightened, as if some great beast had come and knocked the wind out of her lungs.

Fraud. What did it mean? Embezzlement? Theft? False accounting? White-collar crime? The words bounced around her head. The language of newspapers, words without meaning. And then 'crime' brought her up short. Teddy, a criminal? It was impossible to take in. The crowds pushed against her. The whole world seemed to be moving the other way. Her heart thumped. Teddy, a criminal? A thief? She fingered the ring on her finger. The claws that held the diamond in place looked huge. A thought came to her, the same that had come and gone as they had drunk the cold Chablis in the ugly hotel conservatory, when he had given her the ring and she had manufactured some tears; the same thought that had come when he rolled her onto the hotel bed and pounded her until the sweat ran down his face in a stream. The little question that had come and gone while she drew the ring up and down against the bare skin of his back. Why wasn't there a box? Jewellers sell rings in fancy little boxes.

Hugo watched the doctor's car coming up from the road, skirting a stray cow, the easy wave to the compound children who played a kind of hopscotch where the ground was level. The doctor was black, confident with his bag, his stethoscope cold on Hugo's chest. There was talk of the hospital in Liberté.

'None of that. I'm going nowhere.' Squeezing it out between hacks. The parrots on the verandah copied the sound; shrill echoes of his dying.

The doctor pressed the places where the pain lay. Hugo

cursed him. 'It's nothing but a cough. What harm is there in a cough? Look at my bloody leg.' Holding out his foot, the trouser loose on the narrow, twisted limb. 'Look at that if you want to see something real.'

The doctor's hands were soft. 'A chest does not heal like a leg, Mr Ransome. Your lungs will not improve.'

'I have written to England,' Honey interjected. 'There will be help from England.'

Hugo coughed and laughed, a dreadful sound, sawing and braying. 'Your letter will bring nothing.'

When the doctor had gone, leaving his prescription, a letter to the hospital, Honey sat beside him at the table, a box of tissues ready by the plate. *The Times* had come.

'Did you read this newspaper?'

Honey didn't answer. She has read it, thought Hugo. It is clear that she has. A pink flush had appeared under her brown skin, a brightness in her eyes, shock.

The article was on the front page. The name in bold letters.

Hugo coughed. Honey wiped his chin. 'We'll hear nothing now, you know. No-one will answer your letter now.'

Honey buttered a slice of bread. 'Can you eat something, Mr Ransome?'

Hugo pushed the bread away. 'Three quarters of a million pounds!'

Honey persisted with the bread.

'He was bound to go wrong. It was in his blood.' Hugo paused, coughed, spat. 'I'm glad that Winifred is dead, that she did not live to see that she had failed.'

Eventually a corner of bread was taken, chewed. 'I was right to send him away. At least we have not had to live among thieves.'

Hugo swallowed a spoonful of scrambled egg. It was cold, the plate was cold. He barely noticed. He asked Honey to turn the page so that he could see the crossword. Suddenly he looked a little better, as if the news from England had given him zest.

'Will you think about going back now, Mr Ransome?'

'Arrogant and spicy,' he read.

'Will you?'

He was silent, then: 'Tarragon!' Wheezily he laughed. 'Rather clever, don't you think?'

'While you still have the strength for the journey. In England you may be healed.'

'I am not going back to England.'

'There would be *The Times* every day in England,' said Honey.

'I am dying. I shall do it here.'

'And where will you be buried?'

Hugo looked up. 'It concerns you, does it, where to put the old man's body?'

'It will have to be known.'

Hugo tapped his pen on the table, a splash of ink on a side-plate. 'You know the place.'

'Where the hibiscus flowers?'

'Where else? Where else?' Hugo rose, coughing. A stain of blood now, on the napkin.

'And a stone. Hugo – Mr Ransome – what about a stone?'

'That's all? That's all you care for, that she should have a stone?'

'There could be one for you both. It is customary, a man and wife buried . . .'

Hugo was leaving the table, sawing and braying, the pale thunder of his stick on the floorboards. 'A man and his wife? Such a marriage it was, that we must both be dead before we can sleep together in peace?'

Newspapers piled in the hall of her flat, every publication scanned and discarded. A paragraph in the tabloids, a column in the *Evening Standard*, an old photograph of Teddy, like a smug schoolboy. After the first day, the papers lost interest. Without specific enquiries she could discover nothing.

She tried to put him out of mind. It was just an affair – a bad choice. She should forget him, forget she ever knew him.

But she could not take off the ring. The diamond stayed on her finger, a talisman, tying her to him.

Then a message on her desk. *Mr Monday called. Will call again at 2 o'clock.*

It was five to two.

What could she say?

She could refuse to take the call. She could do as others would, and drop him like a hot brick.

I will not consort with thieves.

She tried the sentence aloud. And giggled.

Teddy couldn't be a thief. It was too small a word for him, too petty. If he had committed a crime it would be on the scale of everything else about him – it would have style.

'You must stay away from me. I cannot be associated with you.' That's what she should say. The only sensible thing was to keep away.

But when the telephone rang she said, 'Oh, my darling, what have you done?'

There was silence. She could hear his breath, the faint wheeze that she had heard first in his car, on the first giddy night. It was the same short breath she heard now. Almost the same.

'Annabelle?'

She found herself talking, interrupting, saving him from whatever he felt he had to say. 'I'm so relieved to hear your voice. I've been so afraid –'

'You have nothing to fear, Annabelle. You had no part in this.'

'No, I was afraid you wouldn't phone. That you'd think I would abandon you. I began to think you might do something awful, that I wouldn't have the chance to say – that I – '

'Annabelle, Annabelle.'

'It doesn't matter what you've done. It really doesn't,' she rattled on, 'I want to see you.'

Silence. Nothing but his breathing, slower now.

'Is it possible, Teddy? Are you under . . . guard, or whatever it is?'

'No, my love.' There was a hint of a chuckle. 'I'm not Ronnie Biggs. Nothing will happen until I appear in court.'

'Then I can see you?'

'Now Annabelle, are you being sensible?'

'It doesn't matter.'

'But I have been caught, Annabelle.'

Susan closed the door and put on the security chain. There were large bolts at the top and bottom. Security was important, solid bolts and the alarm system that winked as she passed the stairs.

She put her shopping bag on the table in the small morning room that David used as a dining room. Its doors opened out on to the back yard, where troughs of earth were laid out on concrete. 'Next year we will grow tomatoes and courgettes,' David had said, holding her very tight, hiding her face against his chest so that neither of them might see the horror in her expression. The idea of courgettes in Gro-bags, a concrete yard in place of a kitchen garden.

The alarm winked again as she went upstairs. The shop occupied the ground-floor rooms of a Georgian town house in the heart of Winton Abbas. The kitchen and dining room were part of an extension that ended in a dark lean-to that housed a loo and a washing machine. Upstairs David had converted the back bedroom into a sitting room. His bedroom was at the front; its window looked down on the street.

She had never imagined how it would be, life over a shop; carrying shopping straight in from the supermarket, standing in the busy street fumbling for a key to a door that, as a customer, she had never noticed. She had not thought of the bell on the shop door, ringing out the arrival of customers, the frequency at lunch time.

'I'll help you in the shop,' she'd said, on the first morning, self-conscious in her nightie. David had brought a cup of tea to the spare room where she had spent the night. He stood beside the bed in a pair of old jeans. There were short, reddish hairs on his chest, on his bare feet.

'Did you get any sleep?'

'Yes.'

He handed her the cup. 'You don't look as if you did.'

And her hand going up to her face, remembering the great daubs of mascara that had spread with her tears down her cheeks.

He touched her hair. 'Susan, it doesn't matter. It wouldn't matter how you looked, I'm glad that you are here.'

She'd pulled her dressing gown around her shoulders. 'I must get up. I must phone Crystal.'

167

'Crystal will be all right,' said David.

'How can she be all right, sleeping on a couch in Lucian's bedsit? She should have come with me here.'

'She didn't want to be here.'

'I should have insisted.'

'Susan, she's sixteen years old. You must let her find her own way of dealing with this.'

'But she needs my support.' Susan heard the hesitation in her voice. It was what a mother would say, should think. But of Crystal it might not be true. Who knew what the child felt? Needed?

'Phone her later on,' said David. 'Why not invite her over here at the weekend?'

The shop opened at nine. David sat at his desk at the back of the showroom and a woman came in to dust. Customers crept around as if the showroom were a church. A woman had a clock to sell.

'It's a big one,' she said, her loud voice filling the shop. 'A proper grandfather with a picture on the face. It came down my mother's side. I'd keep it but we haven't the room.'

David marked a date in his diary, writing 'Longcase – painted dial' beside the woman's name.

At eleven o'clock she made coffee and David sat with her in the dining room while they drank it. She started to speak, try to retrieve something from the rush of thoughts and shock and fear that ranged backwards and forwards in her head.

'I don't know what I'm doing here.'

David put his hand on the table, ready to take hers if she should hold it still.

'I should be at home. I shouldn't have abandoned him like that – all of us running away from Chanting Hill as if he had a disease.'

She drummed her fingers, and David's hand lay still on the table. 'I'm only here because I don't want to be there.'

'Yes,' said David, 'I know that.'

'But it's impossible. I can't stay here with you – in your spare room – just because I don't want to be there. It's too much of an imposition.'

168

'It isn't,' said David. 'I don't care how it came about, I just know that this part is right. That now you are here you will stay.'

'I can't. I can't simply leave home!'

'You already have.'

'I'm his wife. I have duties. I can't just abandon him after twenty-three years of marriage.'

'Did Teddy ask you to stay?'

The answer was too hard to think of. She started to cry again, tears coming down her cheeks as she had seen them on Teddy's cheeks, streams of tears, almost without account, without, even, any real sense of sorrow. Just shock, tears of shock that once started were hard to stop, would go on until they were spent.

'No.'

It was the truth. Teddy had not asked her to stay. Had expressed no feeling at all.

She had shouted at him, 'Don't you care?'

'It's all over, Susan. All of it.' Teddy's cheeks had been as wet as her own. 'This began when I was born and now it is over. I am avenged.'

'Don't be ridiculous.' The words came automatically, a reflex response to such melodrama; then the knowledge that the drama was real, the moment deserving of grand statements. She did not, as Crystal had done, call him a thief to his face, but she heard herself say, 'If this is real, if this is really happening, then I do not want to be part of it.'

She had left behind everything of value: all her jewellery and handbags and smart shoes and silk scarves. With only her plainest clothes, packed in an old suitcase of Lucian's, she found herself at David's door, the street door beside the shop window.

David took the case from her hand, led her upstairs. She cried for an hour, two, thoughts bubbling out of her, mostly astonishment, burning, outraged astonishment. 'My husband is a criminal. My husband has been arrested. My husband will go to prison.'

David made coffee and poured brandy and supplied handkerchiefs and rocked her in his arms.

169

'But what am I doing *here*?' A hundred times she asked the question.

'Resting,' said David. 'For now, it is just sanctuary.'

THIRTEEN

A month since she had seen him. It might have been years. A wall of time separated them. Time and anxiety and unbearable ignorance.

The station was no more than a platform and a car-park. She stepped down from the train. Two others disembarked, women in cardigans. They looked like someone's dailies. The older one carried a string bag. They left the station on foot, walking abreast beside the hedgerow.

Annabelle waited until they were out of sight and the noise of the departing train had faded. She could hear birdsong and insects, and sheep braying in the distance.

Even in her dreams she had feared their meeting. Feared that like this, without any glamour, without any of the trappings that had sheltered them from feelings that might have been real, they would be exposed; that now, when it was disastrous, when she should be turning her back on him, she would be unable to be false, that love for him would somehow fall out of her, like belongings from a handbag, all her thoughts and hopes, scattered irretrievably.

Teddy had warned that he wouldn't be there when the train came in. That she should wait. She sat on a stone step and turned her face up to the sun. If she looked relaxed it was a sham. Behind her closed eyes her mind was spinning, the same bewildered thought-stream that spun through all her waking hours: memories, his face, the weight of his body, his kisses.

And superimposed upon those memories, the face in the *Standard*. The word in black lettters. FRAUD.

'They give me their fees and their gratitude.' Teddy's own words – a lifetime ago.

Gratitude.

Was that what it had meant? Was that how he had thought of it? Taking people's money as a kind of gift to himself, a service charge?

There were so many questions. So much she wanted to ask and knew she would not. He had never liked questions. As if she, in her separate compartment, should not stray, even with simple knowledge, into the rest of his life.

Was it to protect her? To keep her safe from the guilt?

A car was turning into the forecourt. A battered, beige Metro. Dazzled by the sun, she couldn't see who was driving. The car pulled up on the far side, out of sight of the road.

And then there he was, emerging, doubled over, like a crouching beast unfolding to stand, to lean on the little car. This pose had no swagger in it, no hint of the old message: This is My Car. Now he leaned as if he needed support, his hand on the roof as if he was afraid to move away.

Annabelle's heels clicked on the stony surface of the road. The clicking quickened; suddenly she was running, her bag banging against her leg. All the usual considerations, wanting to look elegant, to please him, had vanished. She ran like a schoolgirl, arms outstretched.

'Oh!' Her face was against his chest. She could feel his hand on her head, pressing her against him, and then his arms around her waist, gathering her up, kissing her lips, her eyes. Her tongue tasted salt tears on his cheeks. His glasses were adrift. She lifted them off and leaned back.

The same man, but not the same. A thinner face. Still the wide jaw, the heaviness under his chin, but the softness was gone. He looked pale and ill and dazed.

The plastic upholstery felt cold and slippery. There were cassette tapes in the door pocket, empty cigarette packets on the floor. The ashtray was full.

'I'm sorry, I should have cleared it out. You'll have to forgive

172

the car. It's Lucian's. I was going to buy him a new car if he passed his exams.'

Annabelle shook her head. 'The car's fine. It's just the ashtray.'

'I've tried to persuade him to give up. He won't listen to me.'

'What happened to your car?'

'It's gone. So has the Range Rover.'

'So soon?'

'Once we started there was no reason not to go on.'

'Will you have to sell everything?'

'Just about. It's complicated.' He ran his hand through his hair. The gesture was familiar and instantly, in spite of the car, it was the Teddy she knew who sat beside her; the same man, but emptied, as if some essential part had been scooped out of him. She put her hand on his knee and he covered it with his own.

'It's good to have you here, Annabelle.'

'I wanted to come.'

'I don't think I know what to say to you.'

'I don't want you to say anything.'

He smiled.

'But Teddy, I don't want to sit in a car-park all day.'

'No, of course.'

He let go of her hand and started the car. Driving, he was the man she knew, his arm along the back of her seat as they reversed, the easy slip of gears, accelerating away, dragging from the little Metro the feel of the fast, expensive car he had lost.

'Where are we going?'

'There's a pub I know. We can have a drink.'

The pub was old, its dark-timbered front brightened by tubs of flowers and hanging baskets. There were more flowers inside, baskets of begonias crowding the windowsills. Teddy ordered a bottle of house wine and when it came he paid for it with cash. She had never seen him pay for anything with cash. Invariably he had used his plastic cards, or a cheque from a leather folder with the Blairs coat of arms stamped in gold on the front. Cash was something that he kept loose in his pocket, that jangled when he ran, strictly for taxis and collection boxes.

173

They carried the bottle and glasses out to the garden at the rear. There was no-one else there. A picnic table stood in the shade of some trees. Through a belt of undergrowth they could hear the gurgle of a hidden stream. Teddy drank his first glass very quickly and immediately poured himself a refill. They sat in silence for a while. Teddy seemed to be concentrating on the texture of the table.

'It's a lovely place, Teddy.'

'I came here once. A long time ago.'

Annabelle was silent. It was one of their rules, his rules, not to question. Who with? was never asked. Unexpectedly he volunteered the answer. 'I was with Susan. It was she who reminded me of it.' He took a deep gulp of wine. 'She reminded me that we came here once at a time when we were happy.'

Nonplussed, Annabelle looked across the garden. She could see a corner of the car-park and part of the Metro, the back of it visible at the side of the pub. It looked small and dreary. Maybe that's what he wanted now. Not the old flamboyance. Anonymity would be preferable.

'The trouble is, my love, I don't remember it.'

He spoke without looking at her, staring out at the garden. 'She says it was before Crystal was born, but I don't remember it.'

'But you remember the pub itself?'

'Yes, but not her being here with me. I have no recollection of her being here.'

Annabelle could think of nothing to say. He had broken their rule, but then perhaps there were no rules, now. Perhaps he had broken them all.

His glass was empty again. She refilled it and topped up her own. The wine was making her hungry.

'Shall we have something to eat?'

He didn't answer.

'Teddy,' she tugged gently at his sleeve. 'We can't drink all this wine and eat nothing. You won't be fit to drive.'

'No.' He seemed to make an effort to pull himself together.

'Stay here,' said Annabelle. 'I'll go and see what they have.'

The menu was chalked on a blackboard. She ordered two

ploughman's: Stilton for him, Brie for herself. It was easy, picnic food. She asked for extra bread and another bottle of house red.

The publican brought it out on a tray, baguettes with enormous wedges of cheese, sliced tomatoes, and pats of butter in silver paper. The bill was on a spare plate. She put her credit card on top.

Teddy looked at it but made no move to stop her. 'I don't have one of those any more,' he said simply.

'You don't have any cards at all?'

'Nothing. Not even a chequebook. Everything has been frozen.'

'What on earth are you living on?'

'They have my equity stake in the partnership – for the time being I am allowed to receive the interest.'

Annabelle broke off a corner of bread and picked at the crust. Teddy continued speaking, staring at the grass. 'The worst thing is the school fees. Crystal is halfway through her A-levels.'

'Won't the school – '

'At first they said they would. Susan told them we had financial problems. They have some emergency fund for children whose parents get into difficulties. They told Susan she was eligible, that they would waive the fees until Crystal's education is complete. But now the offer is withdrawn. They say there are too many demands on the fund, but it's obvious they've heard about me. They don't want my daughter in their school.'

'What will she do?'

He shrugged. 'She refuses to go to the comprehensive.'

'Could she get a job?'

Teddy shook his head. 'I don't know. We haven't discussed it.'

'She'll adapt,' said Annabelle.

'You think she will?'

'Of course she will.'

'If it were only the school, perhaps she would. But not to all this, Annabelle. We have to ration everything, even the hot water. She's not used to living like that.' He rubbed his hands over his face. 'She won't even speak to me.'

Annabelle took his hands in hers, pulling them down towards

175

her. 'You have to give her time, Teddy. Everyone needs time.'

He let go of her hands and rubbed his eyes. Something inside her squirmed away. She realised that until now his predicament had meant nothing to her – it was just money that he had taken, nothing that could not be replaced. Now here before her was the evidence of what had really happened. Not what he had taken, but what he had lost, wasted. Himself, his sense of himself. She swallowed down her wine and refilled her glass. The wine had a sharp metallic taste and seemed to have no effect on her at all.

'Come on,' she said, in the same calm voice. 'Let's eat.'

He watched her open a pat of butter, slice the baguette and fold in a wedge of Stilton with a sliver of tomato. She held it out. 'Come on, try some.'

He let her feed it to him, taking a bite and then pushing it back so that she should have a mouthful for herself. The cheese was strong and salty. They ate the rest of the baguette together, washing it down with long, brave swallows of wine.

'That's better,' he said, when the plate was empty. 'I'm sorry I flopped like that. It happens sometimes.'

He smiled at her. There was a smear of butter on his chin. She wiped it with a paper napkin and he caught hold of her hand. 'You won't go, will you? Annabelle? You won't be like the rest?'

He was squeezing her fingers. 'Teddy, you're hurting me.'

He let go at once and immediately she wished she had hidden the pain, so despairing was his expression.

'Not everyone can turn their backs. I keep telling myself that not everyone will give up.' He gulped wine. He was well into the second bottle. 'Someone even suggested that I read the Bible. I should read . . . they said, about forgiveness. But isn't there something about casting stones – Let he who has not sinned cast the first stone?' Teddy paused, looking at her very closely. He was a little drunk, his eyes bloodshot, slightly unfocussed. 'There are a lot of non-sinners in Wiltshire. There's a heap of stones around Chanting Hill.'

She ordered coffee, and slices of cheesecake that neither of them ate. The pub stayed open all day but they stayed in the garden, talking of practical things – of how it worked, this sort of crime: fraud as a painless, invisible thing. Of how the City dealt

176

smoothly and facelessly with its own.

A Mareva injunction had been taken out by Harbour Lowe & Robbins, freezing all his accounts. The insurers who underwrote the policy out of which the clients whom Teddy had robbed would be recompensed, had taken possession of all his property – all the pictures and the furniture that were not on the Ransome inventory, everything that he had paid for.

'But they can't take Chanting Hill, can they? Not the house?'

'There's a complication there.'

Teddy went into the details, the lawyer in him surfacing, so that for a time it was as if he was telling her about someone else. She watched his face, saw the life returning to it like a rush of blood, as he explained.

'Chanting Hill belongs to Winifred's estate – she left it to the children. The problem is that a lot of money was spent on the house. The insurers may try to trace it back.'

Annabelle watched rather than listened, and by the end she had only a vague idea of what was happening. The lawyers were building their case. He had been charged with 'specimen' offences and had admitted everything – all that he could remember. 'Nobody will lose out. The firm's insurance will cover every penny.'

'Except you,' said Annabelle.

'What?'

'Surely you have lost something – ?'

'I have lost nothing. Nothing that was ever mine. I was referring to the clients. The old ladies. They will be reimbursed.'

'And the firm – they must suffer the disgrace.'

'Yes.'

'And your family?'

Teddy sighed. The confidence drained from his face. She wanted to ask more, to probe, but he turned away, a gloss of tears on his cheeks.

He drove her back to the station. There was half an hour to wait for the train. They sat in the car.

'You won't be like all the rest, will you, Annabelle?' His fist clutched over hers. The old rules abandoned.

Annabelle turned to the window, confronting her own face,

177

dishevelled and pale. He started to unbutton her blouse, his mouth a line of stubborn appetite.

'Not here, Teddy. Not like this.'

'Don't deny me, Annabelle.'

He had never pleaded with her. Their affair had had no room for such frailty.

She pushed him away, attempted to fasten the buttons as he undid them. His resolve was stronger than hers. And the practice was there, the skill of a hundred undressings. He had hold of her breast. His hands were cold. She shrank away but the car was too small. His other hand cradled her head. 'Don't deny me, Annabelle.'

She stopped resisting. It was a struggle over nothing. The car was too small. Someone walked across the car-park jangling a bunch of keys. The hand on her breast closed tight, as if it were over her mouth, gagging her. From the low windows of the car they saw a raincoat and a briefcase, a man unlocking a car further up the row. He did not drive away but sat inside with the light on. They could see his newspaper.

Releasing her breast, Teddy's hand moved to her thighs, sweeping up in a familiar pattern that in other times had been irresistible.

'Teddy, please.'

'I must, Annabelle. I have nothing else to give you.'

He knew she would not resist for long. She leaned back, let his other hand support her head. She heard herself whimpering; this was sweeter than it had ever been. In a shivering mist of pleasure she heard him speaking low and clear in her ear.

'They cannot take this away from us. This is the truth. This is real.'

He stayed on the platform for as long as she could see him. The wind had set free the hair that he kept so carefully combed. He looked old and ridiculous and sad. As the train began to move he called out: 'You won't be like the rest?'

She didn't answer. The question was too big. The train dragged them apart. She managed a last kiss. A day's growth of beard scratched against her lips. A guard was shouting, 'Stand away!'

Stares in church, in the assembly at school; silences among friends; photographers; men with removal vans, the empty swimming pool littered with fallen leaves. Mercury gone, the door to his stable a blind eye; rationed hot water; men with inventories; arguments about silly things; the Metro an abandoned dog sitting in the great wastes of the garage. Even driving to the village had to be justified, the petrol something to be thought of.

But there was nowhere else. She could not stay in Lucian's bedsit, listening to him hump his girlfriend while she slept on the couch. Graham had been less subtle. After two nights in his flat he simply said, 'Sorry Crystal, my girlfriend's coming back, and she won't want you here.'

There was room in the dealer's flat, but that was out of the question. Even Chanting Hill was better than the sight of her mother lounging on a sofa in a tangerine tracksuit. Dimly, Crystal recognised the urge she felt – the wish to be cut off, to put a distance between what she was and what she had been – but she cried aloud, 'Mother, you can't wear that thing!'

'David bought it for me.'

'But it looks awful.'

'I chose the colour.'

'You can't have done. You look like a woman on a cruise ship.'

'It's been a kind of death, Crystal. The woman I was is no more.'

Crystal cried in her arms. 'I don't want everything to change at once. I can't bear it.'

'My darling, our life was built upon a falsehood. We can't go back.'

'You don't have to go this far.'

'David is being very kind to me.'

'David Bell is a wimp!'

'Papa didn't want me to stay. Even if he did, after all these years of lies, I couldn't trust a word from him. David is honest. I need someone who will tell me the truth.'

There was nowhere to go but back to Chanting Hill, and her

father. She waited until he had gone out before going to the library. It was necessary to find the truth.

Piles of papers on the desk. Pages of typescript, **'Theodore Ransome, (Defendant)'** typed in bold.

A box-file full of letters. The banner of Harbour Lowe & Robbins. Letters from other firms. A bundle marked 'Privileged. Draft schedule of Improper Withdrawals admitted by the Defendant.' The print was very small, a vast amount of material was reproduced on each page: long columns of dates and amounts, with notes down one side. Crystal found herself absorbed, checking the dates against ones she remembered: birthdays, and holidays, the dates of her music exams, the day Lucian passed his driving test.

She remembered an expression people used about money: 'telephone numbers'. There were 'telephone numbers' in the money columns; huge sums, none less than four figures. The highest was six.

Had he truly admitted it all? Could it possibly be true?

Leaving the papers in disarray, making no secret of her snooping, she opened the drawers of his desk. Inside were his old chequebook and a photograph of a girl standing by his car. Under the photograph was an aerogramme, a strip of bright stamps and a smudged postmark.

Dear Mr Teddy,

Your father is ill now. His lungs are bad, and his liver. The Doctor says he must have medicine in England. It is too bad at Mahana for this old white man.

You should come for him now Mr Teddy. Time has passed over the pains of long ago. He is just old and sick and his family must come.

You will forgive that I have not written to you. At first it was forbidden and when it was no longer a concern to be forbidden it was too late. Every day I have prayed for you, every day all these years.

Jaleb writes this letter with me, and Elias. We are all old and the house is falling. You must come to help.

I send you salute from Pentecost. And all the thoughts of these years.

Honey Jellawella

Susan's days acquired a semblance of routine. She shopped in the supermarket, hoovered the flat, ironed David's shirts. Alexander Drayton, Teddy's former senior partner, came with a man from the Law Society. She told them what she knew. Almost nothing. Primarily they wanted to know what property belonged to her. What, of all the things at Chanting Hill, she could claim as her own.

'Nothing,' she said. 'Practically nothing. All of it was either Ransome property or bought with his money. I cannot truly say that any of it was mine.'

Alexander Drayton told her to get some independent advice. He spoke of entitlements – what a wife would be allowed in bankruptcy. She shook her head. 'Nothing at Chanting Hill ever made us happy. All I did was be the wife he wanted.'

A representative from Harbour Lowe & Robbins called on David Bell. More questions; the need to unravel what property belonged to the estate of Winifred Ransome and what could be traced back to funds misappropriated by Teddy.

'There's no question,' said Susan. 'All Winifred's property is on the Ransome inventory. It was there long before we lived at Chanting Hill.'

'We understand that.' The man sighed. 'But a great deal of money has been spent on restoration and repair. It is that expenditure that we would like to quantify.'

'You can look at my accounts,' said David. 'The bills were always paid promptly. All the records are there.'

Susan put her head in her hands. Even David's money was tainted, part of the web.

She telephoned Crystal at Chanting Hill. 'Won't you come over again, sweetheart? What if I just came and fetched you for lunch?'

Susan drove to the house in David's car; waited in the drive for her daughter to come out.

'This is worse than what Papa has done,' Crystal's first words. 'Throwing yourself at David Bell.'

'David has been very kind.'

'He's wet!'

'Please, Crystal,' – this as they parked in a side street near the shop, walked together along the pavement – 'Please don't make it harder than it is.'

'I don't want to be here, Ma.'

She sulked in the upstairs sitting room, curled on David's sofa with her Walkman turned up loud. David chided her gently. 'Your mother really needs to talk to you, you shouldn't defend yourself against her.'

Crystal ignored him, went down to the kitchen where Susan was washing up, her face flushed from the steam.

'I'm going to Pentecost,' she said, defiantly.

'What?'

'I found a letter from someone called Honey Jellawella. She says Hugo is dying.'

'Where did you find the letter?'

'In Papa's desk. He leaves the drawers unlocked now. I found all these papers about his court case, and then this letter begging him to come and help the old man.'

'What was the date of it?'

'Oh, some time ago.' Crystal shook her head. 'Since Winifred died.'

Susan rested her hands in the sink. 'Why didn't he tell us?'

Crystal's face hardened. 'You could ask that about a lot of things. I found a photograph, too. Some woman standing by his car. Quite good-looking. No-one I've ever seen before.'

Tears were rising again in Susan's eyes. She stared fixedly at the foam on the dishes. 'Did he . . . did you ask him about it?'

'Are you serious? Do you seriously think he would tell me the truth?'

Crystal refused to discuss her trip to Pentecost. She put on her jacket. 'I'm going back on the bus.'

'David will take you in his car.'

'No,' she said. 'Let him stay and comfort you.'

'How are you going to manage the fare?'

182

'I've got enough for the bus.'

'No, I meant the fare to Pentecost.'

'I have the proceeds of Mercury. And the tack. You needn't worry, I will go. I won't stick around to get between you and him.'

'Even so – '

That night Susan slept in David's bed for the first time. There was no drama. She simply went there once it was dark. He was lying on his back, his hands behind his head, and when she opened the door, her nightdress ghostly in the light from the street lamp outside, he lifted the corner of the duvet and she slipped in beside him. His lips were cold, his skin was smooth and smelled slightly sweet. She sat astride, as Teddy had always wished she would, and David was strong and straight and slightly narrow inside her. At the end she cried on his chest and he stroked her hair. 'It will get better, Susan,' he said. 'One day you and I will be as happy as two people can be.'

It was more than Teddy had ever promised. Teddy had only said she could have what she wanted.

FOURTEEN

When the day came to leave, Crystal got up early, hoping to go without seeing her father. She switched on the instant heater for the shower. Baths were forbidden. The boiler had been off for weeks.

Downstairs in the kitchen she put on the kettle and crept about, trying not to make a noise. She didn't want him to come downstairs. She couldn't bear his face. All soft and broken. She didn't want to say goodbye, she didn't want any echoes. She couldn't think of anyone in the world she had loved more than she had loved her father. It was she whom he had betrayed. She felt it to be so – that it was she from whom he had stolen, taken her love and offered her only falsehood.

It was the smell of the toast that brought him down, rubbing his hands. He wore his dressing gown and slippers. Had he always shuffled his feet like that? Like an old man?

'Must you go, Crystal?'

'We've had that conversation.'

He put a teabag into a mug. Crystal winced to see him do it. He drank coffee in the morning. It was one of his 'things', fresh ground coffee for breakfast. Now there was no coffee in the house. Nothing but cheap teabags.

'It'll be no good your going out there,' he said. 'He won't want to see you.'

'He's my grandfather.'

'Not quite.'

184

'Quite enough for me,' said Crystal. 'When your real family falls apart you look for the next best thing.'

'I wish you'd stay with me.'

'I don't want to, Papa. Even if I wasn't going to Pentecost I wouldn't stay here.'

'You're too young to go away on your own.'

'I'm sixteen. Old enough to be married, to have kids. I think that makes me old enough to visit my grandfather.'

'No-one's been near him for years. You've no idea what you'll find.'

'He can't be that bad.'

Teddy didn't answer, but gathered his dressing gown more tightly about him. 'And what are you going to do, when you get there?'

'I'm going to do as the letter asks – the letter you've so conveniently ignored all this time. I'm going to pack him up and bring him home.'

'Just like that?'

'Papa, I'm not a child. I know it won't be easy. It might take some time.'

'What about your A-levels?'

'You don't seriously expect me to go back to school, do you? After all this?'

'You'll need your exams, poppet.'

Crystal slammed her knife against her plate. 'Don't call me poppet! Please!'

'I'm sorry, my –' He stopped whatever other endearment had rushed onto his tongue. She could not bear them, these false words. They belonged to another time.

Eventually he said, 'The state schools aren't so bad.'

'Any school would be appalling. I can't stand the whispering. Look at those girls in the riding school, I thought they were my friends – now they are so fucking beastly.'

'Don't use that language, Crystal.'

'I will speak as I wish, and I will do what I want.' She spat out the words, wanting to change the expression on her father's face, to puncture the grey resignation that he wore all the time, his mask. 'You can't tell me anything, Papa. You! Thief!'

For an instant the mask flickered, he closed his eyes.

A taxi hooted in the drive. She ran upstairs for her bag, remembered that she had no earrings. He was there behind her in the mirror as she inserted a pair of bold pink shells.

'Crystal, if you leave me I shall be all alone.'

'I shouldn't think so. There'll be some girl to comfort you. I should take the first one who comes along. You and Mama, you're two of a kind. You just need someone to admire you.'

He stood aside as she hurried down the stairs. The taxi-driver put her case in the boot. She watched the front door, expecting him to come out, wishing he would, fumbling in her heart for the old love for him that she had lost, as one loses things in the dark, knowing they are there but cannot be found.

The door remained closed. She shivered as the taxi pulled away.

The journey to Pentecost seemed endless. Alone at Heathrow, she felt afraid and excited all at once. The plane was full of tourists. The man in the seat beside hers offered her a drink. She stared at a magazine, ignoring him.

From Liberté a battered taxi drove her along a winding coast road through a nameless ribbon of villages, garish shop-fronts, bullock carts carrying tanks of kerosene, tourist hotels, tractor-drawn garbage trucks and glimpses of the sea.

Mahana was big enough to be a town. A row of two-storied shops, a petrol station, vehicle repairs. A wide sidewalk of red earth with a rusty bus shelter. Old tractors parked under a tree. Men on bicycles, two and three to one saddle. The smell of dung and sour milk and steaming puddles.

The shopkeeper's smile was friendly, puzzled. 'It is the old Baton place you want.'

A cow stood in the drive, unmoved by the hooting of the taxi. Eventually the driver took a stick to its back. People gathered to watch and laugh. The garden wall had crumbled away. Coconuts were stacked along the kerb, cowpats on the lawn.

Annabelle turned right after the by-pass into a narrow lane, bordered by fields. Sheep watched her passage, their eyes slow and malevolent. She passed a farm gate and then there was the

186

sign he had promised, old and imposing. *Chanting Hill. Private.* From the road, the house was no more than a lichen-covered rooftop, nestling in a slump in the land.

Her car crunched over gravel. Faded blue hydrangeas leaned towards her. There were no other cars, no sign of life at all. She got out. A small wind played on her face. In the fields around the garden, green grass rose up to the horizon. Skylarks dipped and soared in the air, as if suspended from invisible wires, their kee-kee song high on the breeze. She heard the grate of a bolt. The front door, dark and heavy, swung open.

He was wearing a yellow polo shirt, cotton slacks, tan-coloured soft shoes. His hair had been cut. Unfamiliar scissors had snipped away the lankness. What was left lay soft and wispy about his face. The polo shirt smelled of soap powder and a hot iron.

'It would be better to put your car in the garage. Then if anyone should come . . .'

The garage doors were electrically operated. She parked beside the Metro, two little cars dwarfed by the space.

'Who might come?'

'There have been some reporters. Not many. None this week. I'm not big enough game, it seems. If I'd had a racehorse, or a yacht, I'd have become a celebrity.'

'Eight hundred thousand pounds isn't enough?'

'Is that how much they say?'

'That was the figure in the papers. Have they got it wrong – is there more?'

'I've no idea.' He pushed his glasses up his nose. 'I lost count of it.'

He was so matter-of-fact, so straightforward, that she laughed. He looked down at her, his expression unchanged. And then he laughed too. They walked into the house arm in arm. A clock was striking in the hall. Beside it on a side-table was an empty flower-bowl.

An open door revealed a sitting room. A chest of drawers back to back against a sofa. Marks on the walls where pictures had hung, dents in the carpet, a fine layer of dust. The house swallowed their laughter.

She followed him down a passage, through a dining room, panelled in oak, a heavy chandelier suspended over a huge dining table, so heavy and solid it looked rooted to the floor. In the fireplace was a grate filled with half-burned logs and unswept ash.

A door from the dining room led to the kitchen. Here, for the first time, she felt the presence of others. An array of wooden cupboards glazed in transparent green; a green Aga, a *batterie de cuisine* suspended over the counter, pots and pans in stainless steel and copper. Here was the absence of his wife, and her presence; her presence in the way it was organised: a vaulted skylight that lit the working area, bright cushion seats on chairs around a homely breakfast table, the same bright fabric framing the windows, curtains more for ornament than purpose, matching blinds that would shut out the dark.

And the absence of a wife: a crumple of washing in a basket on the floor. Mugs, two dirty plates, a slice of toast standing in the toaster. A waste bin overflowing, surrounded by empty wine bottles.

The table was littered with papers. The name 'Harbour Lowe & Robbins' caught her eye. And other papers, tattered files held together with rubber bands, a series of box-files in bright colours, labelled in bold felt-tip 'Campaign for Village Schools'.

'Those are Susan's,' he said, seeing her look. 'Those are the things she used to be involved with.' He picked up a file that was heavier than the others: 'St Agnes Restoration Fund'. 'This is the one she really cared about. Everyone who matters in this village sits on the church committee.' The file fell back onto the table with a thud. 'She resents particularly that I have taken these away from her.'

Annabelle did not look at him. She did not want to know these things. She had not come here to talk about his wife.

A fungus of stuffing oozed from the seams of Hugo's chair. He stared out at the garden where the soft, filmy allaca leaves dangled over unmown grass. His eyes were blue and empty, as if he were blind.

Nothing would come of the letter. Jellawella's letter, written in secret and then blurted out after it was sent. 'I have written to Teddy-master.'

He had been so sure. After all these years, with no more than a few cards from Winifred, gossip from the village, her bridge club, the death of the gardener – news from another world. And this year the death of Winifred herself, a letter from a solicitor in Winton Abbas. The last link severed. The sister of the nursery, the garden, Sunday mornings in St Agnes', too long ago to matter.

Nothing would come of Jellawella's letter to England. It was a message into emptiness, into history. No-one would answer and nothing would change. He would continue his quickening journey towards oblivion: drinks at the Club before lunch; a sleep on the verandah in the afternoons. He would feel nothing, notice nothing, not the encroaching compound, children playing in the drive, not the long grass and cobwebs, black faces in the club bar.

Nothing to notice and nothing to hurt him in thirty years.

Until today. This afternoon. A taxi stopping in the drive. The gasp was still sharp in his lungs.

'Clara!'

A girl with Clara's face. Erect, afraid and curious, young, as young perhaps as the girl at the Central Hotel had been. A warm young hand in his. 'I'm Crystal, I'm your grand-daughter. I've come to take you back.'

He laughed, coughed, waved his stick. 'Absurd. Tell the taxi to take you away.'

'I've come all the way from England. We got Honey's letter. I've come to take you home.'

'Home!' Long, choking hacks. The stick waving at the shabby, ruined comfort that surrounded him. 'Did you ever see a man more at home?' The coughing overwhelmed his words.

'Are you all right? Shall I fetch someone?'

Pointing with his stick. 'Sit down,' he gasped. 'For God's sake, sit down.'

'You see – '

'I see nothing.' Clutching his chest. 'Nothing but a ghost.'

The parrots shrieked, their false hilarity swooping around the

189

verandah. The noise brought Honey up from the dhobi, calling as she came through the house, a damp cloth still in her hand.

'What is happening up here? Mr Ransome! Mr Ransome. Who is making this nuisance now?' All said before she came through the door, and then the cloth over her face.

'My God in heaven!'

And the girl going towards her. 'Are you Honey? My name is Crystal. We were so grateful for your letter.'

'My God in heaven!' Honey sitting down, subsiding into a rocker that had broken slats, mended with twine. 'Jaleb! Jaleb! You bring some tea! There is a young lady for tea!'

So alike. Hugo stared, helpless, and he saw that she was accustomed to it. Even at her age, she was accustomed to a man staring.

Jellawella folded her hands in her lap. It was she who made the conversation. There was talk of the journey, the tourists in the aeroplane. The girl chattered, her tongue like a loose coin in a box. Hugo watched, his breath coming short and shallow.

Slender legs, smooth and white. She crossed them as she sat, the material of her loose shorts falling back, showing her thighs. Hugo blinked and Clara was there, the girl by the hibiscus, the wide smile, full of life and hunger and impatience; the girl in the nightdress squirming away from him; the wild, ruthless thing she became, snoring drunk on the verandah. The girl they brought home in the carpenter's van, the poisoned body, swollen with river water.

Crystal chattered. A coin rattled in a box. Hugo stared out at the garden.

'You know the saying, Annabelle – at times like these you learn who your friends are.'

She moved around the table. She was not sure, not a bit sure, where she stood on the question of friendship. She and Teddy had never quite been friends. Lovers, yes; conspirators, yes – but not friends. And now, when the real meaning of conspiracy lay before them, she was not at all sure that she wished to conspire.

He followed her round the table and stood close. Not, she realised, as close as he might have done, but hovering, his polo shirt a yellow blur in the corner of her eye. She touched, at random, one of the heaps of paper on the table.

'You've been working, then?'

'It's not work. I have promised to co-operate with – with all that. I shall be sending these files up soon.'

'And this one?' She was pointing to another box-file, plain grey and unlabelled.

'I bought it the day I went to see my Counsel.'

'What does that mean?'

'A barrister. The one who will represent me in court. There's going to be a lot of paper.' He leaned forward and lifted the lid. 'As you see, it's already filling up.'

'I suppose it will go on for ages?'

'Probably.'

'And then what?' She turned to him, wanting to see his face. 'Will you go to prison?'

He pushed his glasses up his nose. 'That is a possibility.'

Annabelle stifled a sudden urge to run away. She had made the journey knowing, more or less, what she would find. And nothing, so far, had been more or less than she could have expected or predicted (apart, perhaps, from the yellow shirt). She could not run away now, just because it was as she expected it to be.

Teddy was opening a cupboard door. It looked like the rest, matched the kitchen units, but led into a small room. He switched on a light. Inside was a wine store, racks of bottles lined the walls. He looked back at her and smiled. For a moment the file on the table was forgotten, he was his old self, delighted to show something off.

'Come inside. They missed this when they made their inventory.'

She followed him. The store was the size of a large pantry. 'There is room for nearly two thousand bottles in here.' His voice echoed slightly. The air was cool, with the clean, slightly dead smell of air conditioning. 'I've started drinking the really good stuff.'

He consulted an exercise book that hung on a string from a hook.

'I'm surprised you don't keep it all on computer.'

'I did, at first. And then we decided all that high-tech would spoil the fun, so Crystal helped me make up this record book.' He grinned. 'She wanted to introduce some cobwebs, to make it look more authentic.'

He selected a bottle and showed her the label. 'We'll have this with our lunch.'

He pushed the papers to one side, stacked the files on the floor. 'There are knifes and forks in that drawer over there, napkins below. You lay the table while I get cooking.'

He made up a salad, dried leaves of spinach individually on a towel, chopped onions and tomatoes and bright green peppers. The .vegetables were fresh, sprigged with soil, as if he had brought them in that morning from the garden. Every so often he stopped to take a drink of wine, swallowing it as if it were nothing, just supermarket ordinaire. To her the wine tasted of flowers, sweet and slightly scented.

She watched him as he moved back and forth. His trousers were loose, the sleeves of the polo shirt wider than his arms, as if the clothes had been made to fit another body.

Despite the dirty mugs, the cold toast, he had prepared for her coming. Ready in the fridge was a cold omelette, dappled with mushrooms. He cut it into narrow strips and folded them into the salad. Then he fried squares of toast in garlic butter, and finally mixed a vinaigrette.

'There, my love.' The salad was placed before her like a trophy. 'You don't mind the garlic, do you? I thought it would be all right as we're both eating – that is, if you're not going on somewhere else . . .'

'No.' She smiled, feeling in her expression the encouragement she would offer a gawky boy.

He touched her hand across the table. 'I'm so glad you've come.'

She tossed the salad in the vinaigrette and spooned it out onto their plates. The spinach leaves glistened. The dressing smelt sharp and pungent.

'I know what it means – what it has cost you.'

She shook her head. 'I don't yet know that myself.'

'Everyone else has run away, even Crystal.'

'Where is she?'

Teddy shook his head. 'Can you believe it? She has gone to Pentecost.'

'Why?'

'God knows. She wanted to go. Some notion of putting things right – as if Hugo . . .' Teddy lost the sentence, took a sip of wine. 'I don't blame her. I'm not sure whether she understands what has happened. So far all she has done is use foul language – and now this mad trip to Pentecost.'

'She must have a reason for going out there.'

'She found a letter. She went through all my papers one day while I was out. The boys did the same, everyone seems to need to read about what has happened, as if it won't be true until they have seen it written down.

'I'd forgotten about the letter. It arrived in the middle of it all. A letter from a ghost. I just put it to one side, but Crystal doesn't believe that, of course.'

'Who was the letter from?'

'From Honey Jellawella.' He sighed. 'Now, as well as everything else, I am cruel.'

'Who is Honey? What did the letter say?'

Teddy put down his glass. 'She was my ayah. The woman who looked after me before I came to England. I'll show it to you.'

He left her for a moment. There was the sound of a drawer being opened in another room. She took a mouthful of salad. It was sharp and oily on her tongue, the eggs and mushrooms soft against the crisp leaves. She would have liked some bread, but there was none in sight.

He came back with an airletter, edged with red and blue and a blaze of colourful stamps. The creases were muddled, as if it had been read and folded several times. She put down her knife and fork to read.

'You didn't reply?'

'I was going to, but I couldn't think how. I didn't want to bring him back. I didn't want him here, spoiling our lives.'

Annabelle avoided the point, obvious as it was, that their lives were spoiled anyway. Instead, she said, 'But Crystal has gone out there?'

'Imagine it, my little girl with that vicious old man!'

'If she's sixteen, she's not a child, Teddy.'

He put up his hand, as if he could hold back the idea. 'Do you know what her friends asked her?' His voice rose, his face suffused with colour. 'Would she be allowed out of the country? Hadn't her passport been taken away? Can you believe it?'

Annabelle shook her head, but it didn't seem so unreasonable really. A girl whose father had stolen so much that he hadn't counted the total, someone might have reason to want to keep her passport.

Teddy stabbed at his salad with a fork. 'Crystal has done no wrong in her life. It is the same with Susan. How could they even think she was implicated?'

'Susan helped you spend it, Teddy.' Annabelle gestured around her. 'All this – she didn't exactly economise.'

'She had no idea! She would have been aghast! She is – aghast.'

There was a silence. Annabelle took another helping of salad. 'What about your sons?'

'I haven't seen them. Since that first day. Graham won't even speak to me on the phone.'

'What is he doing?'

'I've no idea. Susan mentioned Australia. You see – ?' He flung out his arms. 'They all want to put the greatest distance they can between themselves and their father.'

Annabelle thought of the parallel there was between the two men; the old man left dying in Pentecost, Teddy alone in Chanting Hill.

'I don't blame them,' said Teddy. 'They have my genes, my weak cowardice in their blood.'

'Jellawella has put you up to this.'

'No. It was my idea. I thought,' Crystal pursed her lips, looked into the blue eyes that glared at her, and finished her

194

sentence, 'I thought you would want to come back to Chanting Hill. I thought you'd be glad.'

'Why should I be glad?'

'Well – ' Crystal hesitated.

'For the medicine,' Honey came to the rescue. 'There are better medicines in England for your chest.'

'And what of this place? What would become of it?'

'This house is falling down,' said Honey. 'You do not care for this house.'

Hugo lifted his stick, directing his question to Crystal. 'Who is in there now?'

'Where?'

'At Chanting Hill.' The blunt end of the stick wavered in the air. 'Since my sister died, what has happened to it?'

'She didn't live there. We do – did – '

'Who is we?'

'Mama and Papa and my brothers – all of us.'

'In Chanting Hill?'

'I've never lived anywhere else.'

'*He* lives there?' The question heaved out.

'Who?'

Hugo started to cough. His face was red, a string of mucus on his chin, yellow, speckled with blood. 'Theodore.'

'Yes, I told you.' Crystal changed the subject. 'You must come back, Grandfather. You could live in the Lodge.'

'I could live in the Lodge?'

'It's got central heating now, and a bathroom on the ground floor. But you'd better come soon – '

'You mean the gardener's lodge?'

'Aunty Win lived there, she lived there since before I was born.'

'You want me to live in the gardener's lodge?' The coughing took over, the noise of it roaring around them, phlegm bursting onto a handkerchief, obscene.

Crystal sipped her tea. She had harboured an idea of welcome, of an old man with fluffy white hair opening his arms to greet her. Instead Hugo had shouted at her and coughed his obscene cough, and stared at her with hostile and greedy eyes.

195

Honey had her hand on the old man's back, patting him as the spasm subsided. Hugo stared at Crystal. Honey tried to wipe his mouth, but Hugo pushed her hand away.

'So he has it! He has Chanting Hill?'

Crystal said nothing. Hugo's coughing fit took a long time to die down. The old servant came for the tea tray. She saw him look at her sideways, yellowy eyes bright with interest. The verandah boards groaned as he walked away. Hugo tapped them with his stick. The wood sounded spongy, one board more hollow than the rest.

'Jellawella!'

Honey stirred on her rocker. 'Mr Ransome?'

'These boards are dangerous.'

'Yes, Mr Ransome.'

Crystal had the impression that the exchange was familiar, a ritual. They seemed to have forgotten she was there. Hugo tapped again on the floor and Honey got out of the rocker. 'Here, this one right here.'

Honey stepped on the board where Hugo pointed. It creaked under her weight. 'These woods are damp,' she said. 'It is too much rain.'

Hugo tapped the floor once more. 'Damned monsoon – lasting forever.' He turned in his chair to Crystal and she caught again the shock on his face, the same that had greeted her arrival.

'This will be death, I suppose,' he said, after a moment. 'Like this. Old ghosts and a monsoon that does not end.'

'You're coming back with me, Grandfather. You're not going to die.'

He tapped the loose board again, worrying it, like a bad tooth. 'When you're as old as I am, as ill-used, the idea of death does not frighten you.'

'I'm not afraid, I just – '

'Ah!' He shouted and then again began to cough. Honey put a cloth over his mouth. Crystal wanted to cover her ears but he was still speaking, hurling out the words between gasps. 'No. You never were afraid. Never fearful.' The stick waved out towards the sodden air of the garden, to where the empty green husk of a coconut lay, soft and hollow on the ground. 'You were never anything but empty. As empty as that husk.'

Honey showed her to a room at the back of the house. 'He thinks you are someone else.'

The bedroom smelled of must. A plain iron bed, an empty wardrobe. The bare white walls were finger-marked, stained with damp under the window.

Honey summoned the servant. 'Jaleb, bring us some linen for the bed.'

She hung a mosquito net from a hook on the ceiling. It dangled over the bed like an empty turban. Crystal helped make the bed, trying hard to be neat, to find favour with the housekeeper.

Honey turned down a corner of sheet and patted the pillows. 'Now you can go to bed when you are ready.'

Crystal put out her hand, felt the cool plumpness of the housekeeper's arm. 'Is my grandfather – Hugo – is he going to die?'

'The doctor says there is no more to be done for him. But he would be better in England – there are places there, where he could be treated.'

'I read your letter – I came because of what you said.'

'I wrote to your father.'

Crystal stopped, and then went on to tell the lie that the woman was so clearly waiting to hear. 'But he asked me to come. He told me all about you, Honey. How happy he was when you looked after him.'

'This was a long time ago.'

'Even so, he remembers you – '

'We know he is a thief.'

Stunned, Crystal sat on the bed. 'How do you know?'

'Bad news will always arrive. Even in Pentecost.'

She led Crystal into a bathroom that adjoined the bedroom. A shower-rose the size of a bath-hat was suspended above the bath. There was no shower curtain, but a drain hole in the centre of the floor.

'I will ask Jaleb to bring you towels.'

Crystal ran hot water into the bath and got in. The window was open. She could hear the sounds of the kitchen, the old servant banging pots, Honey by the back door, calling down to someone beyond the garden.

The bathwater was hot and seemingly endless. She wallowed for a long time, occasionally pulling the plug and letting the tub fill again. It seemed an eternity since she had been able to waste anything, to be extravagant, a lifetime since the world had turned upside down.

When at last the water ran cold, Crystal pulled the plug and got out. The towels Jaleb had left were clean but stained and almost threadbare. She put on a fresh pair of jeans and brushed her hair. Honey was waiting in the passage.

'You have used all the hot water. There is only one tank for the house.'

Crystal bit her lip. 'I'm sorry – I didn't think.'

Honey led her to the verandah. 'Mr Ransome will be here shortly.'

Bottles of gin and tonic water on a low table. Slices of lemon in a dish. The tongs for the lemon had the Ransome crest.

The day was almost gone. Neither sunny nor cold, the afternoon subsided into a pale evening grey. Teddy and Annabelle sat on the flagstone terrace outside the kitchen. The still air was filled with the cry of larks and gulls and the bored braying of sheep. He had shown her the walled garden where Susan had grown vegetables and herbs, and beyond it the paddock where Crystal had kept her pony. The stable was swept and empty, bare hooks on the wall where her tack had hung.

'She sold it herself. It wasn't necessary. She could have kept it but she took it out that first weekend and sold it to the riding school for half its proper value.'

Unable to respond, Annabelle turned the conversation to practicalities. 'What happens now, about money?'

'I have none,' he said.

'What are you supposed to live on?'

'There is money in Susan's account. She is expected, while she is my wife, to support me.'

198

'Will you go on the dole?'

'I have already signed on – but you know, it isn't much.'

'Do you need – ' Annabelle stopped. Something, no more than a twitch of muscle, had altered the look on his face. He did not want her to offer him money.

They returned to the terrace. He made tea in a silver pot engraved with an 'R' looped and curled around the sides. They sat in garden chairs. Sparrows gathered at their feet for biscuit crumbs. She watched the elegant way he used tongs to drop cubes of sugar into her cup. For such a big man his movements were light and precise.

'Will you stay the night?'

Quickly, before there was time to think, she shook her head.

'It's very quiet,' said Teddy. 'No-one will disturb us. We could listen to some music.'

In the old days he would have held her eyes, willing her. He would have reached for her hand, even pulled her towards him, denying anything but consent. Now he spoke without looking at her, his hands held in front of him, the fingers clenching and unclenching.

'I don't want to, Teddy. Don't ask too much of me.'

'No. Of course.'

He left her to go to the bathroom. Annabelle sat on outside. The tea had gone cold in the pot. There was a stain in her saucer, used slices of lemon lying limp and brown. The evening began to feel chilly. She had left her jacket inside. She would ask him to bring it out when he came back.

The garden grew quiet, the birds stilling with the fading of the light. Along the wall beside her feet were pots of fuchsia and begonia, a mix of varieties, all in flower, pink and scarlet and purple, faintly obscene.

No sound came from the house. She didn't know the lay-out, which bathroom he might use. Surely the cloakroom downstairs? She could hear nothing, no running water, no gentle swishing in a gutter.

Feeling the chill more keenly, she stacked the cups and carried the tray inside. The kitchen was a dark maze of shadows. At the press of a switch a series of spotlights came on, artfully angled to light the counter, leaving the rest of the room in darkness. She pushed the teabags into the waste disposal unit and for a few seconds the noise of it filled the kitchen. In the following silence she felt the house looming, huge and dark around her. She put the teacups in the dishwasher. Their lunch plates were already inside, waiting for a full load. She wondered if he would be so tidy if he lived alone – really alone, rather than in this temporary aloneness of absence.

Sure that it shouldn't be put in the machine, she washed the teapot by hand. Then she wiped the tray and the counter. Outside, the patio grew dark behind the glass. Perhaps she should go now. Now, before he came down. She could just slip away and not have to say goodbye or promise to see him again.

'I'm sorry I was so long.'

He was standing in the shadows. He'd changed his clothes. The yellow polo shirt was gone, replaced by something soft and black with a high neck. The material – knitted cotton? silk? – had a slight sheen. The contours of his body were caught in the light, his shoulders wide and angular and the new, thin torso.

'It's time I was going, Teddy.'

He stepped forward from the shadow. She could see that he had showered. His hair was wet, his face flushed and shiny. The spots were reflected, like a string of fairy lights, in his eyes.

'You don't have to drive. You could stay.'

'We've already talked about that.' Annabelle smoothed her hands on her jeans. They felt clammy. 'Where's the other light switch? I can't see you properly.'

He pressed a stainless steel panel by the door and a pair of converted oil lamps shed a yellow glow over the kitchen table. He was coming towards her. 'I won't ask any more of you, Annabelle. Only that you stay with me, just for tonight.'

'But you don't need anyone here. This is your home.'

'It isn't a home. I live here now because there is nowhere else. But it is not my home. It never was, it's always just been part of what I could not have, and now it will never be mine at all.'

'Whose fault is that?' The question whipped out, and hearing herself ask it, she felt some relief. Now there would be no more pretence, no skirting round the truth, pretending it was just a

200

misfortune that had brought him to this.

He said nothing for a moment. In the corner of her mind that was still cold, still analysing, not yet swooped up by remorse for wounding him still further, she wondered if his silence was deliberate, intended to give her time to regret the question.

Then he said, 'It depends how far you trace the fault.'

'You can't blame Hugo! Not for this. He didn't make you a thief!'

'Didn't he? Isn't childhood where these things start? Could there be anything more cruel than what he did?'

She wanted to stop it there; to close this Pandora's box, but questions piled on her lips. 'But that didn't make you a thief, a criminal! Why Teddy, why did you do it? You knew it could only ruin you in the end.'

He turned away from her.

'You can't have believed you'd never be caught. It was madness.'

'I may have been mad.' He spoke slowly, defying the harsh rapidity of her questions. 'I may have been mad, but once I started, it became impossible to stop. There might have been a day when I could have put it right. If there was, I missed it. I couldn't see my way out. I couldn't see through the web.'

He was moving forward once more. In his face was an earnest sincerity, an eagerness to explain. She felt a spasm of impatience, distaste. The outrage that had boiled in her unacknowledged since the screen on her desk had first carried its ugly, shocking news, welled up, overcoming compassion.

'How could you do something so low? It is monstrous to steal – to be arrested – to be charged. How can you blame anyone but yourself? I'm not surprised you've been abandoned. Who would stay to comfort a sly thief?'

She was going. The keys were in her hand. In her mind's eye was the car, the drive, the bend in the road. She would go, get out, be gone for good.

But he had walked away from her, sat down at the table.

'I thought you would stay, Annabelle,' he said softly. 'I thought you would – at least for a while – at least until I can get used . . .'

The key-ring dangled from her finger. Against the darkness outside, the great glass doors reflected the kitchen like a stage set. She could see herself hesitating, the keys glinting in her hand, the man at the table, so much older than she, slumped in a chair, an exhausted shadow beside the pool of light.

She watched herself in the glass, walking across the room, the keys safely back in her pocket, walking across to take him in her arms, standing beside the chair, cradling his head against her belly. He looked up at her. 'I don't want to argue with you, Annabelle. I don't want to drag you down with me. I want nothing more from you than that you stay here tonight and take away the silence.'

FIFTEEN

Crystal was efficient and ruthless. Shades of Winifred. Every drawer was opened. Every shelf stripped. Her black hair pinned carelessly on her head.

She carried boxes of rubbish down the garden path. The compound people crowded around at the sight of the white man's rubbish. A request came from the school – if there was anything unwanted; the children were so short. This stopped her. Of course. The papers were sorted a second time; blank pages, bills with nothing printed on the back. The little ones could make use of anything. She came back smiling.

She was efficient and ruthless and kind. And it was Jaleb who voiced the thought. 'You make us sad.'

'Why?'

'With your new face that should be old.'

'I don't mean to do harm, Jaleb. I can't help my face.'

'But you are breaking the house.'

'I don't want to break anything. But Mr Ransome must go home to England now. He needs medicine and care.'

'Honey is caring for him.'

'It isn't enough,' said Crystal.

Jaleb sat in the kitchen shaking his head. 'What is to become of me? What happens to Jaleb now?'

She accompanied Hugo to the Mahana Club. He watched her watching Elias, anxious eyes on the road as they steered round the potholes. She offered him her arm as they picked over the ruts in the car-park.

The District Commissioner, seated with the newspaper, as he always was at that time of day, breaking from his duties for luncheon at the Club, saw them coming up the steps, rose from his chair. 'Commander Ransome.' Holding out his hand.

Hugo puffed his cheeks. It was twenty years since anyone had called him Commander. His visits to the Club were as regular as the Commissioner's, as easily ignored. Hugo Ransome visiting the Mahana Club was no more a matter for comment, for the District Commissioner to stand and greet, than the slide-sweep of the broom-boy on the polished floor or the whine of the barman's cloth shining glasses. No-one had stood up for Hugo Ransome coming into the Club since the British Army had rattled the land with its tanks, since there were still tents on the beach and fresh-eyed Tommies fouling the women – since the District Commissioner had been an Englishman.

The greeting was for the girl, but Hugo shook the hand that was held out to him. It made a second prop as he lowered himself into an armchair.

'I'm Crystal Ransome.' Spoken in a clear voice; Hugo had noted this difference. This voice was stronger – someone else lurking there, a stronger will than Clara's.

'District Comissioner Verinswella.' Hugo managed the introduction before the cough set in, the usual hack, raucously loud, that would bring the gin on a tray and, this time, whisky for the D.C., bottled Martini for the girl, and a dish of limp potato crisps. When the coughing was over, no more than a murmuring tickle in the lower part of his throat, Crystal was smiling at the D.C. Everyone equal now; fresh young women and grizzled Costas.

'Commander Ransome is our last expatriate member,' said Verinswella.

'Is he really – the last one?'

'There is no one left from the old days.' With a gesture of deference Verinswella led her across the club-room, to the old leather Members Book that stood on a lectern by the fireplace. 'There are some Englishmen who still pay their subscription –

but only the non-resident rate. None of them live in Mahana any more'.

Crystal looked at the list. 'But you are still keeping the old traditions.'

'Of course. The Club must continue – though now it is tourists who pay the bills. The club is one of our Pentecost attractions – like an old monument.'

Crystal smiled.

'We are a relic,' Verinswella continued, 'of something so English it can no longer be found in England. All over the world you have left the best parts of your culture behind.'

Without actually taking her arm, he guided her round the club, drawing her attention to the photographs, the coats of arms, the page in the visitors book that bore evidence of a royal visit.

'Charles is not the only prince who has visited us. Many of that family have been. They all love this country. We had everything for them – tea, rubber, cotton, sugar.' Verinswella drew his long fingers together, like a man making a fine philosophical point. 'All the Europeans fought over us. Portuguese and French and English – even, it is said, the Japanese had designs on us. But now we are no longer important. We are left behind with the relics of the conqueror, his clubs, his bureaucracy and his tennis courts.'

'And my grandfather?'

'And men like your grandfather.'

'D'you think he'll leave anything behind? Anything that will be remembered?'

Verinswella looked sly. 'We shall all keep our memories of Commander Ransome – his gin and tonic at a quarter to twelve; his slips, we shall keep some of those.'

'His what?'

'His bar slips. "HR". He has been signing them like that all these years. No matter how many members we have, no matter how many with the same initials, always he puts HR.'

Crystal smiled again.

Verinswella led her into the main bar. He lifted a slip of paper from a spike on the counter. An electronic till had printed out a list of drinks – one gin and tonic, one whisky soda, her own

Martini. At the bottom, as Verinswella had said, was the scrawled acknowledgement: HR. The only white face in the Club, needing no more than a pair of initials to be known by. She looked back at Hugo. His face was pale, splotches of pink on his cheeks.

'He's not well. I've come to take him back to England.'

'It is said that he refuses.'

'I know, but he must. He needs treatment.'

'There are people here who depend on him.'

Crystal nodded. 'Look, I shouldn't ask you, but I'm not sure what should be done – about pensions and that sort of thing.'

Vertinswella patted her hand. 'It is already dealt with. The estate workers are employed by the co-operative.'

'I know, but there are the servants – the housekeeper?'

'I will make enquiries.' He patted her hand again. 'This is not a matter for a young girl's concern. I will make sure the correct steps are taken.'

'And what about the house? It's falling down. He doesn't seem to care.'

'There is no problem about the Baton house. It is a wonderful example of planter architecture. The Government would very much like to turn it into a museum.'

They moved back to where Hugo was sitting, snoring gently, his glass refilled. 'We will be sad when he is gone,' said Verinswella.

Crystal looked into the Costa's eyes. 'And relieved too, I should think.'

He inclined his head. 'Perhaps.'

Felted with dust, pages sealed fast with damp, there were shelves of books that had not been opened for years. Crystal shifted the desk close to the verandah doors and stood on a chair. On the top shelves, high above the books, were small japanned boxes, unlabelled and rusty.

Crystal could not have described the feelings that drove her. Finding Honey's letter, the simple, honest appeal lying among her father's papers, among all the evidence of his betrayal, had seemed to be a sign, a pointer.

She had come to Mahana in search of something more permanent than the confused, shifting world of Chanting Hill. She had hoped for escape and an old man's gratitude, and people who would delight in her, who would show her the affection and admiration in which she had wallowed for all her sixteen years.

What she had found was another trap; a time-cage where old griefs and hatreds had gathered like algae in a stagnant pool. Her noble intentions, such as they were, had no possibility of fulfilment. Even should she succeed in bringing the old man home, there would be no blessing in it. The un-admitted hope she had harboured, the wish for a welcome, for a sudden outburst of love from this forgotten old man, was crushed, crumpled like the rubbish that blew about the compound.

Nothing drove her now but impatience, the desire to get it done, to sort out this impossible house and pack it up, throw out all that was bad or useless and save only that which was real and good.

The base of an ancient cardboard box collapsed in her arms. Jaleb staggered forward, holding his arms up, helpless to prevent the contents cascading onto the floor. A cloud of dust rose. Something scuttled up her arm from the broken cardboard. She slapped out, blindly, jumping down from the chair. There was a smear of blood on her elbow.

'God, how can you stand all these insects?'

Jaleb was on his knees, gathering the scattered contents of the box. 'My skin is not white like yours,' he said.

She licked her fingers and rubbed at the bite. 'What difference does that make?'

'A white skin has more riches. The insects know this.'

Crystal crouched beside him. In his hand was an envelope full of photographs. The flap was torn. Jaleb took one out, and, before she could see it, closed his eyes and hid the picture against his chest.

'I will get Honey.' He stood up.

Crystal's hair hung over her eyes, hot and irritating. She undid the scarf and tied it up again, trying to catch all the loose strands. The air in the house was stifling. She could feel the sweat running inside her shirt. Jaleb had shuffled off in the direction of the kitchen. Gathering up a bundle of envelopes, she went out onto the verandah. Patches of late-afternoon sun lay on the grass. A pair of egrets were picking in the shadows under the trees.

Each envelope contained half a dozen snapshots, curled at the edges. Pictures of a baby. Plump, blue-eyed, ordinary.

Honey came round from the kitchen. 'Jaleb says you have found photographs.'

Crystal handed her an envelope. 'They're just baby pictures.'

'Oh!' Honey touched her lips.

'Who's the baby?'

'It is your father.'

Crystal moved round to look over Honey's shoulder.

'It is Mr Teddy when he was just born.'

Her fingers were shaking. Jaleb kept close. They moved along the verandah to the chairs and slowly, as if a fortune would be told, Honey laid the photographs out on the tea-table. A baby in a cot; a baby in a pram; a young woman smiling.

And others, huddles of strangers. Men in uniform, faces screwed up against the sun.

'Where did you find these?' Honey asked.

'I told you, they were in a box in the dining room.'

'There is more in the box?'

'They're all over the floor.'

'Is there another box?'

'Probably. There are stacks of boxes. It's all old stuff, I haven't really looked.'

'You don't want to look at your grandmother?' Honey held up one of the photographs, keeping it at an angle, so that Crystal was forced to move close in order to see it.

'You see yourself here?'

'Perhaps.' Crystal stared at the face. 'Perhaps a little.'

Honey laughed. 'It is not a little. You are her image.'

'Did you notice? I mean before?'

'Of course.'

'I didn't know,' said Crystal. She could feel her cheeks going pink.

'It is like a ghost,' said Honey. 'But you do not have her voice – and, excuse me, you do not walk as straight as she.'

Crystal straightened her back.

It was difficult, after that, to be so ruthless. The earlier routine of emptying the boxes into plastic sacks was slowed. She found herself looking for pictures. And then there were letters, trivial notes, invitations to dances, a folder of school reports, the Liberté Academy for Young Ladies. 'Clara is a pleasant girl. She can sew very neatly when she tries. Clara should pay more attention in class.'

There were books of accounts. Cash books with bold headings; 'Clara Ransome: Housekeeping Account'. The entries were erratic. And other books, cracking volumes of ledgers labelled 'Baton Estate'. Pages and pages of entries, the names of labourers, wages paid, payments to the bank, interest charges, loan arrangement fees. They stopped in 1946.

And older photographs, brown and faint. Honey pointed out Crystal's great-grandfather, Louis Baton, among a group on the steps of the Mahana Club, men in shorts with long stockings.

Jaleb wept, blowing his nose on a grey rag. Crystal came back to the pictures of Clara.

Party scenes, a girl in a bright yellow dress; a wedding, Hugo just recognisable in uniform, his arms around the bride, clusters of girls with posies in their hair. Then more baby photographs: pictures of Clara with a pram on the verandah.

When it was too dark to see, Honey gathered the photographs together. 'It is time to be cooking, Jaleb.' She followed the servant to the kitchen, the box of photographs in her arms. Crystal went to the bathroom and stood under the shower; the water cascaded over her, alternately cold and scalding as they turned the taps on and off in the kitchen. She could smell rice boiling while she dressed, and baking fish.

There were roasting trays in the sideboard, carving knifes and silver platters, all the paraphernalia of traditional British life, unused. The house diet consisted only of baked fish and nameless stews, spiced to suit Jaleb's tongue, poor quality rice boiled into sudden lumps. Hugo ate with indifference, an airmail copy of *The Times* folded beside his plate, a pen for the

209

crossword. She could see that he would prefer the stews and rice; for these he could dispense with a knife altogether, passing the food into his mouth with a fork without his eyes ever leaving the paper, stopping only to cough. She learned to look away, avoid the scattering of chewed food on the tablecloth.

'Well, you're the golden girl,' he said, the day the photographs were found. He had not looked at them, simply ordered Jaleb to take the boxes away. An extra spoon had been laid at Crystal's place. When the fish was cleared, Honey went out to the kitchen and came back with Jaleb carrying a tray, smiles on their faces.

'Something special for you,' said Honey.

With a stiff bow, Jaleb placed before her a bowl of something white and creamy, and a jug of syrup.

'What is it?' Crystal asked.

'Is curd, madame. Made from the milk of buffalo.'

'And this?' She lifted the jug.

'Is palm syrup.'

'Buffalo curd and palm syrup,' said Honey. 'These foods were once the favourite in this house.'

Crystal turned to Hugo. 'Aren't you having some?'

He didn't answer. His face was bent over the crossword.

The curd was thick and creamy, like a smooth mild yoghurt, the syrup sweet without the sharpness of honey. She ate it all. Smiled at Jaleb. Smiled at Honey.

'It was yummy,' she said.

Hugo looked up. There were tears on the crumpled skin of his cheeks. 'Oh, Clara!'

Closed and shuttered, Crystal had left Clara's bedroom until last. It was the hottest day since she had come. The heat hung in the air like a sound, muffling what was audible; the distant rattle of a radio in the compound, the creak of Honey's chair where she dozed on the verandah, Jaleb humming as he shelled peas on the step.

The bedroom was dark, cluttered, musty. Bottles on the dressing-table, just a dry residue of the contents; old-fashioned underwear in the drawers, moth-eaten, stained with damp.

Crystal stared in the mirror, found herself lifting the silver-backed hairbrush. The hairs still tangled in the bristles were as dark and wiry as her own.

She turned to the wardrobe. There was a hint of scent, stale and flat, mingling with the faint odour of mothballs. Clara's dresses had survived better than her lingerie. Crystal lifted out a scarlet evening dress, silk as frail as paper, with an artificial flower for the cleavage. There were shoes, hardly worn, damp and mouldy. She turned to the mirror. Even the size was right.

On an impulse, she pulled off her shirt, slipped out of her shorts. The old silk rustled against her legs. She stretched back to close the zipper. The bodice fitted her exactly, the false rose was snug between her breasts; the skirt flowed from her waist. There were pearls in a tray in the drawer. She put them on and reached in the cupboard for the shoes. The effect took her breath away. She was the woman in the photographs. Holding her hair aloft, she swayed her hips, dancing before the mirror.

Like a sudden burst of applause, it began to rain. A clatter on the roof, an instant torrent in the gutters, deafening, shutting out the world. Crystal turned this way and that before the mirror, admiring the line of her neck and the colour of the bright silk against her skin. Rain and vanity made her oblivious. She did not hear the car returning from the Club, the thud of Hugo's stick. She heard nothing and did not see him at the open door of the bedroom; did not see the look on his face, in his eyes, his mouth open, the look of surprise and outrage and strangled longing. It was the slamming of another door she heard. When she turned to look, the corridor was empty and dark.

Clara's diary was waiting for her.

So it felt, when she found it. As if the small half-written volume had hung back, waiting for her to be ready for it, to be drawn in as she had not been at the beginning. The dress was back on its hanger, the shoes restored to the rusted rail at the bottom of the wardrobe. There was a shelf above the hanging rail. A dress box, layers of dry tissue and a fold of letters, notes from girlfriends, a postcard from Lisbon:

'We've had three days ashore. It's high summer but feels

cool after Pentecost. Hope you are well. Love Johnny.'

The diary was bound in blue, half a page to a day; large, childish handwriting.

Winifred has written to say the ship arrived safely. Not my son. It was the ship that arrived safely.

The next day was blank, and the next.

I have been up to the grave in Mahana. Papa lies with the other Batons. Were all the Batons cowards? Weak, wicked cowards like me?
There was a Remembrance Day service. Hugo wore his uniform, medals clanking in the place where his heart should be. The Club waiters still call him Commander. It's a joke. He commands nothing. Not even the servants in his own house.
They hate him. All of them, even Jaleb hates him for what he has done.
I look into Honey's eyes and her thoughts are there, the same as mine. How can we go on? How can we all go on like this?
I am drinking more than I should. I can't help it. In the morning I feel so sick. I promise myself that I will stop. For Teddy's sake – for his love, if I can get it back. If one day I can get it back.

Three weeks later she wrote:

My hands shake so. The doctor says I am poisoned. I am poisoning myself. Even his face is closed. He cannot meet my eyes. None of them. How did I do it? How did I allow Winifred to take him away? Who was the woman who went so meekly with her child to the docks? Who wore a new white dress – as if it were for a Communion. Honey knows. For Honey the colour white is for mourning.
They should see that dress now. They should see the tears in it, the blood on the skirt at the back. The girls in the Club would stop their chatter if they saw that dress.
I have been again to the grave in Mahana. Papa lies beside Mama. Louis and Claire-Lise. They share a stone. Everything is forgotten. All their failures and all their joys. All forgiven. Nothing but silence; nothing but the crackle of the palm trees.
It must be a kind of bliss.

212

I have been unwell. I have not behaved as I should. The nursery is empty. Empty. Everything is the same but my little love has gone.

After this there was a gap. Almost five months without an entry. Then a more coherent passage.

There have been riots in Liberté. Hugo has cleaned his guns. The compound boys are wearing tee shirts with Independence slogans. Hugo makes them stand in lines and lectures them on the English code of conduct. Loyalty and punctuality. Pentecost will prosper, he says, if the Costas adopt English values. He is afraid that they will not stay, that they will drift off, that the estate will look bedraggled again and the world will know that it is a sham, that it is only Ransome money that is keeping the place so neat. There is no profit here. My poor dead father told him that. The soil is stripped. There has been no profit in the place for years.

The rain stopped for a while, but it was scant relief. Moisture hung in the air, penetrated every corner of the house. Crystal lay on damp sheets, listening to Hugo cough. She felt hot and cold at the same time, as if she had entered a world halfway between land and water, a steaming cloud where water suspended in the air impeded the breath. Jaleb brought her an old electric fan but its draught only pressed the damp sheets against her skin, chilling her, even in the heat.

She lay naked under the mosquito net, reading the dairy.

Clara's writing grew worse.

The estate sheds are empty. The nursery is empty. There are empty bottles in the kitchen. Our hearts are empty.

I dream of him. Night after night. The way he would smell, clean and powdered after his bath. The mud on his knees when Honey brought him home from school. Honey dreams of him too.

I have been behaving badly. I was sick on the clubhouse floor. I cannot remember the occasion. I have been sick a great deal. I see the satisfaction in Hugo's face. 'Now you will put it right,' he says.

My drinking is the talk of the Club. The doctor says Hugo's baby will be undersized, that it may not survive if I continue to drink like this.

There was nothing more. The rest of the pages in the little book were unmarked.

Crystal arose before it was light. A rooster crowed in the compound. A cluster of dead moths lay on the table under her reading lamp. She went out onto the verandah. Dawn had come pink-silvered into the water-laden garden. Jaleb appeared on the path, carrying his plastic shoes, his sarong gathered high above the mud. At the tap by the kitchen step he stopped to rinse the mud away. His feet left a clean wet trail on the floor.

'Jaleb.'

He stopped. 'Madame.'

'What happened, Jaleb? What happened to Clara?'

The servant dropped his hands. The crushed fabric of his sarong swung down over his knees. 'I am making the morning tea now, Madame.'

'Won't you tell me? How did she die?'

'Is a very long time ago.'

'But she was young.'

Uncomfortably, like a child caught in deceit, Jaleb rubbed his ear on his shoulder.

'Please tell me,' said Crystal.

'It is not Jaleb who can speak of such things.'

'I have no-one else to ask.'

He scuttled away from her, murmuring about the tea. Crystal went back to her room. The water in the bathroom was cold. She splashed her face and slipped on her clothes.

'I have tea for Madame.' Jaleb was in the passage, a laden tray in his hands.

'I don't want any tea.'

Crystal brushed past him, her sandals flapping. Through the kitchen, past a swarm of children eating toast by the back door, down the path. Mud oozed between her toes. A woman was collecting eggs.

'Where does Honey live?'

The woman smiled at her, toothlessly. She pointed to a house near the compound wall. It was part concrete, part a patchwork of corrugated iron and mud.

The door was open. Crystal knocked.

Honey was on her knees before a small statue. She made the sign of the cross and turned.

'I've been reading Clara's diary. She was having another child!'

With an effort, Honey raised herself from her knees. 'What diary?'

'It was with her clothes. With the red dress.'

'And you think it is yours to read?'

'She wrote it. She must have wanted someone to read it.'

Honey dusted down her skirt. 'Is this why you come? To stir up these old sorrows?'

'No.' Crystal stopped. 'I didn't know anything about Clara. My father never talked about her. I came because – '

'Why is it not your father who comes? Why is it a young girl who is sent?'

'No-one sent me. I came because of your letter.'

'It was to your father that I wrote.'

'You know very well he's . . .' Crystal paused. 'He cannot travel abroad. He has committed a crime and they have taken his passport.'

'Is it the truth?'

'What?'

'Is it true that he took money?'

'Yes. He admits it.' Crystal was conscious as she said the words of how small it sounded, for such a vast betrayal.

Honey remained by the statue, standing at the same place where she had been kneeling. 'I pray for him,' she said. 'I have been praying for him for all these years.'

Crystal smiled.

'And you, child. Don't you go reading old diaries now.'

'She was my grandmother.'

'It does not give you right to cause more pain.'

'I only want to know what happened. Why did she send Papa away? How could she let him go?'

'You may ask that question but the answer is not for you to understand. The world of Pentcost was not as it is now. A woman was dependent; the husband ruled.'

215

'But it – it damaged him.'

'And the mother too. Damaged equally. More. Who can say?'

'What happened to her, Honey? It says in the diary that there was another baby. Did she have it? Was there another child?'

Honey's voice was suddenly loud. 'It was not born. She would not bear him a child; she had it in her mind, there was nothing else in her mind, only grief and madness and this one revenge – there would be no more, there would be no true Ransome child born.'

'What did she do?'

Honey continued, her voice loud and harsh, as if now, when at last it was being told, the whole compound should hear it, the whole plantation echo to her deep old woman's cry.

'She took a boat. The child seven months in her womb. She hired a boat from a fisherman. They found it upturned in the mangroves. Clara was underneath, trapped, her feet caught in the roots. At Liberté Hospital they pumped her stomach. There was more gin than water, they say.'

Towards the end of the day, Crystal took the back road across the plantation. The clearing up was finished. Heaps of plastic sacks by the kitchen door. The compound people would take them, sort it through again, take what they could use and burn the rest. She was tired, her legs ached. The bites on her arms were swollen and red.

Workers from the plantation were climbing into the back of a lorry. They wore blue tunics, *Mahana Co-operative* printed on front and back.

She walked all the way to the church. The rain had stopped. The air was clear, with the sweet dark smell of wet earth. In the late-afternoon sun the painted facade of the little church looked like soft ice-cream. A coach was parked on the grass verge and inside, a party of tourists were being lectured on the history of Mahana by a guide who leaned against a glass case in which the old parish register was displayed.

'Before Independence only white persons were registered here,' said the guide. 'Costa births and deaths were recorded by the plantation owners. Only the Batons and the other big white families had their names in this book.'

The tourists' attention was haphazard; they wandered around while he spoke, taking photographs of the plaques on the walls, of the altar with its plain wooden cross, of the open pages of the register which, like everything else on Pentecost, was simple and quaint and easily forgotten.

Crystal waited until the lecture was over and the tourists, guided by their smiling shepherd, returned to their coach. She walked over to the register. The open page was filled with names and dates, some with a comment beside them. A printed card at the foot revealed that this register was closed at Independence. The records of Births, Marriages and Deaths after that date would be found in the Central Registry in Liberté.

Clara's name was halfway down the open page. 'Born 30th January 1925, to Claire-Lise, wife of Louis Baton of Baton Estate, Mahana.'

The Register recorded Clara's marriage, 'on 20th September 1943 to Lt. Commander Hugo Ransome, of Wiltshire, England', and further down the page the birth of a child: '5th September 1946, Theodore Ransome, white, six pounds and nine ounces.'

Clara's death was the last entry. 'On 15th April 1953, in circumstances of tragedy.'

Another coach arrived. Again the church was filled with voices, the click and whirr of cameras. Crystal was on her way out when she saw Honey come in through a side door carrying a duster. Someone filmed her wiping the pews.

Oblivious or indifferent to this, Honey finished the job and then carried a stiff broom out to the yard. Crystal followed her out, watched her sweeping fallen palm fronds from the porch. The housekeeper gave no sign that she had seen her.

Crystal stepped down among the graves. The grass around the stones was tall and brown. Most of the inscriptions were still visible, the name Baton, over and over, the earliest a death in 1824. Honey leaned on the broom handle, her fingers twisting the fringe of her shawl.

'The grave you are looking for is over there,' she said, pointing to a corner where the ground sloped down towards the road. 'Where the hibiscus flowers.'

'There's no headstone?'

'No.'

She walked back the long way round, passing through Mahana, past the big hotel that had gardens down to the beach, the flag of Pentecost like a bright bird on a pole. A small boy ran alongside her, begging for rupees.

Near to the shops she could hear beat music. There were sunhats and beach bags for sale, and paperback books and brash yellow Kodak signs. A bar with a low terrace faced the sea; elderly Costas sat along its wall, a cluster of beer bottles round their feet. In front of them, seated around a table on the pavement, was a group of white tourists, young people, pink from the sun.

As she passed, their talk, that had been loud with beer, fell away. One of the boys stood up. He was tall, clean-shaven, his eyes smiling and honest. 'Would you like to have a drink with us?'

Crystal stopped. 'Why not?'

They made room for her at the table, telling her their names, including her in their easy, holiday banter.

'You're incredibly tanned,' said the first boy. 'How long have you been on holiday?'

'I'm not on holiday,' said Crystal. 'I live here.'

Hugo would die there.

Crystal came to accept it. It would do no good to take him back to England. He was too ill and too old to be moved. And besides, the ramshackle house, surrounded by the plantation, by the noise and life and smells of Pentecost, was his home, as it was becoming hers; an easier place to live, a cradle of warm air and things that mattered.

'It is because of the grave,' Honey told her one day as they shared the task of changing his sheets and washing the wrinkled, grizzle-haired limbs. 'He will not say it, but it is she he wants to lie with in the end.'

The Times still arrived each day, a day or two old. Sometimes he would manage a clue, tapping the pen, blotching the paper with ink. It was Honey who saw the report, a small headline under *Home News*. Home as it was in England, another place from the home that Pentecost was becoming to her.

A photograph of Chanting Hill, taken from the gate, the trees in leaf once more, along the drive. Teddy had pleaded guilty, been sentenced to two years in prison. According to the report Chanting Hill was up for sale. A large proportion of the proceeds would be forfeit, the house having been much improved and enhanced with stolen money.

Honey pointed to the photograph. 'This house? This great house is Chanting Hill?'

'Yes,' said Crystal. 'Actually it's not a very good picture.'

Honey made no mention of the prison sentence – as if only the picture of the house meant anything to her. She fetched scissors from the kitchen and cut out the article. 'He will not see that it has gone,' she said, screwing the clipping into a ball. 'It is better that he reads nothing these days, only the clues.'

With the end of the monsoon, the planter's house reverted. The dampness regressed to the corners, the smell of it going out with the season, leaving only a residue, a fine, sharp must that was strong when the shutters were closed, hardly there when they were open.

Crystal's task was finished. The house was empty of everything except furniture, and treasures, the Ransome silver, a few mildewed watercolours that Crystal thought could be reframed, and two boxes of photographs. And the diary. Crystal wanted to keep the diary for herself.

Verinswella had arranged visits from the Ministry. A Costa with a briefcase spoke about statutory pensions rights; Honey was due to receive a lump sum, and safe tenure of her dwelling place. Jaleb was to have an annuity equal to half his wages, and something for his widow after his death.

Crystal understood enough to coax the writing of cheques.

'Why should I pay this?' Hugo's reluctance was weak, a token.

'They've looked after you all these years. You have a duty.'

A snort, a spasm, bony hands fluttering over the cheque. 'You have it in your blood,' he whispered. 'You have absorbed it from that house, through the walls. You are as obstinate as any

Ransome ever was.'

Crystal chuckled at him. 'Of course I'm a Ransome. What else could I be?'

She had done well. There were new sheets on the bed, new towels in his bathroom; the old remnants sent down to the compound. More cheques to be signed.

Her skin had turned as brown as Honey's. Watching from his chair, Hugo saw how she had settled to the place, the warmth and colour melting into her in a way that made her sweet and familiar.

He had seen the newspaper – the D.C. had brought it to his chair. 'Of course, Commander. The Club newspapers are for us all.' Short though the sentence was, short enough to outrage, it was longer than he had left. Hugo's release would be sooner and more certain. She would stay now, until he was gone. The girl would not go back to a father in gaol.

The thought of it consoled him; her presence consoled him, had become a stole of comfort, a gentle wrap of memories.

Crystal went back to the bar beside the sea. It became a regular thing, after tea, to meet the English boy and the Costas, to drink a beer or two and listen to their stories.

The smell of the stove hung crisp on the evening wind. Tourists came walking down from the hotels, hungry for a taste of real Pentecost, swordfish steaks in unleavened bread, trails of Tabasco on plates of rice, sweet mango and lobster, cardamom and prawns.

Further along the street, in the place where the dhuka used to be, where Bana would wave from his forest of merchandise, a disco opened its doors. Pentecost Nite. The wail of a saxophone as the last wash of light slipped from the sky.

Crystal went to dance. The old Costas tapped their feet. The English boy wore white jeans, clean bright legs in the flash of ultraviolet light.

She did not see them at first: Honey in her shawl by the door, Jaleb and old Justine, the compound people shouting, their ears covered against the boom of the music. Finally someone touched her hand and she saw the throng at the door, eyes

bright with fear.
  'What is it, Honey?'
  'You must come now.'
  'Is it Hugo?'
  'There is fire.'

She ran with them, a shoal of black hands grabbing hers, holding her arms, lifting, her strides made huge by theirs. Honey was behind. Away from the music Crystal could hear her breath, the old woman's lungs heaving.
  'It was the diary. You left it about. And all the photographs.'
  'What do you mean?'
  'He has been in the study. Where all those old things were left. I think he could not bear it.'
  Smoke in the starlight. A pillow of grey over the trees.
  'You mean he started the fire?'
  There was no answer. Honey could run no further. Crystal tore herself away, hurtled towards the house, her sandals pulling and twisting on her feet. The smoke rolled black and poisonous, billowing over the lawn.
  'My grandfather! Where is my grandfather?'
  Faces turned to her, eyes streaming with tears. 'Is too much smoke to see.'
  'Has someone called the fire brigade?'
  There was no answer. Smoke was filling her lungs. 'Please! Has someone called the fire brigade?'
  A voice from the crowd. 'The engine is coming from Liberté.'
  'How long will it take?'
  'Too long for this house.'
  The faces turned away. She had paused on the drive, just at the point where the garden had once been, the grass of the old lawn tall after the monsoon. Crystal pushed through, pressing against bodies, arms and legs and faces turning. She pulled up the neck of her tee-shirt to cover her face. Thick, acrid smoke scorched her throat; she could see bright red flames between the trees.
  All at once she was alone, ahead of them all, with nothing between her and the house but the driveway, and Hugo's

221

ancient motor-car, pitted chrome reflecting the firelight.

The whole building blazed. She could see, in clear silhouette, the parrot cages hanging from the verandah roof, empty, the metal doors hanging open. Someone had set them free. As she reached the car a beam crashed down, showering smuts and fiery solids onto the grass. There was no part of the house that did not belch smoke and flames.

The heat was a wall, holding her back, a terrifying furnace reaching from the steep roof, up into the black night sky. She ran from side to side, like a dog on a chain, helpless to go forward. Behind the house the light of the fire lit the compound: women and children running, clutching possessions, baskets and suitcases, a bed carried aloft, wooden chairs and cooking pots. Minutes passed, minutes that felt like hours, eternities, and then the sound of a siren; a fire engine nudging up through the crowd, its flashing lights and wah-wah wailing incongruous and comforting.

For a moment the wind shifted, pulling the smoke away, like a great curtain drawn back upon a stage. The firemen were smart, badges on their chests, broad yellow helmets. She would learn later, in a welter of the inconsequential, a heap of knowledge, surplus, useless, that Pentecost had been the beneficiary of foreign aid. The firemen had trained in the West; the appliance was as new and smart as any in Europe.

The men put on breathing apparatus, cylinders of air slung on their backs like diving gear. Shiny yellow trousers, blue coats and yellow helmets. The clothes made them huge and reassuring, great boots stirring the dust on the drive. A board was set up, a name scrawled as each man went in. Aluminium ladders were laid against the walls. Flames leaped out at them, like party revellers welcoming new guests.

The tourists started to arrive, drawn from the hotel bar by the noise and the smoke. A man, still in his swimming trunks, had brought his camera case. Without looking at Crystal he opened the lid. The firelight illuminated the contents, storage compartments lined with velvet, cassettes of film, lenses in plastic tubes. The equipment was soon assembled. The camera had the appearance of a weapon, the barrel of a gun or a man rampant.

222

Pressure hoses danced with the flames. The structure of the roof was laid bare; blackened rafters, separated from their moorings by the yellow flames, waved in the heat.

The cameraman covered all the angles – the faces of the crowd, the burning house, the trampled lawn. Behind the house a hydrant had been turned on the path, soaking the ground between the house and the compound. Crystal could see a woman gathering chickens from the coop into her basket. Policemen arrived, adding flashes of blue to the red and gold light that filled the sky. There was little for them to do. Their flat caps and shirt-sleeves looked useless and vulnerable. One of them talked to the cameraman, his hand making a gesture, not to stop, but to be discreet.

From the side of the house came a small explosion; louder than the roar of diesel engines, the hiss and flash of pressure hoses, the breaking of glass and the cascades of roof tiles falling like giant shingle poured into a bucket. The explosion was followed by the long high shriek of a whistle. The policemen stirred. Firemen's boots thundered on the drive. A second wave was to go in. Fresh men struggled into armour as the original fire-fighters emerged, dark faces gleaming. Crystal felt the crowd pressing forward, a heavy stink of sweat mingling with the smoke.

'Is someone hurt?' Two Englishmen stood behind her: assuming her to be one of them, a spectator, she was included in their speculation. Again there was the long shriek of the whistle.

An ancient ambulance, little more than a van, weaved forward, pushing a path through the crowd. Men appeared bearing a stretcher, stained canvas slung between two poles. On the stretcher, incongruously, was a white helmet, the kind worn on building sites, like a soldier's cap at a military funeral. Instead of a flag there was a blanket.

The spectators behind her moved closer. More were coming all the time. People from the village, the estate workers and the tourists, all gathering round the pyre. She caught a glimpse of the boy she had danced with, horror on his face.

High above, against the night sky, the remains of the roof timbers stirred in the hot wind from the fire. The sight had a kind of beauty. Fresh flames leapt out around the gables, gay scarves of red and yellow. Behind them the timbers waved, like amputated limbs. The crowd surged forward; faces bright with excitement, eyes wide, ready for what they might see.

'I've never seen a house burn.'

'They say he stayed with the things he was burning – wouldn't let them drag him away. One of the servants has a burnt hand.'

'You mean the owner is burning in there now?'

'They'll bring him out soon.'

'Do you think so, really?'

'It won't be a pretty sight.'

'They'll cover it up, they always do.'

There were children in the crowd, sheltering between the legs and bodies of the herd. A man in a blue vest held a tiny baby, fast asleep, as soft and vulnerable as a piece of warm cheese in his arms. He rocked his feet from side to side, making of his whole, bullish frame a swaying cradle. His eyes were ahead, fixed on the space where the front doors had been, where firemen were climbing down what remained of the verandah steps. Ambulance men reaching out to take their burden. Something bundled onto the stretcher.

Another noise. Crystal turned. A shouting, louder and higher and more dreadful. A figure pushing through the crowd. Honey had pulled her shawl over her head. Her teeth were bared.

'He is dead, Crystal! Mr Ransome is burned and dead!' She took Crystal's hand, crushing her fingers. 'You must come! You must come with me!'

It was away from the flames that the woman pulled her, away from the people and the excitement. They stumbled over the ground, Crystal's bare feet tearing on roots and shards of rock.

'You must come here and pray.'

The distance was short. A clump of trees, a kind of shelter, smooth waxy leaves against her face. Honey pushed Crystal down onto her knees, pushed her sweat-sodden hair out of her eyes. There was a candle, a statue behind glass.

'Hail Mary, full of grace. Blessed art though among women. Blessed is the fruit of thy womb . . .'

Honey's hands were strong, forcing the rosary between Crystal's fingers.

'I don't do this, Honey. I don't pray.'

'You do, you must. You must pray for them all.'

SIXTEEN

Sodium lights cast a dreary fog of yellow over the car-park. The cars, all old, spattered with rust, looked the same, had the same yellow-brown colour under the feeble glare. She had come by tube, deciding from the address, and, perhaps, the sound of his voice as he gave it to her on the telephone, that this was not a wise place to bring a car, that parking might be scarce and dubious.

She had turned off the High Street into a web of roads shadowed by great squares of concrete, water-stained grey, flat-roofed, serial numbers and graffiti.

He opened the door and smiled. He wore a cardigan, red knitted acrylic. Was it something he had grown used to, learned to like? Did they wear cardigans in prison? Behind him was a living room with a square window and a narrow passage off; a glimpse of the kitchen, cups on a draining board, a washing machine, chipped enamel and bluish paste oozing from the soap drawer.

He said nothing. His glasses were broken, the stylish frames repaired with a caul of Sellotape. He stood aside, made no attempt to touch her. She had a suitcase in her hand, just a small assembly of belongings, not enough for a lifetime, but more than she would need overnight.

She walked along the passage. Three feet wide and no natural light. The suitcase banged her knees.

'It's through here.'

Past the bathroom. White tiles, grouting black with age and grease. The bedroom furniture was incongruous, the wide bed from Chanting Hill, with silk sheets, and curtains hopelessly oversized. On a side table was a pile of books – novels, Penelope Lively and Timothy Mo.

She put her suitcase on the bed. Through the window was a wall of concrete, below them the roof of a pub left standing between the concrete towers, like the survivor of an air-raid. In the distance was the railway line, fast trains passing silently. Paint flaked from the metal window-frame.

'I used to see these flats from the train going home,' said Teddy.

'It's a long way from Chanting Hill,' she said.

'And a long time, too.'

After a pause she said, 'I'm sorry about the visits. I meant – '

'Some of the time I was glad you didn't come. If you'd seen me there . . .' He shrugged. 'You might never have come here.'

'No. It was a gamble. There was a risk that if I didn't see you while you were in prison, I wouldn't see you at all.'

'What were the odds?'

'Evens.' She pressed both catches of the suitcase at once. They sprang open like rapid pistol shots. 'You mustn't think I'm here to stay, Teddy. I can't promise anything.'

'But you'll stay tonight?'

'Is there somewhere I can put my things?'

He sprang to the cupboard, pulled back the sliding door. 'I've kept it clear.'

There were metal hangers on the rack. She started unpacking her clothes and putting them on the hangers.

As if to show her that he could take it, that his new humble world would not destroy him, he fetched fish and chips for their supper and they ate out of the paper and drank cold lager straight from the can. She found herself laughing for the first time.

'What is funny?'

'You,' she said, 'sucking your fingers like that. You were always so well bred.'

He shrugged. 'Prison taught me some new habits.'

227

She watched him for a minute. He finished eating and rolled the fish paper into a ball. She saw that he was aware of her scrutiny but unaffected by it. As if he had nothing at all to hide.

'Aren't you going to eat any more?'

She shook her head. 'It was too much for me.'

He took her debris from her and added it to his, packing it carefully into a plastic bag before dropping it into the bin. 'We don't want to smell it in the morning.'

When it was time for bed he took her hand. 'I'm out of practice, Annabelle.'

But he wasn't. His confidence came back in a moment. Despite the time that had gone by, the place where he had been, the man who took off her clothes was the man she knew of old, sure of himself, slow and irresistible.

She stayed a week, then a fortnight, fetched her car and risked it in the car-park; took his spectacles for repair and bought him a sweater to replace the acrylic cardigan. Every morning she took the tube up to the office, holding her coat aloof from the litter in the streets around the council estate, the stink of the derelicts who gathered on the corner where a van came in the mornings to dispense free tea and toast.

Her flat in Orchard Street was empty. She could take him to live there. The thought was with her all the time. She tried to picture him as a permanent feature; a man without a job, without any family, sitting in her armchair every evening, waiting for her to come home.

No, I must first see if I can love him here. If it is real here, where he deserves to be, then we will survive.

December brought a sudden breath of winter. Frost on the grass between the tower blocks; the derelicts fewer in number. The flat had no central heating, the bathroom was draped with washing that would not dry. I'll think about it after Christmas, she decided. We'll see how it feels to face the New Year with him.

She returned from the office to find him standing in the living room, something in his hand. He held it out to her. A letter from Pentecost.

228

Dear Papa, will you come and visit us for Christmas?

We have a house near the beach. It's very simple but we have lots of space, and there's always someone visiting. People ask me about you, the old ones. How is Master Teddy? they say. You should come before it is too late.

Teddy reached for her. 'I won't go, if you don't think I should.'

'Of course you must,' said Annabelle, gently pulling herself free.

'How long should I stay?'

'As long as you want to, Teddy.'

'Do you suppose Susan has been there?'

Annabelle shook her head. 'Crystal has less reason to ask Susan over there. It is not Susan she needs to forgive.'

The new runway ran parallel with the beach, hot tarmac beside brown-gold sand. A voice filled the passenger cabin, 'Welcome to Liberté', a thick-tongued, round brown accent, washing Teddy with a sweet warm milk of nostalgia.

The seatbelt light went off and he stood up. The aisle seat had been a blessing, despite the disturbances in the night, passengers trundling past to the lavatories, to the spare seats in the smoking section, to ask for glasses of water, whisky, attention. Teddy had moved around too, unable to sleep, to still the restless excitement, fear that cluttered the hours.

How would she be, this daughter whom he no longer knew? Was there anything left of the little girl he had adored? Squeals from the swimming pool, rosettes on Saturdays? Her letter was so short. Could forgiveness be so simple?

He followed the other passengers across the tarmac to the terminal. Heat wafted round his face. A stink of fuel, sweat from a passing mechanic.

More than four decades. He looked up to the hills. Above the trees, above the humps of black rock, the peaks bristled with hardware; huge aerials, multi-shaped antennae, round white buildings like sugared bon-bons. Pentecost had found its destiny as the listening post of the world.

Crystal looked taller. Her legs had filled out, shapely below

229

the denim shorts. Her hair was tied high on her head with a scarlet ribbon. A brisk kiss. 'Have you only one bag?'

He followed her to the car-park. The porters clamouring to take his bag were dismissed, a practised gesture; familiar, something in the flick of the wrist. His heart seemed to pause.

'The rains are just about finished,' she said. 'This year has been particularly bad, silt from the river has stained the beach for miles.'

She spoke as an expert, one who had lived there for years. Three, in fact, thought Teddy. Long enough to compare one year with another. She opened the boot of a battered Toyota.

He put in his case. 'You're driving?'

She smiled, holding up the ignition keys. 'I passed my test first time.' A glimpse of the old Crystal, triumphant. 'I only had one formal lesson – just before the test. Apart from that I learned in William's truck. It's a brute to drive. I reckon I could drive just about anything after that.'

'William?'

'Sahilil's son. He remembers you – just. He's a carpenter.'

She drove efficiently, nosing out onto the main road, cautiously bold. Teddy looked at her profile, a faint cluster of lines at the corners of her eyes. Her nose had straightened out. His Crystal. No longer his.

The road skirted Liberté town, became a dual carriageway.

'This trip is much quicker since they opened the new road. The old coast road used to take forever.'

'Such prosperity,' said Teddy, looking at the tall buildings of Liberté, neon lights, hoardings advertising Coca-Cola and life insurance. 'This is not how I remember it.'

'The Americans have been pouring in aid. Even since I've been here the improvements have been enormous. They've installed so much expensive hardware on the mountains, they want the island to be stable. No coups or revolutions. In their book, stability can be bought with money.' She signalled to turn left. Teddy recognised a steep cluster of black rocks as the dual carriageway looped out over the sea. The old Toyota picked up speed.

'You mentioned a house by the beach?'

'It's just rented – very cheap. The wrong side of town, I guess.'

'How have you been living? I mean, do you have a job?'

She glanced across at him, her look unnervingly mature. 'I work for the manager of the Mahana Palms.'

'The Mahana Palms?'

'It's a hotel. Very smart. Mahana has several.'

Teddy shook his head. Perhaps it would be easier this way. If there was nothing left of the place he remembered.

'I type his letters,' Crystal continued, 'answer the phone, deal with the guests who complain.'

'I didn't know you could type.'

'They taught us at school. It was optional – instead of cookery. The only useful thing I learned for all those fees.' She looked across at him again and he saw what she had left unsaid.

They passed a bright, bold sign. 'Welcome to Mahana.' Clusters of white houses with burglar bars in the windows, tended gardens, swathes of bougainvillea. He looked for the old plantation, for the leaning gates.

'Wasn't it here?'

'Over there.' She gestured with her chin. All Teddy could see was a school; neat, cream-painted two-storey buildings, a tarmac playground, a cricket pitch. Beyond it, behind a tall fence, rows of houses with small verandahs, sprawling veget-able patches for gardens.

'The old *notaire* in Liberté came out the day after the fire. He and D.C. Verinswella are the Trustees of Hugo's will. He left everything for the benefit of the town. Verinswella formed a committee. They opened the school with a great ceremony, on the anniversary of the fire.'

'Were you consulted? As his grand-daughter?'

Crystal smiled again, her lips curling a little with irony. 'Not quite his grand-daughter, you will recall.'

The road curved away from the seafront. She pointed to a turning marked by white painted stones and an archway announcing 'The Mahana Palms Hotel'. 'There it is.'

Teddy wanted to talk about the school. 'Are you on Verins-wella's committee?'

'I declined,' she said abruptly. 'I had to battle to get the legacies paid. Honey was due a sum of money. All the servants were left something. I had to fight for them with Verinswella. You can imagine that this school was not built without some graft, some greasing of palms.'

They had come into the centre of town. Almost unrecognisable. There were pavements, parades of shops. Only the dust was familiar, and the odd donkey cart among the cars, old men sitting in the shade, echoes of the place he remembered, the Pentecost of slumbering afternoons.

She drove straight through, turning down towards the sea and a cluster of eucalyptus trees. 'The house is in the next bay,' she said. 'Do you remember the Mahana Clinic?' Pointing to a long, low building, white paint turned brown with age. 'It's been here forever. The priests run it – for the people who can't get to the free hospital in Liberté.'

She put the car into a lower gear as they left the road, bumping downwards over a barely visible track. 'It's OK now,' she shouted, over the noise of the engine, 'but we could do with the Range Rover during the monsoon.'

Teddy found himself smiling. It was the first time she had made any reference to her old home. The Toyota wound slowly between rocks and then turned sharp right. There, standing outside a ramshackle house, was Honey Jellawella. Old and shrivelled but unmistakable.

Teddy climbed out of the car and took her in his arms.

'Teddy-master, you have come.'

'Yes, Honey.'

'You have sinned, Teddy-master.'

'Yes, Honey.'

'God has punished you.'

Teddy clung to the small, frail woman, his face against her oiled hair.

'God punished Mr Ransome, too. And he punished your poor mother. God has punished you all.'

'Yes.'

Crystal had lifted his bag. 'Come on, Papa. We've put you in the best room.'

He followed her inside the house, to a room with a single bed and virtually nothing else. 'I'm sorry it's a bit sparse,' said Crystal. 'But just look at the view.'

Teddy stood beside her at the window. He could see the great black rocks strung with fishing nets, shallow boats hauled up on the sand, and beyond them, the sea, shining, blindingly blue.

SEVENTEEN

Annabelle stayed in bed until mid-morning, wallowing in the warmth and comfort of the flat in Orchard Street. For once Christmas Day had brought a fall of snow, a white glare through the windows. There were no decorations in the flat, nothing but two red candles on the mantelpiece and a sprig of holly. Pretending another invitation, she had refused the traditional lunch with her father and the other members of her family who gathered each year to cluck about her unmarried state, her childlessness.

They would certainly cluck if they knew the truth, she thought. She washed her hair under the shower, followed her usual ritual of razoring and body lotion. The silent day was an echo of another, years before, that she had spent waiting for his call.

By four o'clock it was dark. She drew the curtains. When the telephone rang she snatched it up after a single ring. 'Hello?'

Her father's sister. 'We wondered how you were, Annabelle. Are you having a nice Christmas?'

Twenty unbearable minutes, smiling falsely into the receiver. Had he tried and missed her? Perhaps he couldn't get to a phone? Crystal's letter had carried only a box number, no mention of a telephone.

She lit the candles on the mantelpiece, watched a carol service on the television with the sound turned down, the mouths of well-scrubbed boys opening and shutting in unison. A film began. The same they had shown last year at Christmas time. She was reaching for the sound button when the telephone shrilled.

'Annabelle?' His voice was perfectly clear, as if he were speaking from the next room.

'Happy Christmas, Teddy.'

'Are you all right?'

She side-stepped the question. 'Are you having a good time? How is Crystal?'

'She's – she's wonderful. All grown up. I've told her about you. We've talked about everything – '

Suddenly Annabelle couldn't bear it. He was too far away. She wanted him right there in the room, sitting in her chair. 'Teddy, when are you coming back?'

There was a hesitation in his voice. 'I wasn't sure. I don't want you to feel . . . What I mean is – '

'I'm perfectly sure,' said Annabelle. 'I want you to come home.'